INSPEC
AND THE STARVEL HOLLOW TRAGEDY

Freeman Wills Crofts (1879–1957), the son of an army doctor who died before he was born, was raised in Northern Ireland and became a civil engineer on the railways. His first book, *The Cask*, written in 1919 during a long illness, was published in the summer of 1920, immediately establishing him as a new master of detective fiction. Regularly outselling Agatha Christie, it was with his fifth book that Crofts introduced his iconic Scotland Yard detective, Inspector Joseph French, who would feature in no less than thirty books over the next three decades. He was a founder member of the Detection Club and was elected a Fellow of the Royal Society of Arts in 1939. Continually praised for his ingenious plotting and meticulous attention to detail—including the intricacies of railway timetables—Crofts was once dubbed 'The King of Detective Story Writers' and described by Raymond Chandler as 'the soundest builder of them all'.

FREEMAN WILLS CROFTS

Inspector French and the Starvel Hollow Tragedy

COLLINS
CRIME
CLUB

COLLINS CRIME CLUB
An imprint of HarperCollins*Publishers*
1 London Bridge Street
London SE1 9GF
www.harpercollins.co.uk

This paperback edition 2017

First published in Great Britain
by Wm Collins Sons & Co. Ltd 1927

Copyright © Estate of Freeman Wills Crofts 1927

Freeman Wills Crofts asserts the moral right
to be identified as the author of this work

A catalogue record for this book is
available from the British Library

ISBN 978-0-00-819064-4

Set in Sabon Lt Std by Palimpsest Book Production Limited, Falkirk, Stirlingshire

Printed and bound by CPI Group (UK) Ltd, Croydon, CR0 4YY

MIX
Paper from
responsible sources
FSC **FSC® C007454**
www.fsc.org

FSC™ is a non-profit international organisation established to promote
the responsible management of the world's forests. Products carrying the
FSC label are independently certified to assure consumers that they come
from forests that are managed to meet the social, economic and
ecological needs of present and future generations,
and other controlled sources.

Find out more about HarperCollins and the environment at
www.harpercollins.co.uk/green

TO
MY WIFE
WHO SUGGESTED THE IDEA FROM WHICH
THIS STORY GREW

Contents

Contents

1

The Tragedy

Ruth Averill moved slowly across the drawing room at Starvel, and stood dejectedly at the window, looking out at the Scotch firs swaying in the wind and the sheets of rain driving across the untidy lawn before the house.

The view was even more depressing than usual on this gloomy autumn afternoon. Beyond the grass-grown drive and the broken-down paling of posts and wire which bounded the grounds, lay the open moor, wild and lonely and forbidding. A tumble of dun-coloured sedgy grass with darker smudges where rock outcropped, it stretched up, bleak and dreary, to the lip of the hollow in which the dilapidated old house had been built.

To the girl standing in the window with a brooding look of melancholy on her pretty features the outlook seemed symbolical of her life, for Ruth Averill was not one of those whose lives could be said to have fallen in pleasant places.

But, in spite of her unhappy expression, she was good to look at as she stood watching the storm. Though rather under medium height she had a charming figure and something of a presence. She was dark, as though in her veins might flow some admixture of Spanish or Italian blood. Her features were small and delicate, but her firmly rounded chin gave promise of character. She scarcely looked her twenty years of age.

But though she had the fresh vitality of youth, there was something old-fashioned in her appearance not out of accord with her surroundings. She wore her long dark hair piled up in great masses over her broad forehead. Her dress was of the plainest, and in the fashion of three years earlier. Though scrupulously neat, it was worn threadbare. Her shoes were cracked and her stockings showed careful darns.

For Ruth Averill was an orphan, dependent on the bounty of her uncle, Simon Averill, for every penny. And Simon Averill was a miser.

Ruth was born in Southern France, and she had dim recollections of a land of sun and warmth, of jolly people and bright colours. But since she had come to this gloomy old house in the wilds of the Yorkshire moors the joy had gone out of her life. Her companions during childhood had been the two not very prepossessing servants and the still less attractive gardener and outdoor man. With her uncle Simon she had nothing in common. Even at the time of her arrival he was elderly and morose, and every day he seemed to grow more self-centred and less approachable.

After some years a break had come in her life; she had been sent to a boarding school. But she had not been happy there, so that when she was 'finished' she was almost glad to return to the dullness and loneliness of Starvel.

There she had found changes. Her Uncle Simon was now an invalid, querulous and solitary, and living only for the accumulation of money. His passion took the form of collecting actual coins and notes and hoarding them in his safe. He made no attempt to cultivate the friendship of his niece, and had it not been that he required her to read to him once a day, she would have seen him but seldom.

At this time also the two old women servants and the gardener had gone, and their places had been taken by a comparatively young married couple called Roper. Though more efficient than their predecessors, Ruth did not take to either of the newcomers, with the result that the fourteen months which had passed since her return from school were lonelier than ever.

Had it not been that Ruth had developed an interest in flowers and gardening, she would have found herself hard put to it to fill her life. Gardening and her friendship with a semi-invalid entomologist who lived close by, together with occasional excursions to the neighbouring market town of Thirsby, were the only distractions she could count on.

But recently another factor had come into her life. She had met on a number of occasions a young man named Pierce Whymper, the junior assistant of an ecclesiastical architect in Leeds. Whymper was acting as clerk of works during some renovations to the parish church at Thirsby, and when Ruth had gone with one or two of the local ladies to inspect the work he had been particularly attentive. He had begged her to come again to see how the job progressed, and she had done so on more than one occasion. Then one day she had met him walking near Starvel, and she had invited him to come in and have tea. This visit had been followed by others and they had made excursions together on the moor. Though no word of love had been spoken during any of these interviews, she knew that he was attracted to her, and though she would hardly admit it to herself, she knew also that she would marry him if he should ask her.

Such was the general condition of affairs in the old house of Starvel on this gloomy September afternoon, an afternoon which was to be remembered by Ruth as the end of her old life and the prelude to a new existence in a different world.

As she was standing, staring mournfully out of the window, the attendant, Roper, entered the room. She did not know then, though she realised it afterwards, that the message he was bringing her was to be the herald of a series of terrible and tragic happenings, so dark and sinister and awful that had she foreseen them she might well have cried out in horror and dismay. But she did not foresee them, and she turned with her instinctive courtesy to hear what the man had to say.

The message, though almost unprecedented, was in itself the reverse of alarming. Roper explained that Mr Averill had instructed him to hand this note, which he had received in a letter to himself, to Miss Ruth, and to say that he hoped Miss Ruth would accept the invitation it contained. Further, that as there would be expenses in connection with the visit, he wished Miss Ruth to have the ten pounds enclosed in this other envelope. She could go in to Thirsby in the morning, get any little thing she might want, and go on to York in the afternoon.

With rapidly beating heart Ruth unfolded the dogeared corner of the note, which was addressed simply 'Ruth,' and read as follows:

> 'Oakdene,' Ashton Drive,
> York, *September 10th*.
>
> 'MY DEAR RUTH,—I hope you will allow me to address you in this way, as your father and I were old friends. I nursed you when you were a baby, and though we

have not met for many years, I do not feel that you are a stranger.

'This is to ask if you will come and stay here for a few days and meet my daughters Gwen and Hilda. I do hope you can.

'Our autumn flower show opens on Wednesday, and the roses are always worth seeing. I am sure you would enjoy it, so try to reach here on Tuesday afternoon and you will be in time to go there with us.

                                   'Yours very sincerely,
                                   'HELEN PALMER-GORE.'

Ruth could scarcely believe her eyes as she read this friendly letter. Mrs Palmer-Gore she dimly remembered as a large, kindly, fussily-mannered woman, whom she had liked in spite of her trick of giving unpleasantly moist kisses. But she had never visited her, or ever been to York, and the prospect thrilled her.

But unexpected as the invitation was, it was as nothing compared to her uncle's attitude towards it. That he should have given her permission to go was surprising enough, but that he should have sent her ten pounds for her expenses was an absolute miracle. *Ten Pounds! What* a sum! Why, she had never had the tenth part of it in her possession before! And *what* she could buy with it! Visions of frocks, shoes, hats and gloves began to float before her imagination. Feeling as he did towards money, it *was* good of her Uncle Simon. She turned impulsively to Roper.

'Oh, how kind of uncle,' she exclaimed. 'I must go up and thank him.'

Roper shook his head.

'Well, miss, I shouldn't if I were you,' he advised in his

pleasant Scotch voice. He came from somewhere in Fife. 'The master's not so well, as you know, and he particularly said he didn't want to be disturbed. I'd wait and see him in the morning before you go. You will go, I suppose?'

'Of course I shall go, Roper.' She hesitated, undecided. 'Well, perhaps if he said that, I'd better see him in the morning, as you suggest.'

'Very good, miss. Then I'd best arrange for a car to take you in to Thirsby in the morning? About ten, maybe?'

'Thank you. Yes, about ten will do. And you might send a telegram to York which I will write for you.'

The man bowed and withdrew, and Ruth gave herself up to glorious dreams of the next few days: not so much of visiting the Palmer-Gores and York, but of getting away from Starvel. Yes, she admitted it to herself at last. It was to get away from Starvel that she really welcomed the invitation. While there had been no chance of quitting it, she had not realised how terribly bitter was her hatred of the place. And not the place only, but of everyone in it. She hated her uncle— in spite of the ten pounds. She hated Roper with his sleek civility, and most of all she hated Mrs Roper, who always treated her with a veiled insolence, as if silently taunting her because of her dependent position. Oh, how splendid it would be to get away from the place and everything connected with it, even for a few days! And she determined she would use the opportunity of this visit to find out what her chances would be of getting some job by means of which she could support herself, so that she might never be forced to return to Starvel or see any of its inhabitants again.

That night she could scarcely sleep from excitement, and next morning she was ready with her shabby little suitcase long before the time at which the car was to arrive.

She was somewhat uneasy about her uncle's condition. For several days he had been ailing, and when she had gone in to say good-bye to him before leaving she had thought him looking very ill. He was asleep, but breathing heavily, and there was something in his appearance which vaguely disquieted her.

'I don't think he's at all well,' she said to Roper when she came down. 'I believe he should have the doctor.'

'I was of the same opinion, miss, and I took the liberty of calling at Dr Philpot's when I went in to order your car. But the doctor's ill. He's got influenza and is confined to bed. I thought of going on to Dr Emerson, and then I thought if it's only influenza that's wrong with Dr Philpot we might just as well wait. He'll likely be about again in a day or two.'

Dr Philpot was Mr Averill's usual attendant. He was a youngish man who had come to the place some three or four years earlier, and who had already built up a reputation for care and skill. The other practitioner, Dr Emerson, was old and past his work, and had retired in all but name.

Ruth paused in some perplexity.

'That's very unfortunate. But I think you are right that if it's only a matter of a day or two we should wait for Dr Philpot. I hadn't heard he was ill.'

'Neither had I, miss. He was all right on Thursday, for he was out that day to see Mr Giles.'

'So I understood. How is Mr Giles today?'

'I haven't heard this morning, miss, but last night he was far from well. Mrs Roper is just going up to see if there is anything wanted.'

'I'll go round to see him on my way to Thirsby,' Ruth decided. 'Can I give Mrs Roper a lift?'

'Thank you, miss, it would be a convenience. I'll tell her.'

Markham Giles, the entomologist, was their nearest neighbour. He was the son of an old friend of Mr Averill's and
lived alone in a little cottage half a mile away across the
moor. He was a pathetic instance of the wreckage left by
the War. Never physically strong, he had been rejected for
the earlier army drafts, but when the struggle had dragged
out and the standard for recruitment had been lowered he
had again volunteered and had got through. He had served
in Flanders, had been badly gassed and wounded, and six
months later had left the hospitals the shadow of his former
self. Being alone in the world and penniless save for his
pension, he had headed north to his father's old friend. A
small cottage belonging to Starvel being then vacant, Mr
Averill had offered it to him at a nominal rent. There he had
since lived, occupying his time by keeping bees and by
studying the insect life of the moor. On this subject he had
become somewhat of an authority, and had written articles
which had attracted attention in entomological circles. He
and Ruth were good friends and she had helped in the capture
and arrangement of his specimens.

Some days previously he had developed influenza, and
though he did not seem seriously ill, he was not shaking it
off. Mrs Roper had been kind in looking after him and Ruth
also had done what she could.

Ten minutes later the two women arrived at the tiny cottage
which lay just outside the lip of Starvel Hollow, the big
saucer-shaped depression in the moor in the centre of which
stood Simon Averill's house. Markham Giles looked worse
than when Ruth had last seen him. He lay with half-closed
eyes and seemed too dull and listless to more than notice his
visitors. But he feebly thanked them for coming and said he
was quite comfortable and wanted nothing.

'If he's not better by tomorrow, I think you should send for Dr Emerson,' Ruth declared as she returned to her car.

'I think so, too, miss. Very good, I'll arrange it. And if he seems bad tonight either John or I will come over and sit with him. I don't like his look this morning somehow.'

'It's very good of you, Mrs Roper. But I expect he'll be all right.'

'I hope so, miss. Good morning, miss.'

Ruth's mind was troubled as she turned away. She had always been intensely sorry for Markham Giles, and now she hated leaving him lying there alone. But there was nothing that she could do, and with a half sigh she re-entered her vehicle and was driven into Thirsby.

There she spent the morning shopping, packing her purchases in her suitcase. This was followed by a frugal meal at the local tea shop, and then arose the question of how she should spend the hour remaining until train time.

She left her suitcase at the tea shop, and sallied forth. Involuntarily her steps turned towards the church, though she assured herself that under no circumstances would she enter the building. There could, however, be no objection to walking past the gate.

What she would have done eventually if left to herself will never be known, as fate intervened and arranged her visit for her. Turning a corner she all but ran into Mrs Oxley, the wife of one of the local solicitors. Mr Oxley had charge of all Simon Averill's business, and on his occasional visits to Starvel he had made a point of asking for Ruth and chatting to her in his pleasant cheery way. Mrs Oxley she had known for years, and had experienced many kindnesses at her hands.

They stopped to talk and Mrs Oxley heard of the visit to York with interest and sympathy.

'Well,' she said, 'if you're not doing anything until half past three, come with me to the church. Boyd, the sexton, promised to send me some of the old flags for the rock garden, and I want to know when I'm likely to get them.'

There was nothing for it but to go, and whether Mrs Oxley had any suspicion of how matters stood, or whether she was genuinely anxious about her paving-stones, Ruth was left alone to talk to Whymper for a good ten minutes. And the young man did not fail to improve the occasion. It appeared that he had to go to the station to make inquiries about a consignment of cement, so it was natural that he should leave the church with the ladies. Mrs Oxley, it then turned out, had business in the opposite direction and to her great regret was unable to accompany the others. So the task of seeing Miss Averill off fell to Mr Whymper.

It was with shining eyes and heightened colour that, half an hour later, Ruth Averill sat in the corner of a third-class compartment, while the train moved out of Thirsby. That Whymper loved her she was now positive. It was true that he had not actually spoken of love, but his every word and look proclaimed his feelings. He had, moreover, insisted on telling her about his family and his position and prospects— a good sign. As to her own feelings, she was no longer in any doubt whatever. She loved him, and in loving him the grey clouds that pressed down upon her life seemed to break and the rosy light of hope to pour in through the rift.

She duly reached York and found Mrs Palmer-Gore waiting for her on the platform. With her for two days she spent a pleasant holiday, enjoying the unwonted good-fellowship. The visit was to have lasted a week, but on the afternoon of the second day, there fell the first of the several blows that she was to experience, and her stay was brought to an abrupt termination.

They had just sat down to lunch when a telegram was handed to her. It was the first she had ever received. Excited and a trifle embarrassed, she hesitated to open it.

But when in answer to Mrs Palmer-Gore's kindly: 'Read it, dear. Don't mind us,' she learned its contents, all thought of herself was swept from her mind.

It was signed 'Oxley,' though whether it came from the solicitor or his wife she could not tell. It read: 'Terrible accident at Starvel. Your uncle injured. Return Thirsby and stay night with us.'

It was characteristic of the girl that her thoughts and feelings were all for old Simon Averill. Was the poor old man badly injured? Was he suffering? Could she do anything to help him? It was kind of the Oxleys to ask her to stay the night, but of course she could not do so. She must go out to Starvel and help with the nursing. Not one thought of the possible effect on herself of the disaster entered her mind. That the old man might die of his injuries and that she might be his heir never occurred to her. Nor did she repine at the cutting short of her first real and altogether wonderful holiday.

By Mrs Palmer-Gore's advice she wired to the Oxleys that she would be with them at 5.40 p.m., and after a hurried lunch she found herself once more in the train. During the journey she had time to ponder over her news. A 'terrible accident' at Starvel! What *could* have happened? It must surely be bad or that ominous word 'terrible' would not have been used. She began to invent possibilities. Had her uncle taken the wrong medicine, perhaps some awful burning stuff that would hurt him horribly? Or had he fallen downstairs or into the fire? Or cut himself and been unable to summon help?

She gave full rein to her imagination, but when she learned the truth she found it vastly more terrible than anything she had thought of. The Oxleys met her at the station, and having driven her to their home, broke the news.

It seemed that when about eleven o'clock that morning the baker was approaching Starvel to make his customary Thursday call, he had noticed a faint pall of smoke hanging in the sky above the hollow. On crossing the shoulder he had glanced down as usual into the curious circular dell, and had instantly been overwhelmed with incredulous amazement. There were the trees, the thin, stunted pines which surrounded the old house, but—*the house was gone!* The long line of slated roof which had stood out above the trees had absolutely vanished. No trace remained. At first sight the man thought that the entire building had disappeared, but a closer approach revealed blackened windowless walls surrounding a still smouldering interior, all that remained of the old place.

No sign of life appeared about the ruins, and the horror-stricken man was forced to the conclusion that all three occupants had lost their lives in the flames.

He drove hurriedly into Thirsby and gave the alarm, and soon Sergeant Kent of the local police force with some of his men, Dr Emerson, Mr Oxley and a number of others were hastening to the scene. They found matters as the baker had described, the smouldering ruins standing gaunt and sinister at the bottom of the dell, lonely and deserted, hidden from the surrounding country by the rim of the strange natural Hollow.

The fire had evidently raged with extraordinary fury. With the exception of an outhouse separate from the main building not a scrap of anything inflammable remained. Floors, roof, staircase, window sashes, all were gone. And in that glowing mass of red-hot debris within the blackened and twisted walls lay, almost certainly, the bodies of Simon Averill, and of John and Flora Roper.

Anxious that Ruth should not have to learn the terrible news from the papers, Mr Oxley had returned to Thirsby and sent his wire. He had thought it best to make this only a preparation, intending that the full story should be broken more gently on the girl's arrival.

Ruth was terribly shocked and upset. It was the first time, since reaching years of discretion, that she had been brought in contact with tragedy and death, and she was appalled by its horror. She begged to be allowed to go out to Starvel, but neither of the Oxleys would hear of it, pointing out that a visit would only harrow her feelings, and that she could do nothing there to help.

As the long evening dragged away she found herself hoping against hope that Whymper would call. But there was no sign of him and she supposed he had not heard of her return.

Sergeant Kent, however, had heard of it, and about eight o'clock he called and asked to see her. He was a tall, rather brusque man, though in Oxley's presence he was polite enough. He questioned her as to the household and its personnel, but she had nothing to tell him which could throw any light on the tragedy.

The next day it was found possible to attempt some research work among the ruins, and by ten o'clock a number of men were engaged in removing the cooler portions of the débris. Ruth insisted that she must see the place for herself, and the Oxleys, not liking to let her go alone, drove her out in their car. But the terrible picture which met her eyes and the thought of what lay below the sinister mound where the men were working made her feel almost sick with horror. Her feelings too, had changed. Gone was her hatred of the place, and particularly of the three poor people who had met with such an appalling fate. She felt she had been wicked to hate them. Her uncle had been a recluse and fond of money no doubt. But in his own way he had always been kind to her. He had opened his door to her when she was a homeless child, and had since supported her without grudging the money she must have cost him. And he had been ill—continuously ill; and when people are ill they cannot help being depressed and a little trying to others. And the Ropers, had she not misjudged them also? In their own way, they, too, had always been kind to her. For the first time, Ruth saw that the lives of the couple must have been as dull and grey as her own. Though their jobs were underpaid, and rather thankless, they had not complained. And she, Ruth, had never shown an appreciation of their services. She saw now that she had really had no reason at all for hating them, and when she thought of their terrible death, her tears flowed. In silence she allowed Mrs Oxley to lead her back to the car and drive her to Thirsby.

On their way to the little town the second blow fell on the young girl, and coming so quickly on the first, left her weak and trembling. As they mounted the rim of the Hollow they saw a funeral approaching along a converging road. It was a sorry procession; only the hearse, and the vicar and Dr Emerson in the former's car. As the two ladies drew up for it to pass, the vicar also stopped, and he and the doctor came over to express their sympathy with Ruth.

'You will be sorry for poor Mr Giles, also, Miss Ruth,' the vicar went on. 'I understood you were kind enough to help him in his scientific researches.'

Ruth stared at him in horror.

14

'You don't mean,' she stammered, 'that Mr Giles is—is dead?'

'He died the day before yesterday, I'm sorry to say. After a short illness he passed away in his sleep. He had no suffering. But, only thirty-six! Truly, another tragedy of the War.'

Ruth was stunned. Markham Giles, also! To lose at one blow all four persons whom she had known best—the only four persons in the world she had known at all well! It was too much.

She pulled herself together, however, and insisted on following her friend's body to its last resting-place, but when she reached the Oxleys' house she broke down altogether. Mrs Oxley put her to bed and at last she sobbed herself to sleep.

That evening the charred remains of three human bodies were found within the tragic walls of Starvel.

2

The Inquest

When Ruth Averill awoke next morning she found that the overwhelming sense of sick horror which had weighed her down on the previous evening had lightened. She had been worn out in body from the shock and the nervous strain, but sleep had restored her physical wellbeing, and her mind reacted to her body. She was young, she was in perfect health, and—she was in love.

While her feelings of compassion for the trio who had lost their lives in so terrible a way was in no whit lessened, she would have been less than human had she not begun to look upon the tragedy as it affected herself. And here at once was something exciting and a little terrifying. What would happen to her now? She had hated her life at Starvel; would the life that lay before her be better or worse? Scarcely worse, she thought; any change must surely be for the better. She had intended while at York to make some inquiries about earning her own living so that she might leave Starvel. Now this was no longer a matter of choice; in some way she must learn to support herself. Vaguely she wondered if any of her uncle's money would come to her. But she dismissed the idea as too good to be true. Perhaps with luck there might be enough to keep her until she could train for some post, but even about this she could not be certain. However, Mr Oxley was kind and clever. She need not worry overmuch. He would advise her.

While making up her mind to rise and face what the day might bring forth, Ruth was greatly comforted by a visit from Mrs Oxley. That lady presently knocked to inquire if her charge were awake, and she was so kind and understanding and kissed her in such a motherly way that Ruth felt a glow of warmth in her heart. Mrs Oxley brought with her a tiny tray with the daintiest little tea service and the thinnest of bread and butter, and while Ruth enjoyed this unheard of luxury the elder woman sat on the bed and proceeded to feed the girl's mind with healing news. She mentioned, casually and yet with such a wealth of detail, that Mr Whymper had called on the previous evening to inquire for Miss Averill. With really praiseworthy ingenuity she spun out the subject for nearly ten minutes, then she went on to tell something of almost—though of course not quite—equal importance. Mr Oxley had wished her to say, in the strictest confidence—no one at this stage was supposed to know anything about it—but in order to relieve Ruth's mind, he thought he might tell her—that she was not to worry as to her future. He had drawn up old Mr Averill's will and there would be some money. Mr Oxley had not said how much, but Mrs Oxley was sure there would be enough. At all events Ruth was not to worry. And now, breakfast would be ready in half an hour and there was plenty of hot water in the bathroom.

During the morning Ruth went down into the little town

and engaged in the melancholy business of buying mourning. Mr Oxley had lent her twenty pounds, explaining that she could repay him when she got her own money. This prospect of money coming to her made Ruth feel excited and important, and she could not refrain from day-dreaming about all the wonderful things she would do when she received it. It was well for her indeed that she had something so absorbing to take her mind off the ghastliness of the tragedy which surrounded her. In fact, if only Pierce Whymper had come to see her again, she would have been really happy. But, as she afterwards learned, the young architect was out of town on business all that morning.

During Sergeant Kent's call on the evening after the tragedy he had warned Ruth that she would be required to give evidence at the inquest. Now he came round to say that this was to be held in the courthouse at three o'clock that afternoon, and that she must be sure to be there in good time. The girl was naturally nervous at the prospect of giving evidence, which she had always heard was a terrible ordeal. But Mrs Oxley reassured her in her kindly way, explaining that she had nothing to do but answer the questions she was asked, and promising that Mr Oxley would see that nothing untoward befell her.

Shortly before the hour, therefore, the little party approached the courthouse. The building was already crowded, but Mr Oxley's position as the leading solicitor of the town and Ruth's as one of the most important witnesses procured them an immediate entrance and places on the seats usually reserved for counsel. As Ruth looked round the small old-fashioned building she saw many familiar faces. There, surrounded by policemen and looking weighed down with importance and responsibility, was Sergeant Kent. He was moving restlessly about, whispering to various persons and consulting at times a sheaf of papers he held in his hand. Some of the policemen she recognised also. There was the young smiling one with the light blue eyes whom she had met so many times when shopping in the town, and his companion with the long drooping nose and the hollow cheeks. In the seat behind was Mr Snelgrove, the butcher, and Mr Pullar, of the shoe shop. That tall very thin man with the little moustache and the bald head was Mr Tarkington, the bank manager, and the slight, medium-sized man beside him was Mr Bloxham, the clerk whom he used to send out to Starvel with Mr Averill's money. The venerable-looking old gentleman with the short white beard who was just pushing to the front was Dr Emerson. And there—how could she have failed to see him before?— there, at the back of the court, was Pierce Whymper. He looked anxious and troubled, and though when she caught his eye and smiled, he smiled back, there was a something of embarrassment or reserve in his manner that seemed to her strange and disquieting. And just beside him—but a sudden shuffle took place about her, and looking in front of her, she saw that a stout thick-set man with a square face and a walrus moustache had entered from some invisible side door and was taking his seat in the judge's chair.

'Dr Londsale, the coroner,' Mrs Oxley whispered, and Ruth nodded. She was surprised to find that the affair began so tamely. She had expected an elaborate and picturesque ritual, but nothing of the kind took place. The coroner opened his bag, and taking out some papers, began to turn them over. Other persons sitting round the table before her also took out papers and shuffled them, while Sergeant Kent, turning round, shouted out 'Robert Judd!' so suddenly and loudly that Ruth jumped. Someone at the back of the court answered

'Here!' and was promptly ordered to come forward and enter the jury box. Other names were called—to some of which there was no reply—until all the places in the box were occupied. Then all stood up and stared vacantly at Kent while he murmured something about 'justly try and true deliverance make,' after which everyone sat down again.

'Have the jury viewed the remains?' asked the coroner, and Kent, answering, 'They're going to do it now, sir,' shepherded his charges out of the box and away through a door just behind it. Everyone began conversing in low tones except the coroner, who kept on steadily writing. Presently the jury trooped in again and the proceedings began in real earnest.

'Call Peter Spence!' Sergeant Kent shouted.

'Peter Spence!' repeated two or three policemen, and a stout redfaced man pushed to the front, and entering the witness box, was sworn.

Spence told his story in great detail. In answer to the sergeant's questions he explained that he drove a breadcart belonging to Messrs Hinkston of Thirsby, and that for over twelve years he had, three times a week, delivered bread at Starvel. He remembered the day before yesterday. On that day, about eleven in the morning when he was approaching Starvel to deliver bread, he had observed a cloud of smoke in the sky. On crossing the lip of the Hollow he happened to look down at the house. He was amazed to notice that the roof, which formerly showed up above the surrounding trees, had totally disappeared. He drove on quickly to the place, and then he saw that the house had been burnt down. Only the walls were standing. There was no one about. He hurried into Thirsby, and reported the matter to Sergeant Kent.

Simple as these facts were, their recital was a lengthy

business. After each question a pause ensued while the coroner wrote a précis of the man's reply. Finally Dr Lonsdale, after vainly inviting the jury to ask the witness any questions, read over what he had written. Peter Spence, having agreed that it was a correct transcript of his evidence, was asked to sign the document, and then allowed to step down.

The next witness was a lugubrious looking man in grey tweeds. He deposed that his name was Abel Hesketh, and that he was Town Officer of Thirsby. He also acted as chief of the fire brigade. On the Thursday in question he received a telephone message from Sergeant Kent, informing him that Starvel had been burnt down. He inquired if he should get the brigade out, but the sergeant answered that it would be of no use, the damage being already done. Sergeant Kent asked him to go with him to see the place. He did so, and he would describe what he saw. The entire buildings at Starvel were gutted except a detached outhouse at the opposite side of the yard. He had never seen such complete destruction. Nothing that could be burnt was left. Between the walls the débris was still a red-hot glowing mass. In answer to the coroner, he thought it quite impossible to say either where or how the fire had originated. There was no wind that night, and the outbreak, once started, would creep through the entire building.

Hesketh went on to say that the very heavy rain which fell on the following night had cooled down the red-hot interior, enabling his men to search the ruins. They had come on the charred remains of three human beings. Yes, he could say just where the remains were found. The house was in the shape of the inverted letter 'ר' with the shorter wing pointing to the west and the longer to the south. At the extremity of the shorter wing—in the north-western corner—were two bodies. The third body was about ten feet from the end of the southern wing. All the bodies were unrecognisable, but he assumed they were those of the three inmates of the house.

After the bodies had been removed he continued his investigations, but he found nothing of interest except a safe, which was in the southern wing, not far from the single body. It was locked, and he had set it up on a pile of débris so that the expert that he understood Sergeant Kent was getting to open it should be able more conveniently to carry out the work.

Sergeant Kent corroborated the evidence of the last two witnesses in so far as their testimony concerned himself, and added that an expert from Hellifield had that morning opened the safe. In it he had found £1952 in sovereigns and a mass of burnt papers.

'It seems to me an extraordinary thing,' the coroner remarked when he had noted these details, 'that a fire of such magnitude could take place without being seen. I quite understand that the Hollow is deep enough to hide the actual flames, but there must have been a tremendous glare reflected from the sky which would have been visible for miles round. How do you account for that, Sergeant, or can you account for it?'

'As a matter of fact, sir, it was noticed by at least three people, and I have one of them here in case you would like to call him. But I agree with you, sir, that it is very strange that it was not more generally observed. All I can suggest is that it was a clear night with a quarter moon, and there wouldn't, therefore, be such a glare as if it had been quite dark or if there had been clouds to reflect the glow. Then, as you know, sir, this is a quiet district, and it would be only by chance that anyone would be awake or looking out at the time.'

'Who were the three who saw it?'

'First, sir, there was James Stokes, a tramp. He was sleeping in one of Mr Herbert Reid's outhouses at Low Tolworth, about a mile and a half to the west across the moor. He said nothing about it at the time because he thought it wasn't his business and he didn't want his whereabouts inquired into. But he mentioned it in Thirsby in the morning and it came to my ears, though not before the baker had reported. I have Stokes here, if you wish to call him. Then, sir, it was seen by Mrs Eliza Steele, a labourer's wife living just outside the town on the Hellifield Road. Her husband was ill and she was sitting up attending to him. She did nothing about it because she was busy with her husband and the glare looked far away. She said she thought those nearer it would do all that was possible. The third party, or rather parties, were the two Miss Lockes, elderly ladies who live alone about a mile on the road to Cold Pickerby. Miss Julia saw the glare and awoke her sister Miss Elmina, but they thought the same as Mrs Steele, that they were not called on to do anything, as they would only get to the town to find that everyone knew about it and that the brigade had gone out.'

'I can understand that attitude,' the coroner admitted. 'It is a pity, however, that no one noticed it in time to give a warning, though indeed it is doubtful whether a warning would have been of any use. I will hear the man Stokes.'

But the tramp had little to say, and nothing which threw any light on the subject of the inquiry. He had seen a glow through the door of the outhouse and had looked out. From the direction of Starvel great masses of smoke were belching up, with a bright flickering glare and occasional jets of fire.

23

The night was calm, and even at the distance of a mile and a half he could hear the roaring and crackling of the flames. That was about four in the morning.

Ruth's feelings were harrowed by these recitals, which seemed to bring home the tragedy to her in all its grim starkness. But she had not time to dwell on the terrible pictures, as after the tramp had signed his deposition and stepped down from the box, her own name was called.

With her heart beating rapidly she left her seat and entered the little pulpit-like enclosure. There she stood while the sergeant repeated a phrase about truth, and then, having given her name, she was told to sit down. The coroner bent towards her.

'I am sorry, Miss Averill,' he said kindly, 'to have to ask you to attend and give evidence in this tragic inquiry, but I promise you I shall not keep you longer than I can help. Now, Sergeant.'

In spite of this reassuring beginning, Ruth soon began to think Sergeant Kent's questions would never cease.

Half the things he asked seemed to have no connection whatever with the tragedy. She stated that she was the late Simon Averill's niece, the daughter of his brother Theodore, that she was aged twenty, and that she had come to Starvel when she was four. She told of her schooldays in Leeds, saying that it was now over a year since she had returned to Starvel and that she had lived there ever since.

Her uncle had recently been in very poor health. She thought his heart was affected. At all events, to save climbing the stairs he had had a room on the first floor fitted up as a bed-sitting room. For the last year he had not been downstairs and some days he did not get up. Recently he had been particularly feeble, and she told of his condition when she saw him two mornings before the tragedy. Then she described her visit to York, mentioning Mrs Palmer-Gore's invitation and the episode of the ten pounds.

There seemed no end to Sergeant Kent's inquisition. He switched over next to the subject of the house and elicited the facts that her uncle's and the Ropers' beds were situated in the extremities of the southern and western wings respectively.

'You heard the last witness describe where the bodies were found,' he went on. 'Would I be correct in saying that if Mr Averill and the Ropers had been in bed when the fire took place their bodies would have been found in just those positions?'

Ruth assented, and then the sergeant asked how the house was lighted. There was oil, Ruth told him, oil for the lamps other than Mr Averill's and for the cooker which was used sometimes instead of the range. There was also petrol. Her uncle's sight was bad and he used a petrol lamp. The oil and petrol were kept in a cellar. This cellar was under the main building, and if a fire were to start there, in her opinion the whole house would become involved. The lamps were attended to by Roper, who had always been most careful in handling them.

'Now Miss Averill,' the sergeant became more impressive than ever, 'I think you said that during the last fourteen months, when you were living at Starvel, Roper and his wife were in charge of the house?'

'Yes, they were there when I came back from school.'

'Now, tell me, during all that time have you ever known either of them the worse for drink?'

'Oh, no,' Ruth answered, surprised at the question. 'No, never.'

'You have never even noticed the smell of drink from either of them?' the sergeant persisted.

'No.' Ruth hesitated. 'At least—that is—'

'Yes?' went on the sergeant encouragingly.

'Once or twice Roper has smelt of whisky, but he was never the least bit the worse of it.'

'But you have smelt it. Was that recently?'

'Yes, but Roper explained about it. He said he felt a cold coming on and had taken some whisky in the hope of getting rid of it.'

'Quite so. And how long ago was that?'

'A couple of times within the last fortnight, perhaps once or twice before that.' But to Ruth her answer did not seem quite fair, and she added: 'But he was as sober as you and I are. I never saw him the least bit drunk.'

'I follow you,' the sergeant answered, and began to ask questions about Mrs Roper. Here Ruth could truthfully say that she had never even smelled drink, and she insisted on giving each of the deceased an excellent character.

The sergeant next attempted to draw from her an opinion as to how the fire might have originated. Did Mr Averill read late in bed? Might he have knocked over his petrol lamp? Could he have fallen in the fire? Did he take a nightcap of whisky? And so forth. But Ruth had no ideas on the subject. Any accident might have happened, of course, but she didn't think any that he had suggested were likely. As to her uncle taking drink, he was a strict teetotaller.

This ended Ruth's examination. None of the jurors wished to ask her any questions, and after her evidence had been read over to her and she had signed it, she was allowed to return to her seat with the Oxleys.

Dr Emerson was the next witness. He deposed that he had

26

examined the remains disinterred from the debris. It was, of course, quite impossible to identify them, but so far as he could form an opinion of the body found in the southern wing it was that of an elderly, tall, slightly built man and the others were those of a man and a woman of medium height and middle age. These would correspond to Mr Averill and the Ropers respectively, and so far as he was concerned he had no doubt whatever that the bodies in question were theirs.

Questioned as to the conditions obtaining at Starvel before the fire, Dr Emerson said that for the last four years he had not attended Mr Averill. At his advancing age he found it too much to visit outlying patients, and Dr Philpot had taken over almost all of them.

'Is Dr Philpot here?' the coroner asked.

'Dr Philpot is suffering from influenza at present,' Dr Emerson returned, though it was to Sergeant Kent that the question had been addressed. 'I saw him this morning. He wished to attend, but I persuaded him not to run the risk. It would have been most unwise. He had a temperature of over 101.'

'I'm sorry to hear he is laid up. But I don't suppose he could have helped us. I should have liked to ask him about Mr Averill's condition and so forth, but it doesn't really matter.'

'Well,' Dr Emerson returned, 'I can tell you a little about that, if I should be in order in mentioning it. I attended him for some eight years, during the last two of which he aged very considerably, growing slowly and steadily weaker. Without going into details I may say that he had an incurable complaint which must eventually have killed him. Four years ago he was already feeble, and since then he can only have become gradually worse.'

'Thank you, Dr Emerson, that was what I wanted to know. Would you say that his condition rendered him liable to sudden weakness during which he might have dropped his lamp or had some similar accident?'

'I should say so decidedly.'

A Miss Judith Carr was next called. She proved to be a rather loudly-dressed young woman whom Ruth had not seen before. She was pretty in a coarse way, and entered the witness-box and took her seat with evident self-confidence.

Her name, she admitted heartily, was Judith Carr, and she was barmaid at the Thirsdale Arms, the largest hotel in Thirsby. She knew Mr Roper, the attendant at Starvel. He occasionally called for a drink, usually taking one or at most two small whiskies. She remembered the evening of the fire. That evening about seven o'clock Mr Roper had come into the bar. He seemed to have had some drink, but was not drunk. He asked for a small Scotch, and believing he was sober enough she had given it to him. He had taken it quickly and gone out.

The last witness was a young man with bright red hair who answered to the name of George Mellowes. He was, he said, a farmer living at Ivybridge, a hamlet lying some miles beyond Starvel. On the day before the tragedy he had been over in Thirsby on business, and he had left the town in his gig shortly after seven to drive home. He had not passed beyond the lights of the town when he had overtaken Mr Roper, whom he knew. Roper was staggering, and it was not difficult to see that he was drunk. The deceased was by no means incapable, but he had undoubtedly taken too much. Mellowes had stopped and offered him a lift, and Roper had thanked him and with some difficulty had climbed into the gig. He had talked in a maudlin way during the drive.

Mellowes had gone a little out of his way and had set the other down at the gate of Starvel. Roper had opened the gate without difficulty, and had set off towards the house, walking fairly straight. Mellowes had then driven home. That was close on to eight, and there was no sign then of a fire.

When Mellowes had signed his deposition and returned to his seat, the coroner made a little speech to the jury. He said that everyone must feel appalled at the terrible tragedy which had happened so near to them all. The police had been unable to find relatives of any of the deceased other than Miss Averill, who had given evidence that day, and he took that opportunity of conveying to her their respectful sympathy in her loss. He would remind the jury that their duty on this occasion was threefold: first, to state the identity of the deceased if they were reasonably convinced by the evidence on this point; second, to find the cause of death in each case, and third, to state whether, in their opinion, blame attached to any person or persons, and if so, to whom. He did not think their task would be difficult. On neither of the first two points was there any doubt. He had only one observation to make with regard to the third point—the fixing of responsibility for the catastrophe. It had been shown that the manservant, John Roper, had been to some extent under the influence of drink on the evening in question. The suggestion, of course, was that some careless act of Roper's might have caused the fire. Now, while he approved the action of the police in bringing out this matter—they could not have done anything else—he must point out to the jury that there was no evidence that Mr Roper's condition had had anything to do with the fire. If anything, the evidence tended in the opposite direction. The position of the remains suggested that the three unfortunate people had been burnt in their beds, and if this was so it seemed to involve the presumption that they had been suffocated by the smoke while asleep. If the jury accepted this view they would see that it ruled out the possibility of any accident with lamps, or by falling in the fire or by igniting petrol or paraffin oil. The argument was, of course, not conclusive, but he thought it tended as he had said. In any case he should be sorry that a slur should be cast on the memory of Mr Roper, to whose zeal and efficiency different witnesses had testified, unless that slur were really deserved. It was, of course, for the jury to decide, but he suggested that they might find that Simon Ralph Averill, John Roper and Flora Roper had lost their lives in a fire at Starvel on the night of the fifteenth of September, the cause of which there was no evidence to show.

Without leaving the box the jury found as the coroner directed, the verdict was entered on the records and signed, and the inquest was over.

3

Mr Tarkington Develops a Theory

As Ruth emerged from the comparative gloom of the courthouse into the bright September sunshine her spirits seemed to rise. A reaction had set in from the strain of the inquiry, with its continuous suggestion of the hideous details of the tragedy. Now with the ending of the inquest it seemed to her that the terrible affair was all but over. The final episode, the funerals, would not be anything like so harrowing. Not since the first hint of disaster had come in the shape of Mr Oxley's telegram to York had she felt so lighthearted and in love with life. She seemed to have awakened from an evil dream.

It was therefore no indication of heartlessness that she should glance eagerly around as she and her friends advanced from the shadow of the old building into the little square. She was young and the claims of the living were more to her than those of the dead. And who will reproach her for the thrill of pleasurable excitement which she experienced as the sight she was hoping for met her eyes? There was Pierce Whymper evidently waiting for a chance of speaking to her. With a smile she invited him over, and he came and joined her. At the same moment Mr Tarkington, the thin hawk-like bank · manager, whom she had seen in the courthouse, approached and spoke to Mr Oxley.

'Will you go on?' the latter said to his wife. 'I want to go round to the bank with Mr Tarkington. I'll follow in a few minutes.'

Mrs Oxley, Ruth and Whymper moved off in one direction, while Mr Oxley and Mr Tarkington disappeared in the other. For a time the trio chatted with animation, then Ruth grew gradually more silent, leaving the burden of the conversation to the others. She was in fact puzzled and a little hurt by a subtle change which she felt rather than noticed in Whymper's manner. He seemed somehow different from the last time she had seen him—that time in another existence when she had left Thirsby for her visit to York. Then he had been obviously eager for her company, anxious to talk to her, even before Mrs Oxley making no secret of his admiration and regard. But now, though he was just as polite as ever, his manner was less spontaneous, indeed at times she thought it almost embarrassed. It occurred to her that possibly the change might be in herself, and even when their ways parted at the turn to the church she had not completely made up her mind. But whatever the cause, a certain disappointment remained, and when she went up to change for dinner she had lost a good deal of the lightheartedness she had felt on emerging from the courthouse.

Mr Oxley, when he arrived shortly after, also showed a change of manner. He was a kindly, jovial man, fond of a joke and the sound of his own voice, but during dinner he was strangely silent and wore an expression of concern and disappointment. But he did not offer any explanation until the meal was over, and then he followed the ladies into the drawing-room and unburdened his mind.

'I am awfully sorry, Miss Ruth,' he began hesitatingly, 'but I am afraid I have brought you some more bad news. It's about money,' he added hurriedly as the girl turned a piteous glance towards him. 'I'll tell you exactly what has happened. You know, or perhaps you don't, that in spite of the way he lived, your uncle was a rich man. As his solicitor I have known that for many a year, but I had no idea of just how much he had. Tarkington knows I was his solicitor and he was talking about it just now. He tells me that Mr Averill must have been worth between thirty and forty thousand pounds when he died. Of course one would naturally suppose that the money was in securities of some kind, but here is my terrible news. Tarkington assures me that it was not, that practically the whole sum was in Mr Averill's safe.'

'Oh, Arthur!' Mrs Oxley burst out. 'You can't mean that it's gone.'

'I'm afraid I do,' her husband answered. 'It's awful to think about, but there were only some five hundred pounds in the bank. The rest was in Mr Averill's safe in notes and gold. The nineteen hundred odd pounds in gold are there all right, but the whole of the paper money has been destroyed.'

'Oh, how perfectly dreadful! But surely it can be replaced? Surely something can be done by the bank?'

Mr Oxley shook his head.

'Nothing, I'm afraid. I talked it over with Tarkington. The money is a total loss.'

Mrs Oxley took Ruth into her arms.

'You poor child,' she commiserated. 'I just can't tell you how sorry I am.'

But Ruth took the news coolly.

'Dear Mrs Oxley,' she answered. 'How kind you are! But indeed I look upon this as a comparatively little thing. I shall have far, far more than I ever expected. I want to get some work, and I shall have plenty to support me while I am training and perhaps even a little after that. I am more than content.'

Mrs Oxley kissed her and commended her spirit, though she felt the girl's attitude was due more to her unworldliness and ignorance of life than to courage under disappointment. She wished to change the subject, but Ruth asked to have her position made clear to her and begged the others' advice as to her future. The Oxleys, delighted by her common sense, willingly agreed to discuss the situation, and after a long talk a proposal of Mr Oxley's was provisionally agreed to.

It appeared that, assuming the old man's money had really been lost, Ruth's capital would amount to about £2400. Of this Mr Oxley was to invest all but £100, so as to bring Ruth about £130 per annum. The remaining £100 was to be spent in taking a secretarial course at one of the London training colleges. With the backing of the £130 a year and what she could earn for herself she ought, Mr Oxley believed, to be quite comfortably off. 'But you must,' Mr Oxley went on, 'stay here for as long as you like, until you have rested and got over the shock of this terrible affair.'

Mrs Oxley warmly seconded this invitation, and Ruth thankfully accepted it. It was true that she was anxious to start work as soon as possible, and life in London and the undergoing of the course of training appeared to her as a glorious and thrilling adventure. But even more anxious still was she to meet Pierce Whymper and find out if there really was a change in his feelings towards her. At the time she had imagined that there was, but now she thought that perhaps she had been mistaken and that after the inquest he had simply been suffering from a headache or some other trifling indisposition. That he loved her she had not the slightest doubt, and she could not bring herself to go away until she was sure that no stupid, unnecessary misunderstanding should have been allowed to come between them.

Two days later she met him in the main street of the little town. She stopped to chat and he turned about and walked with her, and presently they had tea at the local confectioner's. But the interview left her more puzzled than ever. Her belief that Whymper loved her was confirmed beyond any doubt by his manner, by the way he looked at her, by the tones of his voice. But it was evident to her that something was weighing on his mind which prevented him making the proposal which, if the truth must be admitted, she had been expecting. He gave her the impression that he would speak if he could, but that he was being held back by matters outside his own control. And the same state of mind was evident at their subsequent encounters, until Ruth's pride asserted itself and she grew colder and more distant and their intimacy bade fair to come gradually to an end.

She would have made a move for the metropolis to begin her course of training had not Mrs Oxley, from what was probably a quite mistaken sense of kindliness, suggested that a rest would be good for her after the shocks she had experienced. On the excuse of desiring the girl's assistance in the remodelling of her garden, which, owing to the difficulty of obtaining labour, she was doing with her own hands, the good lady invited her to stay on for a few weeks. Ruth did not like to refuse, and she settled down with the intention of remaining at Thirsby for at least another month.

During the month the little town also settled down again after its excitements and alarms, and events once more began to pursue the even tenor of their ways. The Starvel Hollow

Tragedy ceased to be a nine days' wonder and was gradually banished from the minds of the townspeople, until an event happened which was to bring up the whole matter again, and that in a peculiarly sensational and tragic manner.

One morning in mid-October, some five weeks after the fire, Mr Tarkington called to see his friend Oxley. The bank manager's thin face wore a serious and mystified expression, which at once informed Mr Oxley that something out of the ordinary had occurred to disturb the other's usual placid calm.

'Good morning, Oxley,' said Mr Tarkington in his thin, measured tones. 'Are you busy? I should like a word with you.'

'Come along in, Tarkington,' the solicitor rejoined heartily. 'I'm not doing anything that can't wait. Sit you down and have a spot.'

'Thanks, no, I'll not drink, but I'll take one of these cigarettes if I may.' He drew the client's big leather covered chair nearer to Mr Oxley and went on: 'A really extraordinary thing has just happened, Oxley, and I thought I'd like to consult you about it before taking any action—if I do take action.'

Mr Oxley took a cigarette from the box from which the other had helped himself.

'What's up?' he asked, as he struck a match.

'It's about that terrible Starvel affair, the fire, you know. I begin to doubt if the matter is really over, after all.'

'Not over? What on earth do you mean?'

'I'll tell you, and it is really a most disturbing thought. But before you can appreciate my news I must explain to you how Averill carried on his bank business. The poor fellow was a miser, as you know, a miser of the most primitive kind.

He loved money for itself—just to handle and to look at and to count. His safe was just packed full of money. But of course you know all this, and that it was through this dreadful weakness of his that that poor girl lost what should have come to her.'

'I know,' Mr Oxley admitted.

'Averill's income passed through the bank, and that's how I come to be aware of the figures. He had between sixteen and seventeen hundred a year and it came from three sources. First he had a pension; he had held a good job with some company in London. That amounted to about three hundred pounds. Next he had an annuity which brought him in £150. But the major portion came from land—land on the outskirts of Leeds which had been built over and which had become a very valuable property. In this he had only a life interest— not that that affects my story, though it explains why that poor girl didn't get it.'

'I know about that property,' Mr Oxley interjected. 'I've had a deal to do with it one way and another. The old man got it through his wife and it went back to her family at his death.'

'I imagined it must be something of the kind. Well, to continue. Averill's income, as I said, was passed through the bank. He received it all in cheques or drafts and these he would endorse and send to me for payment. He had a current account, and my instructions were that when any cheque came I was to pay in to this account until it stood at some-thing between £40 and £60—whatever would leave an even £20 over—and I was to send the surplus cash in £20 notes out to Starvel. Averill evidently looked upon this as a sort of revenue account and paid all his current expenses out of it. It never of course rose above the £60 and seldom fell below £20. To carry on my simile, any monies that were over after raising the current account to £60 he considered capital, and they went out to swell the hoard in the safe at Starvel. In addition he kept a sum of £500 on deposit receipt. I don't know exactly why he did so, but I presume it was as a sort of nest-egg in the event of his safe being burgled. You follow me?'

'I follow you all right, but, by Jove! it was a queer arrangement.'

'Everything the poor old man did was queer, but, as you know, he was—' Mr Tarkington shook his head significantly. 'However, to go on with my story. These monies that were to be sent out to Starvel I used to keep until they reached at least a hundred, and then I used to send a clerk out with the cash. The mission usually fell to Bloxham—you know Bloxham, of course? Averill liked him and asked me to send him when I could. Bloxham has seen into the safe on two or three occasions, and it is from him I know that it was packed with notes as well as the gold.'

'I never can get over all that money being burnt,' Mr Oxley interjected. 'It makes me sick to think of even now. Such stupid, needless, wicked waste!'

Mr Tarkington took no notice of this outburst.

'It happened that about a week before the tragedy, he went on in his precise manner, 'a cheque for £346 came in from the Leeds property. The current account was then standing at £27, so I paid £26 into it, raising it to £53, and sent Bloxham with the balance, £320, out to Starvel. The money was in sixteen twenties, the numbers of which were kept. As I said, it was one of the old man's peculiarities that he liked his money in £20 notes. I suppose it made it easier to hoard and count. Bloxham saw Averill lock these notes away in his safe and brought me the old man's receipt.'

Mr Tarkington paused to draw at his cigarette, then continued:

'In my report about the affair to our headquarters in Throgmorton Avenue, I mentioned among other things that these notes, giving the numbers, had been destroyed in the fire. Well, Oxley, what do you think has happened? I heard from headquarters today and they tell me that one of those notes has just been paid in!'

Mr Oxley looked slightly bewildered.

'Well, what of it?' he demanded. 'I don't follow. You reported that these notes had been destroyed in the fire. But wasn't that only a guess? How did you actually know?'

'It was a guess, of course, and I didn't actually know,' Mr Tarkington agreed. 'But I think it was a justifiable guess. I am acquainted with Averill's habits; he made no secret of them. Monies he paid out he paid by cheque on the current account—everything that one can think of went through it, even the Ropers' salaries. The cash sent out to Starvel went into the hoard.'

'All of it didn't.'

'Why, what do you mean?'

'The ten pounds to Ruth Averill didn't.'

Mr Tarkington seemed slightly taken aback.

'Well, that's true,' he admitted slowly. 'I forgot about the ten pounds. I—'

'And there's another twenty that didn't,' Mr Oxley continued, 'and that's the twenty that turned up in London. I don't get your idea, Tarkington. Just what is in your mind?'

Mr Tarkington moved uneasily in the big arm-chair.

'It seems far-fetched, I know, and I hardly like putting it into words, but are you satisfied in your own mind that business was all just as it appeared to be?'

39

'What? The fire? How do you mean "as it appeared to be"?'

'That it really was the accident we thought it.'

Mr Oxley whistled.

'Oh, come now, Tarkington, that's going a bit far, isn't it? Do you mean arson? What possible grounds could you have for suggesting such a thing?'

'I don't exactly suggest it; I came to ask your opinion about it. But what passed through my mind was this: There have been several burglaries lately—skilful burglaries, and, as you know, the police have been completely at fault. Averill was universally believed to be wealthy—the legend of the safe was common property. Is it impossible that some of these burglars might have decided to make an attempt on Starvel? Remember the situation was one of the loneliest in England. Assume that they got in and that something unexpected happened—that they were surprised by Roper, for example. In the resulting disturbance Roper might easily have been killed—possibly quite accidentally. The intruders would then be fighting for their lives as well as their fortunes. And in what better way could they do it than to murder the other members of the household; lay them on their beds and burn the house down?'

Mr Oxley did not reply. The idea was chimerical, fantastic, absurd, and yet—it was certainly possible. There *had* been a number of daring burglaries within the last few months, which were generally believed to be the work of one gang, and in no single instance had the police been able to effect an arrest. The belief in the old miser's hoard *was* universal, and from the point of view of the thief, Starvel would be one of the easiest cribs to crack. Moreover, on second thoughts Tarkington's suggestion as to the origin of the fire was not so fanciful, after all. The safe containing the money was in Averill's bedroom, and the old man would have to be quieted in some way before it could be opened. Roper's attention might easily have been attracted, and the burglars, either by accident or in self-defence, might have killed him. If so, the fire would be their obvious way of safety. Yes, the thing was possible. All the same there wasn't a shred of evidence that it had happened.

'But, my dear fellow,' Oxley said at last, 'that's all my eye! Very ingenious and all that, but you haven't a scrap of evidence for it. Why invent a complicated, far-fetched explanation when you have a simple one ready to hand? Sounds as if you had been reading too many detective stories lately.'

Tarkington did not smile with his friend.

'You think it nonsense?' he asked earnestly. 'You think I needn't tell the police about the note?'

'I don't think you have any evidence: not evidence to justify even a suspicion. You've no real reason to suppose Averill did not hand that twenty-pound note to someone from whom it passed to the man who paid it in.'

'To whom, for example?'

'I don't know. Neither of us knows what visitors the old man might have had. But that doesn't prove he had none.'

Mr Tarkington seemed far from satisfied. He threw away his cigarette and took another from the box, handling it delicately in his long, thin fingers. He moved nervously in his chair and then said in a low voice:

'I suppose then, Oxley, I may take it that you were quite satisfied about that business—I mean at the time?'

Mr Oxley looked at his friend in surprise.

'Good gracious, Tarkington, what bee have you got in your bonnet? Do you mean satisfied that the fire was an accident and that those three poor people were burned? Of course I was. It never occurred to me to doubt it.'

The other seemed slightly relieved.

'I hope sincerely that you're right,' he answered. 'But I may tell you that I wasn't satisfied—neither at the time nor yet since. That's the reason that when I heard about the note I came at once to consult you. There's a point which you and the coroner and the police and everyone concerned seem to have overlooked,' he dropped his voice still further and became very impressive. 'What about the papers that were burnt in the safe?'

Mr Oxley was surprised at his friend's persistence.

'Well, what in Heaven's name about them? For the life of me I don't see what you're driving at.'

'Haven't you ever been in Averill's bedroom?'

'Yes. What of it?'

'Did you notice the safe?'

'Not particularly.'

'Well, I've both been there and noticed it,' He bent forward, and his thin face seemed more hawk-like than ever as he said impressively: 'Oxley, that safe was fireproof!'

Mr Oxley started.

'Good Heavens, Tarkington! Are you sure of that?' he queried sharply.

'Not absolutely,' the other replied. 'It was certainly my strong opinion and if I had been asked before the fire I should have had no doubt. When I heard the evidence at the inquest I concluded I had made a mistake. But now this affair of the twenty-pound note has reawakened all my suspicions.' He paused, but as Oxley did not reply, continued: 'Perhaps I've got a bee in my bonnet as you said, but I'm now wondering if Roper's drunkenness doesn't support the theory? Could he not have been enticed into Thirsby by some member of the gang and treated so as to make him sleep well and not hear what was going on? Remember, he was an absolutely temperate man.'

'Not absolutely. Ruth had smelt drink on other occasions.'

'You are right. Perhaps that is a trifle far-fetched. But what do you think on the main point, Oxley? Ought I to tell the police of my suspicions?'

Mr Oxley rose and began to pace the room. Then he went to the window and stood for some moments looking out. Finally he returned to his chair, and sat down again.

'I declare, Tarkington, I think you ought,' he said slowly. 'When you first made your—I might perhaps say—your amazing suggestion I confess I thought it merely grotesque. But if you are right about the safe it certainly puts a different complexion on the whole business. I take it it's not too late to ascertain? The safe is not too much damaged to trace the maker and find out from him?'

'I should think the police could find the maker quite easily.'

'Well, I think you should tell them. If you are wrong no harm is done. If not, there are murderers to be brought to justice and perhaps a fortune to be recovered for Ruth.'

Mr Tarkington rose.

'I agree with you, Oxley. I'll go down to the police station and tell Kent now.'

Mr Oxley waved him back into his seat.

'Steady a moment,' he said. 'Don't be in such a hurry.' He drew slowly at his cigarette while the other sat down and waited expectantly.

'It seems to me,' went on Mr Oxley, 'that if your suspicions are correct the thing should be kept absolutely quiet. Nothing should be said or done to put the criminals on their guard.

Now Kent, you know as well as I do, is just a bungling ass. My suggestion is that we both take the afternoon off and go see Valentine. I know him pretty well and we could ring him up and make an appointment.'

'Valentine, the chief constable of the County?'

'Yes. He's as cute as they're made and he'll do the right thing.'

'Kent will never forgive us if we pass him over like that.'

'Kent be hanged,' Mr Oxley rejoined. 'Can you come in by the three-thirty?'

'Yes, I'll manage it.'

'Right. Then I shall ring up Valentine.'

Five hours later the two friends found their way into the strangers' room of the Junior Services Club in Leeds. There in a few moments Chief Constable Valentine joined them, and soon they were settled in a private room with whisky and sodas at their elbows and three of the excellent cigars the chief constable favoured between their lips.

Mr Tarkington propounded his theory in detail, explaining that he was not sure enough of his facts even to put forward a definite suspicion, but that he and his friend Oxley agreed that Major Valentine ought to know what was in his mind. The major could then, if he thought fit, investigate the affair.

That the chief constable was impressed by the statement was obvious. He listened with the keenest interest, interjecting only an occasional 'By Jove!' as Mr Tarkington made his points. Then he thanked the two men for their information, and promised to institute inquiries into the whole matter without delay.

Two days later Mr Tarkington received a letter from Major Valentine saying that he thought it only fair to inform him in the strictest confidence that his belief that the safe was fireproof was well founded, that he, the chief constable, strongly suspected that more had taken place at Starvel on that tragic night than had come out in the inquest, and that as he considered the matter was rather outside the local men's capacity he had applied to Scotland Yard for help in the investigation.

Mr Tarkington, honouring the spirit rather than the letter of the chief constable's communication, showed the note to Mr Oxley, and the two men sat over the former's study fire until late that night, discussing possible developments in the situation.

4

Inspector French Goes North

The stone which Messrs Tarkington and Oxley had thrown into the turbid waters of the British Police Administration produced ripples which, like other similar wave forms, spread slowly away from their point of disturbance. One of these ripples, penetrating into the grim fastness of the Criminal Investigation Department of New Scotland Yard, had the effect of ringing the bell of a telephone on the desk of Detective Inspector Joseph French and of causing that zealous and efficient officer, when he had duly applied his ear to the instrument, to leave his seat and proceed without loss of time to the room of his immediate superior.

'Ah, French,' Chief Inspector Mitchell remarked on his entry. 'You should be about through with that Kensington case, I fancy?'

'Just finished with it, sir,' French answered. 'I was putting the last of the papers in order when you rang.'

'Well, you've had a lot of trouble with it and I should have liked to have given you a breather. But I'm afraid I can't.'

'Something come in, sir?'

'A Yorkshire case. A place called Thirsby, up on the moors not far, I understand, from Hellifield. We've just had a request for a man and I can't spare anyone else at present. So it's you for it.'

'What is the case, sir?'

'Suspected murder, robbery and arson. The people there appear to know very little about it and the whole thing may turn out a mare's nest. But they're darned mysterious about it—say they don't want it to be known that inquiries are being made and suggest our man might go to the Thirsdale Arms, the local hotel, in the guise of an angler or an artist. So, if you're a fisherman, French, now's your chance. You're to call down at the police station after dark, when Sergeant Kent, who's in charge, will give you the particulars.'

It was with mixed feelings that Inspector French received his instructions. He delighted in travelling and seeing new country, and the Yorkshire moors comprised a district which he had often heard spoken of enthusiastically, but had never visited. He was by no means averse, moreover, to getting away from town for a few days. It would be a welcome break in the monotony of the long winter. But on the other hand he loathed working away from headquarters, bereft of his trained staff and of the immediate backing of the huge machine of which he was a cog. Local men, he conceded, were 'right enough,' but they hadn't the knowledge, the experience, the technique to be really helpful. And then the 'Yard' man in the country was usually up against jealousies and a more or less veiled obstruction, and to the worries of his case he had to add the effort always to be tactful and to carry his professed helpers with him.

However, none of these considerations affected his course of action. He had his orders and he must carry them out.

He completed the filing of the papers in the Kensington murder case, handed over one or two other matters to his immediate subordinate, and taking the large despatch case of apparatus without which he never travelled, went home to inform his wife of his change of plans and pack a suitcase with his modest personal requirements. Then he drove to St Pancras and caught the 12.15 p.m. restaurant car express to the north.

He was neither an artist nor an angler, and in any case he considered the month of November was scarcely a propitious time for worthies of either type to be abroad. Therefore beyond dressing in a more countrified style than he would have effected in town, he attempted no disguise.

He changed at Hellifield and took the branch line which wound up in a north-easterly direction into the bleak hills and moors of western Yorkshire. Six o'clock had just struck when he reached the diminutive terminus of Thirsby.

A porter bearing the legend 'Thirsdale Arms' on his cap was at the station, and having surrendered his baggage, French followed the man on foot down the main street of the little town to a low, straggling, old-fashioned building with half-timbered gables and a real old swinging sign. Here a stout and cheery proprietor gave him a somewhat voluble welcome, and soon he was the temporary tenant of a low and dark, but otherwise comfortable bedroom, while an appetising odour of frying ham indicated that the *pièce de résistance* of his supper was in full preparation.

He smoked a contemplative pipe in the bar, then about half past eight took his hat, and passing the landlord at the door, gave him a cheerful goodnight and said he was going for a walk before bed.

While he did not intend to hide the fact of his visit to

Sergeant Kent, he had no wish to draw attention thereto. He believed that in a small town such things invariably get out, and to shroud them in an air of mystery was only to invite publicity. He therefore did not ask for a direction, but instead strolled through the streets until he saw the police station, walking quietly but openly to the door, he knocked. Two minutes later he was shaking hands with the sergeant in the latter's room.

'I'm sure I'm grateful to you for giving me the chance of a change from London,' French began in his pleasant, cheery way as he took the chair the other pulled forward to the fire. 'Will you join me in a cigar, or do you object to smoking in the office?'

The sergeant dourly helped himself from French's case, and gruffly admitted he was not above the use of tobacco after office hours. French seemed in no hurry to come to business, but chatted on about his journey and his impressions of the country, drawing the other out and deferring to his views in a way that was nothing less than flattering. Before ten minutes Kent had forgotten that his visitor was an interloper sent to him over his head because his superiors imagined that he was not good enough for his own job, and was thinking that this stranger, for a Londoner and a Yard man, was not as bad as he might reasonably have been expected to be. Under the soothing influences of flattery and good tobacco he gradually mellowed until, when French at last decided the time had come, he was quite willing to assist in any way in his power.

At French's request he gave him a detailed account of the tragedy together with a copy of the depositions taken at the inquest, and then went on to describe the bomb which Mr Tarkington had dropped when he mentioned his theories to Major Valentine.

'Chief Constable, he told me to find out what kind of safe it was in the house,' the sergeant went on. 'I knew, for I had seen it at the time, but I went out again to make sure. It was made by Carter & Stephenson of Leeds, number—' he referred to a well-thumbed notebook—'12,473. I went down to Leeds, and saw the makers, and they said the safe was twenty years old, but it was the best fireproof safe of its day. I asked them would the notes have burned up in it, and they said they wouldn't scarcely be browned, no matter how fierce the fire might be.'

'And what exactly was in the safe?'

'Just paper ashes and sovereigns. No whole papers; all was burned to ashes.'

'Could I see those ashes? Are any of them left?'

'I think so. We took out the sovereigns and left the rest. The safe is lying in the rubbish where we found it.'

French nodded, and for some minutes sat silent, drawing slowly at his cigar while he turned over in his mind the details he had learned. As he did so the words of Chief Inspector Mitchell recurred to him: 'The people down there don't appear to know much about it, and the whole thing may turn out to be a mare's nest.' Now, having heard the story, he wondered if this was not going to be another of his chief's amazing intuitions. It certainly looked as like a mare's nest as anything he had ever handled. The only shred of evidence for foul play was the safe builder's statement that their safe would protect papers even in the fiercest fire, and that statement left him cold. What else could the builders say? They had sold the thing as fireproof; how could they now admit they had made a false claim? And this Tarkington's theory of the twenty-pound note was even less convincing. There was no real reason to believe that Averill had not handed it to his servant or to a visitor or sent it away by post. In fact, the whole tale was the thinnest he had listened to for many a day, and he saw himself taking a return train to St Pancras before many hours had passed.

But he had been sent up to make an investigation, and make an investigation he would. He rapidly planned his line of action. The first thing to be done was to get rid of this sergeant. He might be right enough for his own job, but French felt that he would be no help in an affair of this kind. Left to himself, he would go out and examine the house and then interview Tarkington. By that time he should have learned enough at least to decide whether or not to go on with the case. He turned to Kent.

'Your statement, Sergeant, has been so very complete that I do not believe there is anything left for me to ask you. But I think I should understand the affair even better if I went and had a look at the house. I'll do that tomorrow. But, much as I should like your company, I cannot ask you to come with me. I entirely agree with and admire your wisdom in keeping the affair secret, and if we were seen together the cat would be out of the bag. I will give out that I am a representative from the insurance companies and I think no suspicion will be aroused. If now you will kindly tell me where the place lies, I think that's all we can do in the meantime.'

Five minutes later French turned from the main street into the door of the Thirsdale Arms. The landlord was standing in the hall and French stopped in a leisurely way, as if ready for a chat. They discussed the weather for some moments, and then French asked the other if he would join him in a drink.

It was not long before they were seated before a glowing fire in the private bar, when French proceeded to account for himself.

'I like your country,' he began, 'what I've seen of it. I've been a bit run down lately, and though it's not the time one would choose for a holiday, my doctor thought I should take a week or two's rest. So, as I had a bit of business here I thought I would kill two birds with one stone and do my business and take my holiday at the same time. And about that bit of business I thought that if you would be good enough you could maybe give me some help.'

The landlord, evidently curious, was anxious to do anything in his power, and French, following out his theory that where absolute truth is inadmissible, deviations therefrom should be as slight as possible, went on confidentially:

'It's about a place called Starvel where there was a big fire recently. You know all about it, of course.' The landlord nodded eagerly. 'Well, I may tell you strictly between ourselves that I am a detective. A fire unaccounted for is a very disturbing matter to insurance companies, and I have been sent down to try to find the cause of the outbreak. I've seen the police sergeant, and he has very kindly promised to show me his notes of the inquest, but I should like more general information than that. I wondered if you could, perhaps, tell me something about the affair; about the people who lived in Starvel, and so on?'

With this beginning, and the help of whiskies and sodas and two more of his cigars French was soon in possession of all the landlord knew and surmised about the Starvel Hollow tragedy. But he learned nothing helpful. The man's story agreed with that of Sergeant Kent, though it was obvious that the idea of foul play had never entered his mind.

One thing he remarked on which Kent had not mentioned—about which indeed, as French afterwards learned, Kent knew nothing—and that was the incipient affair between Ruth

Averill and Pierce Whymper. When French learned later on how slight this affair had been he was filled with amazement, as he had been so many times before, at the range and exhaustiveness of local gossip.

'Nice young fellow, Mr Pierce Whymper,' the landlord went on. 'He's a son of Mr Stephen Whymper, the Leeds surgeon, and a junior assistant of Nixon and Arbuthnot's, the church architects. He's here as clerk of works of the renovation of the church—a fine old church, this of ours! I got to know Mr Whymper a bit, for he stayed here for a few days when he came first, and before he got lodgings. Our terms are a bit high for him, you know, for a constancy. They don't overpay these young fellows that are just starting on their jobs.'

'It's a fact,' French admitted. 'And how is the affair with the young lady getting on?'

'No one rightly knows. It seemed to be going on thick enough before the fire and then, somehow, it seemed to be cooled off. I suppose one of these here lovers' quarrels,' and the landlord smiled tolerantly, as one man of the world to another.

But whether or not the landlord was a man of the world, there was no doubt whatever that he was a thoroughly accomplished and successful gossip. French soon found that by the mere interjection of an occasional phrase he could obtain a detailed description of the life, habits and character of any of the inhabitants of Thirsby that he cared to name. Very willingly, therefore, he suggested more whisky and proffered further cigars, while he sat registering in his memory the impressions of his neighbours which the other sketched with such evident relish.

He was a likeable old fellow, the landlord, or so French

thought. Though a gossip first and always, he was something of a philosopher and his outlook was human and kindly. The people he spoke of were real people, and French could picture them living in the little town and going about their businesses, with their loves and hates, their ambitions and their weaknesses. Old Mr Averill—well, the landlord hadn't a great opinion of him. He was dead, and one didn't ought to say too much about the dead, but there was no denying that he was mean—a regular miser, he was. The way he had treated that niece of his—as nice a young lady as ever stepped—was just a fair scandal. A young lady just grown up, like Miss Ruth was, should have a bit of pleasure sometimes, and the poor girl hadn't even decent clothes to wear. Mean, the landlord called it. And what use, he asked, growing oratorical, was the old man's money to him now? That was what he said—and he waved his cigar to give point to his remark—that was what he said: What had the old man got for all his screwing and saving? It would have paid him better . . .

French insinuated the idea of Roper.

Roper, the landlord did not know so much about, though he had to confess he had not particularly liked him. Roper had a squint, and if French took the landlord's advice, he would just keep his weather eye open when dealing with a man with a squint. Roper was quiet enough and civil spoken, and they said he was good enough at his job, but he was close—very close. Sly, the landlord would call it, though, mind you, he hadn't known anything wrong about the man. Mrs Roper? He had only met her once. He didn't know much about her, but she was well enough spoken of. Neither of them could have had much of a time out at Starvel, but they had served the old man well and made no complaint.

About Tarkington, the landlord waxed almost lyrical.

Tarkington was a white man, straight as a die and no fool neither. He was more than a bank manager. He was, so French gathered, a sort of financial father confessor to the neighbourhood. Everyone trusted Tarkington, and took their difficulties to him for help and advice. And Tarkington gave both, in good measure pressed down and shaken together. He did not spare himself, and if he could help a lame dog over a stile, he did it. What Tarkington said went, as far as most things were concerned.

The landlord also approved of Oxley. Oxley would have his joke, if he was to be hung for it the next minute, but he was a very sound man and a good lawyer. If you had Oxley on your side he would make a keen fight for you, and for all his jokes and his breezy manner he wouldn't give nothing away. Oxley was well liked and he deserved it.

Of the medical profession in Thirsby the landlord was equally ready to impart information. Dr Emerson was a good doctor and well respected, but he was growing old. He hardly did any work now, but he had made plenty and he could afford to retire. Not that he had been a money-grubber—the landlord had known many a case where he had treated poor patients free—but until Dr Philpot had come he had the whole of the practice, and he hadn't done badly with it. The landlord wished that hotel keeping was half as profitable. Well off, Dr Emerson was.

French next murmured Dr Philpot's name, but the landlord spoke with more reserve. He was a clever man, first rate at his job, the landlord believed, though he was thankful to say he hadn't ever needed to call him in. But he had made some good cures and people that had had him once wouldn't have anybody else. And he was pleasant spoken and likeable enough, and there was no reason why he shouldn't have done extra well at Thirsby, for there was an opening for just such a man on account of Dr Emerson's age. But—the landlord sank his voice and became more confidential than ever—the truth was he had made a muck of things, and no one would be surprised to see him take down his plate any day. He was all right in every way, but the one—he was a wild gambler. Fair ruining himself, he was. Horses mostly. It was a pity, because he was well liked otherwise. But there you were. The landlord had nothing to say about backing an occasional horse—he did it himself—but, systematic gambling! Well, you know, it could go too far.

French was interested to learn that Sergeant Kent was a fool. The landlord did not put it quite in those words, but he conveyed the idea extraordinarily well. Kent was bumptious and overbearing, and carried away by a sense of his own importance. French, the landlord was afraid, wouldn't get much help there.

The landlord showed signs of a willingness to go on talking all night, but by the time eleven-thirty had struck on the old grandfather's clock in the hall French thought he had all the information that was likely to be valuable. He therefore began insinuating the idea of bed, and this gradually penetrating to the other's consciousness, his flow of conversation diminished and presently they separated.

The next day was Sunday, and after a late breakfast and a leisurely pipe, French asked for some sandwiches, saying he was going out for a long tramp over the moor. Having thus explained himself he strolled off and presently, by a circuitous route, reached the lip of Starvel Hollow.

In spite of the fact that his professional and critical interests were aroused, French could not help feeling impressed by the isolation of the ruins and the morbid, not to say sinister atmosphere which seemed to brood over the entire place. Around him were the wild rolling spaces of the moor, forbidding and desolate, rising here into rounded hills, dropping there into shallow valleys. The colouring was drab, in the foreground the dull greens of rushes and sedgy grass, the browns of heather and at intervals a darker smudge where stone outcropped, on the horizon the hazy blues of distance. Scarcely a tree or a shrub was to be seen in the bare country, and the two or three widely separated cottages, crouching low as if for protection from the winds, seemed only to intensify the loneliness of the outlook.

At French's feet lay the Hollow, a curious, saucer-like depression in the moor, some quarter of a mile or more across. Its rim looked continuous, the valley through which it was drained being winding and not apparent at first sight. In the centre was the group of pines which had surrounded the old house, stunted, leaning one way from the prevailing wind, melancholy and depressing. Of the walls of the house from this point of view there was no sign.

French walked down toward the ruins, marvelling at the choice which would bring a man of means to such a locality. He could understand now why on that night some five weeks earlier a building of the size of this old house could be burned down without attracting more attention. The Hollow accounted for it. Even flames soaring up from such a conflagration would not surmount the lip of the saucer. Truly a place also, as Tarkington had pointed out, where burglars could work their will unseen and undisturbed.

French had seen the remains of many a fire, but as he gazed on the wreckage of Starvel he felt he had never seen anything quite so catastrophic and complete. He felt a growing awe as he began to examine the place in detail.

The walls were built of stone, and except these walls and the small outhouse at the opposite side of the yard, nothing remained standing. The house was two storied and 'L' shaped, with the remains of a single story porch in the angle of the two wings. French compared the ruins with the sketch plan given him by Kent and identified the places where the bodies had been found. Then after a general survey he stepped through the gaping hole that had evidently been the front door and ploughed his way across the debris to the safe.

It was red with fire and rust, but the maker's name and number, in raised letters on a cast iron plate, were still legible. The safe had been lifted upright and fixed on a roughly built pile of stones, as the town officer of Thirsby had deposed at the inquest. The doors were now shut, but with some diffi- culty owing to the rusty hinges French was able to swing them open. Inside, as he had been told, was a mass of paper ash.

Fortunately it was a calm day or the heap might have whirled away in dust. As it was, French sat down on a stone, and putting his head into the safe, began to examine the ash in detail.

The greater part had been ground to dust, doubtless by the fall of the safe from the second story, and the churning of the sovereigns, though there still remained a number of small flakes of burnt paper. These French began to turn over with a pair of forceps, examining them at the same time with a lens.

He was delighted to find that on nearly all he could distin- guish marks of printing. But, as he turned over piece after piece he became conscious of growing astonishment. For this printing was not the printing of bank notes. Rather it seemed to him like newspaper type. Wrapping paper, he supposed.

But why should the contents of the safe have been wrapped up in newspapers? More important still, why should portions of the newspapers rather than of the notes have been preserved?

His interest keenly aroused, he set to work in his careful, methodical way to check over all the fragments he could find. As he did so something very like excitement took possession of him. There were no fragments of notes! Every single piece that bore any marking was newspaper!

What, he asked himself, could this portend? What other than robbery? And if robbery, then murder! Murder and arson! Could Tarkington and the chief constable be right, after all? Certainly, after this discovery he couldn't drop the investigation until he had made sure.

He had brought with him a small case of apparatus, and from this he now took a bottle of gum and some thin cards. Painting over the cards with the gum, he laid on them such flakes of ash as bore legible words. From one piece in particular he thought he might be able to identify the newspaper of which it had been a part. It was a roundish scrap about the size of a shilling, along the top of which were the words: '—ing as we—' in small type, with below it in capitals, as if the headline of a small paragraph: 'RAT-CATCHER'S F—'

French secured the cards in a case specially designed to preserve specimens, and re-closed the safe. It certainly looked as if Tarkington's suggestions might be true, and as he put the case away in his pocket, he wondered if there was any further investigation he could make while he was on the ground.

Stepping outside the building, he considered how a hypothetical burglar might have forced an entrance. The window frames and doors were all gone; moreover, any marks which might have been made approaching them must long since have been defaced by time and the footprints of sightseers and workmen. French, nevertheless, walked all round the house and about the grounds, looking everywhere in the hope of coming on some clue, though he was scarcely disappointed when his search ended in failure.

He was anxious, if possible, to find out what newspaper had been burned. He did not think the point of vital importance, but on general principles the information should be obtained. There was no knowing what clue it might not furnish. On his way back to Thirsby, therefore, he turned aside to Mr Oxley's house and sent in his card.

In the privacy of the solicitor's study French introduced himself and in confidence declared his mission to the town. He apologised for troubling the other on Sunday, but said that at the moment he wished only to ask one question: Could Mr Oxley tell him, or could he find out for him from Miss Averill, what daily paper the late Mr Averill had taken?

Mr Oxley did not know, and excused himself to interrogate Ruth. Presently he returned to say it was the *Leeds Mercury*.

Next morning French took the first train to Leeds, and going to the *Mercury* office, asked to see the files of the paper for the month of September. Commencing at the 15th, the day of the fire, he began working back through the papers, scrutinising each sheet for a paragraph headed 'RAT-CATCHER'S F—'

He found it sooner than he had expected. Tucked in among a number of small news items in the paper of Tuesday, 14th September, he read: 'RAT-CATCHER'S FATAL FALL.' And when he saw that the type was similar to that on the burnt scrap and the last line of the preceding paragraph was 'Mr Thomas is doing as well as can be expected,' with the '—ing as we—' in the correct position relative to the 'RAT-CATCHER'S F—' he knew he had really got what he wanted.

French was extraordinarily thorough. Long experience had taught him that everything in the nature of a clue should be followed up to the very end. He did not therefore desist when he had made his find. Instead he worked on to see if he could identify any of the other scraps he had found. And before he left he had found eight out of the eleven he had mounted, and proved that the burnt papers were those of the 13th, 14th, and 15th; the three days before the fire.

So far, then, the indications were at least for continuing the investigation. Leaving the *Mercury* office, French walked up the Briggate to Messrs Carter & Stephenson's, the makers of the safe. He asked for one of the principals, and was presently shown into Mr Stephenson's room. Introducing himself in the strictest confidence in his true guise, he propounded his question: Was the safe absolutely fireproof?

Mr Stephenson rose and went to a drawer from which he took a number of photographs.

'Look at those,' he invited, 'and tell me was the fire at Starvel any worse than those fires?'

The views were all of burnt-out buildings, most of them completely gutted and resembling the wreckage of Starvel. French assured him that the cases seemed on all fours.

'Very well, there were safes in all those fires—safes just the same as that at Starvel, and all those safes had papers in them, and there wasn't a single paper in anyone of them so much as browned.'

French took out his burnt fragments.

'Look at those, Mr Stephenson,' he invited in his turn. 'Suppose there were newspapers in that safe before the fire, could they have come out like that after it?'

'Not under any conceivable circumstances,' Mr Stephenson declared emphatically, 'that is, of course, unless the door had been left open. With the door shut it's absolutely impossible. And I'll be prepared to stand by that in any court of law if you should want me to.'

The man's manner was convincing, and French saw no reason to doubt his statement. But he saw also that its truth involved extremely serious consequences. If Mr Stephenson was right the newspapers had not been burnt during the Starvel fire. They could only have been burned while the safe door was open. But the door was locked during the fire; Kent had had to get an expert to open it. They must therefore have been burned before it was locked. A sinister fact truly, and terribly suggestive!

On his way back to Thirsby French sat smoking in the corner of a carriage; weighing in his mind the significance of his discoveries. He considered the points in order.

First. Old Averill was a miser who had filled up his safe with notes and gold. The notes had been seen on more than one occasion by Mr Tarkington's clerk, Bloxham, the last time being only a few days before the tragedy. Mr Tarkington estimated there must have been some £30,000 to £40,000 worth of notes in the safe, though this was probably only a guess. But it was at least certain that before the fire it contained a very large sum in notes.

Second. After the fire the gold was intact, or at least part of it was there, but there was no trace of the notes. It was perfectly true that a number of notes might have been burned and been crushed to powder by the falling sovereigns. But it was straining the probabilities too far to believe that no single fragment of anyone note should remain. On the other hand fragments did remain—but these were all of newspapers.

Third. The newspapers, according to Mr Stephenson's evidence, were burned before the door of the safe had been closed.

Gradually French came to definite conclusions. As far as his information went the following facts seemed to be established:

First. That the safe was unlocked, and the notes were taken out before the fire.

Second. That three or four newspapers were put in to replace them.

Third. That the newspapers were set on fire and allowed to burn to ashes while the safe door was open.

Fourth. That after they were burned the safe was locked.

If these conclusions could be sustained it unquestionably meant that French was on to one of the most dastardly and terrible crimes of the century. He felt the sudden thrill of the hunter who comes across the fresh spoor of some dangerous wild beast. But he did not disclose his feelings. Instead he kept his own counsel, simply reporting to headquarters that the case seemed suspicious and that he was remaining on to make further inquiries.

5

French Picks Up a Clue

The more Inspector French pondered over the problems which his discoveries had raised, the more difficult these problems seemed to grow. There was so desperately little to go on. It was a common enough trouble in detective work certainly, but this business was worse than the average. He could not recall a case which offered fewer clues or 'leads.'

As he turned over in his mind all that he had learned it seemed to him indeed that there was but one channel to be explored, and that a channel which offered a very poor chance of success—the £20 bank note. If he were unable to trace the £20 bank note, and the odds were enormously against his doing so, he did not see what other line of inquiry he could follow up.

Of course, there was the usual police question: Who was seen in the vicinity of the crime at the time of its commission? But he had already put this inquiry to Kent and the answer had been: 'No one.'

If, as seemed likely, Tarkington's theory were true and this crime had been committed by the burglars who had already brought off so many *coups* in the district, French was up against a very able gang. For over six months the police had been searching for these men and they seemed no nearer finding them now than in the beginning.

The bank note, then, appeared to be the only chance, and French decided that he would begin operations by trying to trace the passer, trusting that if this line failed, some other would by that time have opened out.

The night was still young, and desiring to lose no time, French left his comfortable corner in the bar and went out to call on Mr Tarkington.

The bank manager was greatly interested when French revealed his calling and mission. He willingly repeated all he knew about old Simon Averill and his finances and explained his theories at length.

'The only other thing I wish to ask you,' French remarked when the other showed signs of coming to an end, 'is about previous sums sent out to Starvel. Your clerk kept a record of the numbers of all the twenty-pound notes sent in the last consignment, but have you a similar record of former consignments?'

Mr Tarkington nodded.

'I early appreciated that point and made inquiries,' he replied in his precise, measured tones. 'By my own instructions it has been the practice to keep such records of all notes over ten pounds in value, and this was done in the case of those sent to Starvel. The records, however, are not retained very long, and I did not hope to be able to lay my hands on those of earlier consignments. But by a piece of pure chance my clerk, Bloxham, found some earlier records in an old notebook, and I am able to give you the numbers of the notes of eleven; not consecutive consignments, but stretching at intervals over nearly five years. They cover £3860, all of which was sent to Starvel in twenties; that is 193 twenties. I have their numbers here.'

'That's a piece of luck for me,' French commented, as he pocketed the list which the other passed him. 'Curious that Mr Averill collected twenty-pound notes. Why not fifties or hundreds or tens?'

Mr Tarkington shook his head.

'Like most of us,' he said, a hint of human kindness showing beneath his rather dry manner, 'the poor old fellow had his weakness. Why he should prefer twenties to notes of other denominations I don't know. I can only record the fact that he did.'

The next morning French occupied in making the acquaintance of the obvious *dramatis personæ* in the case. He paid a long visit to Ruth Averill, hearing her story at first hand and questioning her on various details which occurred to him. Oxley he saw at his office and the lugubrious Abel Hesketh, the town officer, he found at the toll room in the markets. He was waiting for Dr Emerson as the latter concluded his morning round, and he went to the trouble of an excursion over the moor to interview the red-haired farmer, George Mellowes, who had driven Roper home on the fatal night. Dr Philpot he also called on, to obtain his impressions of the Starvel household.

Lastly, he saw the bank clerk, Bloxham, who struck him at once as a man of character. Though seemingly not more than thirty, he had a strangely old face, sardonic and determined looking, almost sinister. He gave his testimony with a refreshing restraint of words, and seemed to have observed carefully and to know just what he had seen. He said that on three occasions when he was at Starvel Mr

Averill had opened his safe and he had had a glimpse of its contents. From the size of the stacks of notes he would estimate that these contained possibly 1500 separate notes. If these were twenties that would mean £30,000. There was also a cardboard box of sovereigns. If he had not heard the number he would have estimated that it contained about two thousand.

To all of these people, except Oxley, who already knew the truth, French accounted for himself by the story of the detective employed to ascertain the cause of an unexplained fire. All seemed anxious to help him, but unfortunately none could tell him anything more than he already knew.

Having thus completed the obvious local inquiries he felt free to follow up the matter of the £20 note. He therefore left Thirsby by the afternoon train and late that night reached St Pancras. Next morning saw him at the headquarters of the Northern Shires Bank in Throgmorton Avenue. In five minutes he was closeted with the manager, who shook his head when he heard what was required of him.

'I naturally imagined some such question might arise,' the manager said, 'and I questioned the clerk who had received the note. At first he was unable to give me even the slightest hint, but on thinking over the matter he said the balance of probability was in favour of its having been paid in by the messenger from Cook's office in Regent Street. He explained that in Cook's deposit, which was an unusually heavy one, there were no less than seventeen notes for twenty pounds, and he remarked to the messenger: "You're strong in twenties today." It was shortly afterwards that the clerk discovered he held one of the numbers sent in by Mr Tarkington. He had twenty-two twenties in hand when he made his discovery and he believed he had not parted with any since the Cook lodgment, therefore, the chances that the note came from Cook's are as seventeen to five.'

'There is no certainty about that,' said French.

'No certainty, but a good sporting chance,' the manager returned with a smile as he bade his visitor good day.

The next step was obviously Cook's office. Here again French asked for the manager, and here again that gentleman shook his head when French stated his business.

'I should be only too glad to help you, Mr French,' he declared, 'but I fear it is quite impossible. In the first place we don't know the numbers of any of the notes which passed through our hands, and we don't, therefore, know if we had the one in which you are interested. Apparently you don't even know it yourself. But even if we did know, we couldn't possibly tell you who paid it in. So much money comes in over the counter that individual notes could not be traced. And then we have no idea of the date upon which we received this one, if we did receive it. You think we lodged it yesterday week. We might have done so and yet have received it weeks before. You see, we keep a fairly large sum in our safe in connection with our foreign exchange department.'

'Do you give receipts for all monies received?'

'For most transactions. But not all. If a man came in for a ticket to Harrogate, for example, we should hand him the ticket, and the ticket would be his receipt. Again, no note other than that of the actual sums passing is taken in our exchange department.'

French smiled ruefully.

'It doesn't seem to get any more hopeful as it goes on, does it?' he remarked, continuing after a moment's silence. 'You see what I'm trying to get at, don't you? If I could look over your receipts for some time prior to yesterday week I might find a name and address which would suggest a line of inquiry.'

'I follow you,' the manager returned. 'It is just possible that you might get something that way, though I must warn you it's most unlikely. You see, the balance of the payments in notes would not, in the nature of things, require receipts, and conversely most of the accounts requiring receipts are paid by cheque. However, if you wish to make a search, I am prepared to help you. How far back do you want to go?'

'The note in question was known to be in the possession of the dead man on Friday, 10th September. It was discovered in the bank here on Monday, October 18th. That is,' he took out his engagement book and rapidly counted, 'thirty-three working days: a little over five weeks.' He looked deprecatingly at the other, then added: 'Rather a job to go through all that, I'm afraid.'

'It'll take time,' the manager admitted. 'But that's your funeral. If you wish to see our books I shall be pleased to facilitate you in every way I can.'

French thanked him and a few minutes later was hard at work under the guidance of a clerk going through interminable lists of names and addresses, For two hours he kept on steadily, then suddenly surprised his companion by giving a muttered curse. He had come on a name which dashed all his hopes and showed him that his one clue was a wash out. The item read:

'Oct. 5th. Pierce Whymper, Oaklands, Bolton Road, Leeds,—£16 8s. 4d.'

'Curse it!' French thought. 'There goes all my work! There's where the twenty-pound note came from all right. That young man has been out at Starvel before the fire and Averill has given him the note for some purpose of his own.'

French was disgusted. Though he had known his clue was weak, he had, nevertheless, subconsciously been building on it, and now that it was gone he felt correspondingly at a loss. However, thoroughness before all things! He continued his study of the books, working through the period until he reached the end, but nowhere else did he get any hint of a possible connection with the tragedy.

But the same habit of thoroughness prevented his dropping the matter until he had explored its every possibility. He asked the clerk to take him once again to the manager.

'Your kind help, sir, and this young gentleman's, has not been wasted,' he began. 'I've almost certainly got the man who gave you the note. Unfortunately, however, he turns out to be someone who could have obtained it from its owner in a perfectly legitimate way. So I fear its usefulness as a clue is nil. At the same time I should like to follow up the trans-action and make quite sure it is all right. It is this one that I have marked—name of Whymper.'

'Fortunately,' the manager answered, 'that is an easier proposition than the last.' He directed the clerk to conduct French to a Mr Bankes. 'Mr Bankes will give you details about that case,' he went on, 'and if there is anything further you require, just come back to me.'

Mr Bankes proved most willing to assist, and in a few moments the whole of the transactions between Mr Pierce Whymper of the one part and Messrs Thos. Cook & Son of the other part, stood revealed. They were as follows:

On Saturday, 18th September, the day of the inquest at Thirsby, Whymper had written to ask the cost of a second class return ticket from London to Talloires, near Annecy, Savoy, and to know if a passport would be necessary for the journey, and if so, where such was to be obtained. This letter was received at Cook's on Monday evening and replied to on Tuesday 21st. Two days later Whymper wrote asking Messrs Cook to provide the tickets as well as various coupons for meals, etc., en route, which, he said, he would call for on the afternoon of Wednesday, October 6th. He evidently had done so, as on that date a receipt had been made out to him for the £16 8s. 4d.

'What was the route covered?' French inquired.

'Dover-Calais, Paris Nord, Paris P.L.M., Bourg, Amberieu, Culoz and Aix-les-Bains. Return the same way. Meals on the outward journey were included as well as three days' pension at the Hotel Splendid, Annecy.'

'I don't know Annecy at all. What kind of place is it?'

'Delightful little town on the lake of the same name. A tourist place, becoming better known in recent years. I could recommend it for anyone who liked a fairly quiet change.'

'But surely October is too late for it?'

'Well, yes, it's rather late. Still, I have no doubt it would be pleasant enough even then.'

Next day French travelled back to Thirsby. He was in a very despondent frame of mind, for he did not see a single clue or line of inquiry which might lead to the solution of his case. He would, of course, interview Whymper and follow up the affair of the bank note, but he felt certain that the young man had obtained it in a legitimate way, and that his inquiries would lead nowhere.

From the talkative Miss Judith Carr, the barmaid at the Thirsby Arms, French learned that Whymper had lodgings on the outskirts of the town, at 12 Stanhope Terrace, and when dusk had fallen he went out to make the young man's acquaintance.

Whymper was at work on some plans when French was

shown into his sitting-room. He was a typical, healthy-looking Englishman of the upper middle class. French observed him with some favour, as not at all the type to be mixed up in criminal enterprises. He rose on French's entry, and with a slight look of surprise, indicated an arm-chair at the fire.

'Mr Pierce Whymper?' French began with his pleasant smile. 'My name is French, and I called to see you on a small matter in which I am going to ask your kind help.'

Whymper murmured encouragingly.

'I must explain in the very strictest confidence,' French went on, glancing searchingly at the other, 'that I am an inspector in the Criminal Investigation Department of New Scotland Yard, and it is in connection with an investigation I am making that I want your assistance.'

As he spoke French had been watching his companion, not with inimical intent, but as a matter of mere habit. He was surprised and interested to notice a look of apprehension amounting almost to fear in the young man's eyes, while his face paled perceptibly, and he moved uneasily in his seat. French decided at once to be more careful in his examination than he had intended.

'I have been,' he resumed, 'working at Messrs Cook's office in Regent Street. I need not go into details, but there has been a robbery, and they have been handling some of the stolen money. Your name appeared among others who had been dealing with them during the period in question, and I am trying to find out if you or these others could unwittingly have passed in the money.'

That Whymper was experiencing considerable relief French was sure. He did not reply, but nodded expectantly.

'I can ask everything I want in a single question.' French's voice was friendly and matter of fact, though he watched the other intently. 'Where did you get the twenty-pound note with which you paid for your trip to Annecy?'

Whymper started and the signs of uneasiness showed tenfold more strongly.

'Where did I get it?' he stammered, while French noted the admission his bluff had drawn. 'Why, I couldn't tell you. I had it for a considerable time. It probably came in my pay.'

'You get your pay in notes?' French's voice was stern.

'Well, sometimes—that is, I may have got the note from my father. He makes me an allowance.' The young man twisted nervously in his chair and gave every sign of embarrassment. French, whose experience of statement makers was profound, said to himself: 'The man's lying.'

It did not occur to him that this thoroughly normal looking youth could be guilty of the Starvel Hollow crime, but it suddenly seemed possible that he might know something about it.

'I should like you to think carefully, Mr Whymper. The matter is more serious than perhaps you realise. You handed Messrs Cook a stolen twenty-pound note. I am not suggesting that you stole it or that you are in any way to blame for passing it. But you must tell me where you got it. You cannot expect me to believe that you don't know. Twenty-pound notes are too uncommon for that.'

Rather to French's surprise the young man began once more to show relief.

'But that's what I must tell you, Inspector,' he declared, but he did not meet French's eye, and again the other felt he was lying. 'I have had that note for a long time and I don't really remember how it came into my possession.'

'Now, Mr Whymper, as a friend I should urge you to think again. I am not making any threats, but it may become very awkward for you if you persist in that statement. Think it over. I assure you it will be worth your while.'

French spoke coaxingly and the other promised he would try to remember. He seemed to French like a man who felt he had been exposed to a danger which was now happily past. But if he thought he had got rid of his visitor he was mistaken.

'When were you last at Starvel, Mr Whymper?'

At this question Whymper seemed to crumple up. He stared at his questioner with an expression of something very like horror. When he answered it was almost in a whisper.

'The day after the fire. I have not been there since.'

'I don't mean that. I mean, when were you last there before the fire?'

Whymper's composure was coming back. He seemed to be nerving himself for a struggle. He spoke more normally.

'Really, I couldn't tell you, Inspector. It was a long time ago. I was only there half a dozen times in my life. Once it was by Miss Averill's invitation, the other times on the chance of seeing her.'

'Were you there within a week of the fire?'

'Oh no. The last time was long before that.'

'Had you any communication with Mr Averill—I mean within a week of the fire?'

'No. I never had any communication with Mr Averill. I have never seen him.'

'Or with anyone in the household; either by letter, telegram, telephone, personal interview or in any other way whatever?'

'Yes. I met Miss Averill accidentally on the day before the fire. Mrs Oxley, the wife of a solicitor here, came round to the church where I am working to see about some stones she was buying, and Miss Averill was with her. Miss Averill was on her way to stay with some friends and I saw her to the station.'

'Did she give you the twenty-pound note?'

'She did nothing of the kind,' Whymper returned with some heat.

'Was Miss Averill the only member of the Starvel household with whom you communicated during the week before the fire?'

Whymper hesitated and appeared to be thinking.

'Well, Mr Whymper?'

'I met Roper, Mr Averill's valet and general man, for a moment on the evening of the fire. We met by chance and merely wished each other good-evening.'

'Where did you meet him?'

'On the street just outside the church gate. I was leaving work for the night.'

'At what hour was that?'

'About half past five.'

'And do you assure me that you had no other communication with any member of the Starvel household during the period in question?'

'None.'

'Nor received any message through any third party?'

'No.'

'Well, Mr Whymper, it is only fair to tell you that the note in question was in Mr Averill's safe five days before the fire. You will have to explain how it came into your possession, if not to me, then later on in court. Now think,' French's voice was suave and coaxing, 'would you not rather tell me here in private than have it dragged out of you in the witness box?'

'I would tell you at once, Mr French, if I had anything to

tell, but I've nothing. There must be some mistake about the note. The one I gave to Messrs Cook couldn't possibly have been in Mr Averill's safe at any time.'

The words sounded reasonable, but Whymper's manner discounted them. More than ever was French convinced that the man was lying. He pressed him as hard as he could, but Whymper stuck to his story and nothing that French could say shook him. French, of course, could only bluff. He was quite unable to prove that Whymper had really passed the stolen note, and though he believed he had done so, he fully realised that he might be mistaken.

Recognising he had failed for the moment, French set himself to calm the other's anxieties before taking his leave. He pretended to accept the young man's statement, saying he was afraid his journey had proved a wild-goose chase, and that he would now have to interview the other persons whose names he had obtained from Cook's. Whether his efforts were successful he wasn't sure, but the look of relief on Whymper's face made him think so. Outwardly at all events both men seemed to consider the incident closed when, after French had again warned the other as to secrecy, they bade each other goodnight.

But to French it was very far indeed from being closed. He saw that the matter must be probed to the bottom. There was, however, nothing he could do that night except to take one obvious precaution. Whymper must be watched, and going to the police station he surprised Sergeant Kent considerably by asking him to put the young man under careful surveillance.

This precaution was a bow drawn at a venture, but to French's surprise and delight, on the very next day it proved that the arrow had found its way between the joints of

Whymper's harness. While he was breakfasting a note was brought to him from Kent. In it the sergeant said that as a result of the order to put a watch on Whymper, Constable Sheldrake had made a statement which he, Kent, thought the inspector should hear. Sheldrake said that on the evening of the fire he had spent a couple of his free hours in taking a walk in the direction of Starvel with a friend of his, a young lady. Between half past nine and ten the two were approaching the junction where the Starvel lane diverged from the road which circled round the outside of the hollow, when they heard steps approaching. Not wishing to be observed, they had slipped behind some bushes, and they had seen a man coming from the Starvel lane. He had passed close to them, and by the light of the moon Constable Sheldrake had not only recognised Whymper, but had seen that his face bore an expression of horror and distress. At the time there was no suspicion either of Whymper or of foul play at Starvel, and the constable, not wishing to be chaffed about the girl, had not mentioned the matter. But now he believed it to be his duty to come forward with his report.

Here was food for thought. The Starvel lane after passing through the Hollow almost petered out. As a rough track it wound on past one or two isolated cottages, debouching at last into a cross road some four miles farther on. It was therefore most unlikely that Whymper could have been coming from anywhere except Starvel. But if he had been coming from Starvel he had lied, as he had stated that he had not been there within a week of the fire.

This fact made French's next step all the more imperative. He went down to the police station and saw Kent.

'Look here, Sergeant,' he explained, 'I want to search that young man's rooms and I want your help. Will you do two things for me? First, I want you to find out at what time he goes home in the evening and let me know, and second to make some pretext to keep him half an hour later than usual at the church tonight. Can you manage that?'

'Of course, Mr French. You may count on me.'

Kent was as good as his word. When French returned to the hotel in the afternoon a note was waiting for him, saying that Whymper always reached home about six. Accordingly ten minutes before six found French once more knocking at the door of 12 Stanhope Terrace.

'Has Mr Whymper come back yet?' he asked the stout, good-humoured looking landlady.

She recognised her visitor of the night before and smiled.

'Not yet, sir. But he won't be long. Will you come in and wait?'

This was what French wanted. It was better that she should suggest it than he. He paused doubtfully.

'Thanks,' he said at last, 'perhaps it would be better if you think he won't be long.'

'He might be here any time. Will you go up, sir? You know your way.'

French thanked her and slowly mounted the stairs. But once in Whymper's sitting-room with the door shut behind him his deliberation dropped from him like a cloak and he became the personification of swift efficiency. Noiselessly he turned the key in the lock and then quickly but silently began a search of the room.

It was furnished rather more comfortably than the average lodging-house sitting room, though it retained its family resemblance to the dreary species. In the centre was a table on half of which was a more or less white cloth and the preparations for a meal. Two dining-room chairs and two easy chairs, one without arms, represented the seating accommodation. A sideboard, a corner cabinet laden with nondescript ornaments, a china dog and a few books, together with a small modern roll-top desk completed the furniture. On the walls were pictures, a royal family group of the early eighties and some imaginative views of sailing ships labouring on stormy seas. A gilt clock with a bell glass cover stood on the chimney-piece between a pair of china vases containing paper flowers.

French immediately realised that of all these objects, only the desk was of interest to him. It was evidently Whymper's private property, and in its locked drawers would be any secret documents the young man might possess. Silently French got to work with his bunch of skeleton keys and a little apparatus of steel wire, and in two or three minutes he was able to push the lid gently up. This released the drawers, and one by one he drew them out and ran through their contents.

He had examined rather more than half when he pursed his lips together and gave vent to a soundless whistle. In a small but bulky envelope at the back of one of the drawers was a roll of banknotes. He drew them out and counted them. They were all twenties. Twenty-four of them—£480.

With something approaching excitement French took from his pocket the list given him by Tarkington of the numbers of the twenty-pound notes sent to Starvel. A few seconds sufficed to compare them. Every single one of the twenty-four was on the list!

6

Talloires, Lac D'Annecy

Having noted the twenty-four numbers, French hurriedly replaced the notes and with even more speed looked through the remaining drawers. He was now chiefly anxious that Whymper should not suspect his discovery, and as soon as he was satisfied that he had left no traces of his search, he silently unlocked the door and then walked noisily downstairs. As he reached the hall the landlady appeared from the kitchen.

'I'm sorry, ma'am,' he said politely, 'that I cannot wait any longer now. I have another appointment. Please tell Mr Whymper that I'll call to see him at the church tomorrow.'

The door closed behind him, but he made no attempt to return to the hotel. Instead he hung about the terrace until he saw Whymper approaching in the distance. Then walking towards him, he hailed him as if their meeting was accidental.

'Good evening, Mr Whymper. I've just been calling at your rooms to ask if you could see me at the church tomorrow. One or two points occurred to me in connection with our discussion of last night, and I wanted to get your views on them. Unfortunately I have an appointment tonight, and cannot wait now.'

Whymper, evidently not too pleased at the prospect, curtly admitted he would be available, and with a short 'Goodnight,' passed on.

French went his way also, but when in a few seconds the shadowing constable put in an appearance, he stopped him.

'Look here, Hughes. I have a suspicion that Whymper may try to get rid of some papers tonight. Be specially careful if you see him trying to do anything of the kind, and let me hear from you about it in the morning.'

He reached the hotel and in his pleasant way had a leisurely chat with the landlord before turning in. But when once he reached his room for the night he lit a cigar and settled down to see just where he stood.

It was obvious in the first place that the evidence which he had obtained against Pierce Whymper would have been considered by most police officers sufficient to justify an arrest. To find a man suspected of the theft with the stolen property in his possession was usually reckoned an overwhelming proof of his guilt. And if to this be added the fact that the accused was seen in the neighbourhood of the crime about the time of its commission, having previously denied being there, and further, that his whole bearing when questioned was evasive and embarrassed, any lingering doubt might well have been swept away.

But French was not wholly satisfied. A ripe experience had made him an almost uncanny judge of character and he felt a strong impression that Pierce Whymper was not of the stuff of which thieves and murderers are made. That the young man knew something about the crime he had no doubt; that he was guilty of it he was not so certain.

He racked his brains as to whether there was no other statement of Whymper's which he could check. Then he remembered that the young architect had admitted having seen Roper on the afternoon of the tragedy. This was a point of contact with Starvel, and French wondered whether more might not have passed between the two men than Whymper had divulged. He decided that it would be worth while trying to find out.

According to his own statement Whymper had met Roper outside the church gate at about 5.30 on the evening in question. Next morning therefore French strolled to the church, and getting into conversation with one of the workmen, learned that the sexton was usually waiting to lock up when the men left at 5.15. From the notice board he learned the sexton's address, ran him to earth and explained that he wished to speak to him confidentially.

To his customary story of the insurance company who wished to discover the cause of the Starvel fire he added some slight embroidery. At the inquest a suggestion was made of contributory negligence—in other words, drink—and his instructions were to find out what he could about this possibility.

Now he had heard that Roper was seen outside the church gate about 5.30 on the afternoon of the tragedy and he, French, wondered whether the sexton might not have noticed him when locking up.

It was a long shot, but rather to French's surprise, it got a bull's eye. The sexton *had* seen Mr Roper. Mr Whymper, the young gentleman in charge of the renovation, had been ten or fifteen minutes late finishing up that evening and he, the sexton, had waited by the gate till he should leave. While there he had noticed Roper. The man seemed to be hanging about as if waiting for someone, and when Mr Whymper appeared, Roper went up and spoke to him. The two men talked together as if Roper were delivering a message, then they separated, walking off in opposite directions. They talked, the sexton was sure, for two or three minutes. No, he did not observe the slightest sign of drink on Mr Roper. As a matter of fact the man wished him good-evening and he could swear he was then perfectly sober.

'Well, I'm glad to know that,' French declared, 'though I suppose it is really against my company. But I expect we shall have to pay in any case. Now, I think I'd best see this Mr Whymper you speak of, and get his confirmation of your views.'

'You'll find him in the church, probably in the north transept where they're rebuilding the window.'

French did not, however, go immediately to the north transept of the church. Instead he found his way to the residence of a certain Colonel Followes, a prominent magistrate with a reputation for discretion, whose name had been given him by Sergeant Kent. He took the colonel into his confidence, made the necessary formal statement and obtained a warrant for the arrest of Pierce Whymper. Whether or not he would execute it would depend on the young man's answers to his further questions, but he wished to be able to do so if, at the time, it seemed wise.

Returning to the church, French found his quarry superintending the resetting of the stone mullions of the beautiful north transept window. He waited until the young man was free, then said that he would be glad if they could now have their talk.

'Come into the vestry room,' Whymper returned. 'I use it as an office and we won't be disturbed.'

Of all the sights which the groined roof of the old vestry had looked down on during the three centuries of its existence, none perhaps was so out of keeping with the character of the place as this interview between a detective of the C.I.D. and the man whom he half suspected of murder, arson, and burglary. And yet there was nothing dramatic about their conversation. French spoke quietly, as if their business was everyday and matter of fact. Whymper, though he was evidently under strain, gave none of the evidence of apprehension he had exhibited on the previous evening. Rather had he the air of a man who feared no surprise as he had braced himself to meet the worst. He waited in silence for the other to begin.

'I am sorry, Mr Whymper,' French said at last, 'to have to return to the subject we discussed last night, but since then further facts have come to my knowledge which render it necessary. I think it right to tell you that these facts suggest that you may be guilty of a number of extremely serious crimes. I am, however, aware that facts, improperly understood, may be misleading, and I wish, therefore, to give you an opportunity of explaining the matters which seem to incriminate you. I would like to ask you a number of questions, but before I do so I must warn you that if your answers are unsatisfactory I must arrest you, and then anything you have said may be used in evidence against you.'

Whymper had paled slightly while the other was speaking. 'I shall try to answer your questions,' he said in a low voice, and French resumed:

'The main question is, of course, the one I asked you last night: Where did you get the twenty-pound note with which you paid Messrs Cook? You needn't tell me that you don't know. Apart from the improbability of that I have absolute proof that you know quite well. Now, Mr Whymper, if you are innocent you have nothing to fear. Tell me the truth. I can promise you I will give your statement every consideration.'

'I have already explained that I don't know where the note came from.'

French paused, frowning and looking inquiringly at the other.

'Very well,' he said at last, 'let us leave it at that for the moment. Now tell me: Did you receive any other money from Mr Averill or Miss Averill, or Roper or Mrs Roper within three or four days of the fire?'

'None.'

'There was a matter of a certain £500. It was in Mr Averill's safe four days before the fire. All but twenty pounds of it was in your possession last night. Now where did you obtain that money?'

In spite of his being prepared for the worst, Whymper seemed completely taken aback by the question. He did not answer, but sat staring at the inspector, while an expression of utter hopelessness grew on his face. French went on:

'You see, Mr Whymper, I know all about your having that money. And I know that you were at Starvel on the night of the fire. I know also that your interview with Roper outside the church on that same evening involved a good deal more than a mere exchange of goodnights. Come now, I want to give you the chance of making a statement, but I don't want to press you. If you would like to reserve your replies until you have consulted your solicitor, by all means do so. But in that case I shall have to take you into custody.'

For some moments Whymper did not speak. He seemed overcome by French's words and unable to reach a decision.

French did not hurry him. He had sized up his man and he believed he would presently get his information. But at last, as Whymper remained silent, he said more sternly:

'Come now, Mr Whymper, you'll have to make up your mind, you know.'

His words seemed to break the spell and Whymper replied. He spoke earnestly and without any of the evidences of prevarication which had marked his previous statements. 'The truth this time,' said French to himself, and he settled down to listen, thinking that if the other really had a satisfactory explanation of his conduct, it was going to be worth hearing.

'I wanted to keep this matter secret,' Whymper began, 'for quite personal reasons. The £500 you speak of, of which the money I paid to Cook was a part, was not stolen. It never occurred to me to imagine I could be accused of stealing it. I don't see now what makes you think I did. However, I see that I must tell you the truth so far as I can and I may begin by admitting that what I have said up to now was not the truth.'

French nodded in approval.

'That's better, Mr Whymper. I am glad you are taking this line. Believe me, you will find it the best for yourself.'

'I'm afraid I can't take any credit for it. I needn't pretend I would have told you if I could have helped myself. However, this is what happened:

'On that Wednesday evening of the fire, as I left the church about half past five, I saw Roper outside the gate. He seemed to be waiting for me and he came up and said he had a message for me from Mr Averill. Mr Averill wasn't very well or he would have written, but he wanted to see me on very urgent and secret business. Roper asked could I come out that night to Starvel and see Mr Averill, without mentioning my visit to anyone. I said I should be out there shortly after eight o'clock, and we parted.'

Again French nodded. This was a good beginning. So far it covered the facts.

'I walked out as I had promised. Roper opened the door. He showed me into the drawing-room and asked me to wait until he had informed Mr Averill. He was absent for several minutes and then he came back to say that Mr Averill was extremely sorry, but he was feeling too ill to see me. He had, however, written me a note, and Roper handed me a bulky envelope.

'I was fairly surprised when I opened it, for it contained banknotes, and when I counted them I was more surprised still. There were twenty-five of them and they were all for £20: no less than £500 altogether. There was a note with them. I don't remember the exact words, but Mr Averill said he was sorry he was too unwell to undertake what must be a painful interview, that he didn't wish to put the facts in writing, that Roper was entirely in his confidence in the matter and would explain it, and that as I should want money for what he was going to ask me to do, he was enclosing £500, to which he would add a further sum if I found I required it.

'Roper then went on to tell me a certain story. I can only say that it is quite impossible for me to repeat it, but it involved a visit to France. Mr Averill would have preferred to have gone himself, but he was too old and frail, and he could not spare Roper. He asked me would I undertake it for him. The money was for my expenses, if I would go. The matter was, however, very confidential, and this I could see for myself.

'I agreed to go to France, and took the notes. I left Starvel

87

about half past nine, and walked back to my rooms. Next day came the news of the tragedy. This put me in a difficulty as to the mission to France. But I saw that my duty would be to go just as if Mr Averill was still alive. So I went, as you seem to know, but I was unable to carry out the work Mr Averill had wished me to do. Instead, therefore, of spending four or five hundred pounds as I had expected to, the trip only cost me my travelling expenses, and I was left with £480 of Mr Averill's money on my hands. At first I thought I had better hand it over to Mr Oxley, Mr Averill's solicitor, but afterwards I decided to keep it and go out again to France and have another try at the business.'

French was puzzled by the story. It certainly hung together and it certainly was consistent with all the facts he had learned from other sources. Moreover, Whymper's manner was now quite different. He spoke convincingly and French felt inclined to believe him. On the other hand, all that he had said could have been very easily invented. If he persisted in his refusal to disclose his business in France, French felt he could not officially accept his statement.

'That may be all very well, Mr Whymper,' he said. 'I admit that what you have told me may be perfectly true. I am not saying whether I myself believe it or not, but I will say this, that no jury on the face of this earth would believe it. Moreover, as it stands, your story cannot be tested. You must tell the whole of it. You must say what was the mission Mr Averill asked you to undertake in France. If I can satisfy myself about it there is no need for anyone else to know. Now, be advised, and since you have gone so far, complete your statement.'

The hopeless look settled once more on Whymper's face.

'I'm sorry,' he said despondently. 'I can't. It's not my secret.'

'But Mr Averill is now dead. That surely makes a difference. Besides, it is impossible that he could wish to get you into the most serious trouble any man could be in because of even a criminal secret. Tell me in confidence, Mr Whymper. I'll promise not to use the information unless it is absolutely necessary.'

Whymper shook his head. 'I can't tell,' he repeated.

French's tone became a trifle sterner.

'I wonder if you quite understand the position. It has been established that some person or persons went to Starvel on the evening we are speaking of, murdered Mr Averill and Roper and his wife,' Whymper gave an exclamation of dismay, 'stole Mr Averill's fortune and then set fire to the house. So far as we know, you alone visited the house that night, some of the stolen money was found in your possession, and when I give you the chance of accounting for your actions, you don't take it. Do you not understand, Mr Whymper, that if you persist in this foolish attitude you will be charged with murder?'

Whymper's face had become ghastly and an expression of absolute horror appeared on his features. For a moment he sat motionless, and then he looked French straight in the face.

'It's not my secret. I can't tell you,' he declared with a sudden show of energy and then sank back into what seemed the lethargy of despair.

French was more puzzled than ever. The facts looked as bad as possible, and yet if Whymper's tale were true, he might be absolutely innocent. And French's inclination was to believe the story so far as it went. The secret might be something discreditable affecting, not Mr but Miss Averill, which would account for the man's refusal to reveal it. On the other hand, could Whymper be hiding information about the Starvel crime? Was he even shielding the murderer? Could he, learning what had occurred and finding proof of the murderer's identity, have himself set fire to the house with the object of destroying the evidence? Somehow, French did not think he was himself the murderer, but if he knew the identity of the criminal he was an accessory after the fact and guilty to that extent.

Whether or not he should arrest the young man was to French a problem which grew in difficulty the longer he considered it. On the whole, he was against it. If Whymper turned out to be innocent such a step would, of course, be a serious blunder, but even if he were guilty there were objections to it. Arrest might prevent him from doing something by which he would give himself away or at least indicate the correct line of research. Free, but with arrest hanging over him, the man would in all probability attempt to communicate with his accomplice—if he had one—and so give a hint of the latter's identity. French made up his mind.

'I have more than enough evidence to arrest you now,' he said gravely, 'but I am anxious first to put your story to a further test. I will, therefore, for the present only put you under police supervision. If you can see your way to complete your statement, I may be able to withdraw the supervision. By the way, have you got the note Mr Averill enclosed with the £500?'

'Yes, it is in my rooms.'

'Then come along to your rooms now and give it to me. You had better hand over the notes also, for which, of course, I'll give you a receipt. I shall also want a photograph of yourself and a sample of your handwriting.'

When French reached the hotel he took out some samples

90

of Mr Averill's handwriting which he had obtained from Mr Tarkington and compared them with that of Whymper's note. But he saw at a glance that there was nothing abnormal here. All were obviously by the same hand.

That evening after racking his brains over his problem it was borne in on him that a visit to Annecy was his only remaining move. It was not hopeful, but as he put it to himself, you never knew. He felt there was nothing more to be learned at Thirsby, but he *might* find something at Annecy which would give him a lead.

He saw Sergeant Kent and urged him to keep a close watch on Whymper's movements, then next day he went up to town and put the case before Chief Inspector Mitchell. That astute gentleman smiled when he heard it.

'Another trip to the Continent, eh, French?' he observed dryly. 'Fond of foreign travel, aren't you?'

'It's what you say, sir,' French answered, considerably abashed. 'I admit it's not hopeful, but it's just a possibility. However, if you think it best I shall go back to Thirsby, and—'

'Pulling your leg, French,' the chief inspector broke in with a kindly smile. 'I think you should go to France. You mayn't learn anything about the tragedy, but you're pretty certain to find out Whymper's business and either convict him or clear him in your mind.'

That evening at 8.30 French left Victoria and early next morning reached Paris. Crossing the city, he bathed and breakfasted at the Gare de Lyon, and taking the 8.10 a.m. express, spent the day watching the great central plain of France roll past the carriage windows. For an hour or two after starting they skirted the Seine, a placid, well wooded stream garnished with little towns and pleasant villas. Then through the crumpled up country north of Dijon and across more plains, past Bourg and Amberieu and through the foothills of the Alps to Culoz and Aix. At Aix French changed, completing his journey on a little branch line and reaching Annecy just in time for dinner. He drove to the Splendid, where Whymper had stayed, a large hotel looking out across a wide street at the side of which came up what looked like a river, but which he afterwards found was an arm of the lake. Scores of little boats lay side by side at the steps along the road, and on the opposite side of the water stood a great building which he saw was the theatre, with behind it, the trees of a park.

After dinner French asked for the manager, and producing his photograph of Whymper, inquired if anyone resembling it had recently stayed at the hotel. But yes, the manager remembered his guest's friend perfectly. He had stayed, he could not say how long from memory, but he would consult the register. Would monsieur be so amiable as to follow him? Yes, here it was. M. Whymper?—was it not so? M. Whymper had arrived on Friday the 8th of September and had stayed for three nights, leaving on Monday the 11th. No, the manager could not tell what his business had been nor how he had employed his time. Doubtless he had gone on the lake. To go on the lake was very agreeable. All the hotel guests went on the lake. By steamer, yes. You could go to the end of the lake in one hour, and round it in between two and three. But yes! A lake of the greatest beauty.

French had not expected to learn more than this from the manager. He remembered that in his original letter to Cook Whymper had asked for Talloires, and he now spoke of the place. Talloires, it appeared, was a small village on the east side of the lake, rather more than half-way down. A picturesque spot, the manager assured him, with no less than three hotels. If monsieur wished to visit it he should take the steamer. All the steamers called.

Next morning accordingly French took the steamer from the pleasant little Quay alongside the park. French thought the lake less lovely than that of Thun, but still the scenery was very charming. High hills rose up steeply from the water, particularly along the eastern side, while towards the south he could see across the ends of valleys snow peaks hanging in the sky. Villas and little hamlets nestled in the trees along the shore.

Right opposite the pier at Talloires was a big hotel and there French, having ordered a drink, began to make inquiries. But no one had seen the original of the photograph, or recollected hearing a name like Whymper.

Another large hotel was standing close by, and French strolled towards it beneath a grove of fine old trees which grew down to the water's edge. This hotel building had been a monastery and French enjoyed sauntering through the old cloisters, which he was told, formed the *salle à manger* during the hot weather.

Having done justice to an excellent *déjeuner*, he returned to business, producing his photograph and asking his questions. And here he met with immediate success. Both the waiter who attended him and the manager remembered Whymper. The young architect had, it appeared, asked to see the manager and had inquired if he knew where in the neighbourhood a M. Prosper Giraud had lived. When the manager replied that no such person had been there while he had been manager—over five years—Whymper had been extremely disconcerted. He had then asked if a Mme. Madeleine Blancquart was known, and on again receiving a negative reply, had been more upset than ever. He had left after lunch and the manager had heard that he had repeated his questions to the police.

In ten minutes French was at the local gendarmerie, where he learned that not only had Whymper made the same inquiries, but had offered a reward of 5000 francs for information as to the whereabouts of either of the mysterious couple. Interrogations on the same point had been received from the police at Annecy, so presumably Whymper had visited them also.

This supposition French confirmed on returning to the little town. Whymper had made his inquiries and offered his reward there also and had seemed terribly disappointed by his failure to locate the people. He had left his address and begged that if either of the persons were heard of a wire should be sent him immediately.

As French made his way back to London he felt that in one sense his journey had not been wasted. Whymper's actions seemed on the whole to confirm his story. French did not believe he would have had the guile to travel out all that way, and to show such feeling over a failure to find purely imaginary people. He felt sure that M. Prosper Giraud and Mme. Madeleine Blancquart did really exist and that Mr Averill had mentioned them. If Whymper had invented these people he would have spoken of them so that his inquiries might be discovered in confirmation of his statement. If Whymper, moreover, had had sufficient imagination to devise such a story, he would certainly have had enough to complete it in a convincing manner.

The more French considered the whole affair, the more likely he thought it that there really was a secret in the Averill family, a secret so important or so sinister that Whymper was willing to chance arrest rather than reveal it. And if so, it could concern but one person. Surely for Ruth Averill alone would the young man run such a risk. And then French remembered that until the fire, that was, until Whymper's visit to Starvel, the courtship of the young people had been going strong, whereas after the tragedy the affair had seemed at a standstill. There was some secret vitally affecting Ruth. French felt he could swear it. And what form would such a secret be likely to take? French determined that on his return he would make some guarded inquiries as to the girl's parentage.

But when he reached London he found a fresh development had taken place, and his thoughts for some time to come were led into a completely new channel.

7

Posthumous Evidence

The cause of Inspector French's change of outlook on the Starvel case was a note from Sergeant Kent which was waiting for him on his arrival at Scotland Yard. The sergeant wrote enclosing a letter addressed to 'The Heirs or Assigns of the late Mr John Roper, Starvel, Thirsby, Yorkshire, W.R.' The postmaster, he explained, had shown it to him, asking him if he knew to whom it should be forwarded. Though he did not suppose it could have anything to do with the tragedy, the sergeant thought that French should see it.

'No good,' French thought. 'Nothing to me.' Nevertheless he slit open the envelope and withdrew the contents.

It was a letter headed 'The Metropolitan Safe Deposit Co., Ltd., 25b King William Street, City,' and read as follows:

'DEAR SIR OR MADAM,—We beg to remind you that the late Mr John Roper of Starvel, Thirsby, Yorkshire, W.R., was the holder of a small safe in our strong-rooms. The rent of the safe, 30/- (thirty shillings stg.) is now due, and we should be glad to receive this sum from you or alternatively to have your instructions as to disposal of its contents.

'Yours faithfully,
'For The Metropolitan Safe Deposit Co., Ltd.'

To French it seemed a rather unusual thing that a man in Roper's position should require the services of a safe deposit company. He could not but feel a certain curiosity regarding the object which required such careful guarding. As things were he supposed he had as much right as anybody to deal with the affair, and as it was but a short distance to King William Street, he decided he would go down and investigate.

Half an hour later he was explaining the position to the manager. As far as was known, Roper had no relatives or heirs. His safe would therefore be given up, and on behalf of Scotland Yard, he, French would take charge of its contents.

The contents in question proved to be a small sealed envelope, and when French had once again reached the seclusion of his own office he tore it open and ran his eye over its enclosure. As he did so his eyes grew round and he gave vent to a low, sustained whistle. To say that he was at that moment the most astonished man in London would be a very inadequate description of his sensations.

The enclosure consisted of a single sheet of grey notepaper with an address, 'Braeside, Kintilloch, Fife,' printed in small embossed letters at the top. One side was covered with writing, a man's hand, cultivated, but somewhat tremulous. It read:

'15*th May*, 1921.

'I, Herbert Philpot, doctor of medicine and at present assistant on the staff of the Ransome Institute in this

97

town, under compulsion and in the hope of avoiding exposure, hereby remorsefully confess that I am guilty of attempting the death of my wife, Edna Philpot, by arranging that she should meet with an accident, and when this merely rendered her unconscious, of killing her by striking her on the temple with a cricket bat. I do not state my overwhelming sorrow and despair, for these are beyond words.

'May God have mercy on me,

'HERBERT PHILPOT.'

French swore in amazement as he read this extraordinary document. Dr Herbert Philpot! Surely that was the Thirsby doctor? He turned to his notes of the case. Yes, the name was Herbert all right. Presumably it was the same man. At all events it would be easy to find out.

But what under the sun did the document mean? Was it really a statement of fact, a genuine confession of murder, written by Philpot? If so, how had it fallen into the hands of Roper, and what had the man been keeping it for? Had he been blackmailing Philpot? Or was the whole thing a forgery? French was completely puzzled.

But it was evident that the matter could not be left where it stood. It must be gone into and its monstrous suggestion must be proved or rebutted.

French's hand stole toward his pocket and half unconsciously he filled and lit his pipe, puffing out clouds of blue smoke while he thought over this latest development. *If* the confession were genuine and *if* Roper were blackmailing Philpot, Philpot would want to get rid of Roper. Could it therefore be possible that Philpot was in some way mixed up with the Starvel crime? Not personally of course; there was medical evidence that the doctor was ill in bed at the time of the tragedy. But could he be involved in some way that French could not at the moment fathom? It seemed too far-fetched to consider seriously, and yet here was undoubtedly a connection with Roper of the most extraordinary kind.

But this was sheer idiocy! French pulled himself together. An inspector of his service ought to know better than to jump to conclusions! Hadn't bitter experience again and again taught him its folly? Let him get hold of his data first.

And then French recalled the statement of the landlord of the Thirsdale Arms in Thirsby. He had taken all that the landlord had said with a grain of salt—gossips were seldom entirely reliable—but if Philpot *had* been gambling to the extent of embarrassing himself financially . . . It was worth looking into any way.

Obviously the first thing was to make sure that the Philpot of the confession really was the Thirsby doctor. This at least was easy. He sent for a medical directory and traced the Thirsby man's career. A few seconds gave him his information.

Herbert Philpot was born in 1887, making him now 39 years old. He passed through Edinburgh University, taking his final in 1909. For a year he was at sea and for two more years he worked in one of the Edinburgh hospitals. In 1913 he was appointed junior assistant at the Ransome Institution at Kintilloch, where he remained for eight years. In September 1921—four months after the date of the confession, French noted—he set up for himself in Thirsby.

So that was that. French's interest grew as he considered the matter. If the confession were genuine, the affair would be something in the nature of a scoop, not only for himself personally, but even for the great organisation of the Yard.

It would create a first-class sensation. The powers that be would be pleased and certain kudos and possible promotion would be forthcoming.

French left the Yard and drove to the office of the *Scotsman* in Fleet Street. There he asked to see the files of the paper for the year 1921, and turning to the month of May, he began a search for news of an accident to a Mrs Philpot at Kintilloch.

He found it sooner than he had expected. On the 17th May, two days after the date of the confession, there was a short paragraph headed 'Tragic Death of a Doctor's Wife.' It read:

'The little town of Kintilloch, Fife, has been thrown into mourning by the tragic death on Tuesday evening of Mrs Edna Philpot, wife of Dr Herbert Philpot, one of the staff of the Ransome Institute. The deceased lady in some way tripped while descending the stairs at her home, falling down the lower flight. Dr Philpot, who was in his study, heard her cry and rushed out to find her lying unconscious in the hall. She was suffering from severe concussion and in spite of all his efforts she passed away in a few minutes, even before the arrival of Dr Ferguson, for whom Dr Philpot had hurriedly telephoned. Mrs Philpot took a prominent part in the social life of the town and her loss will be keenly felt.'

'It's suggestive enough,' French thought, as he copied out the paragraph. 'It looks as if she had been alone with him in the house. I must get more details.'

He returned to the Yard and put through a telephone call to the Detective Department of the Edinburgh police, asking

100

that any information about the accident be sent him as soon as possible.

While he was waiting for a reply his thoughts reverted to Whymper. He was rather troubled in his mind about the young architect. While he was now strongly inclined to believe in his innocence, he was still not certain of it, and he hesitated upon starting off on this new inquiry until he had made up his mind definitely about the other matter. But some further thought showed him that there was no special reason for coming to an immediate decision about Whymper. Sergeant Kent was keeping him under police supervision and might well continue to do so for a day or two more.

Two days later French received a voluminous dossier of the case from the authorities in Scotland. There were cuttings from several papers as well as three columns from the *Kintilloch Weekly Argus*. There was a detailed report from the local sergeant embodying a short history of all concerned, and a copy of Dr Ferguson's certificate of 'death from concussion, resulting from a fall.' Finally there was a covering letter from the head of the department, marked 'confidential,' which stated that, owing to some dissatisfaction in the mind of the local superintendent, the matter had been gone into more fully than might otherwise have been the case, but that this inquiry having evolved no suspicious circumstances, the affair had been dropped.

Considerably impressed and beginning to think he was on a hot scent, French settled down to study the documents in detail. And the more he did so, the more determined he became that he would sift the affair to the bottom. Apart from the possible murder of Mrs Philpot and the bringing of her murderer to justice, he saw that if such a crime had been committed it might have a very important bearing on the Starvel tragedy. Roper might have been blackmailing Philpot, and though he did not see how, Philpot might have some association with the crime. Therefore, from two points of view it was his duty to carry on.

By the time he had read all the papers twice he had a very good idea in his mind of what at least was supposed to have taken place. Dr Philpot was third in command on the medical staff of the Ransome Institute, a large mental hospital about a mile from Kintilloch, a small town in Fifeshire. He was a man of retiring disposition, neither popular nor exactly unpopular, and pulling but a small weight in the public and social affairs of the little township. In May 1914 he had married Miss Edna Menzies, the daughter of the manager of a large factory near Dundee. Miss Menzies was a pretty young woman with a vivacious manner and was a general favourite, particularly among the athletic and sporting sets of the community.

The Philpots, who had no children, lived at Braeside, a small detached house some half-mile from the town and a few hundred yards from the gate of the Ransome Institute. The only other member of the household was a general servant, Flora Macfarlane, who had been with them for over three years at the date of the tragedy and who was believed to be an efficient servant. But she was 'ay one for the lads,' as the local gossips expressed it, and though the breath of scandal had so far passed her by, dark hints were given and heads shaken when her doings came under review.

This girl, Flora, lived only a short distance from Braeside. For some weeks before the tragedy her mother had been ailing, and she had formed the habit of running over to see her for a few minutes when her duties permitted. About 5.30 on the afternoon of the accident she had asked and obtained permission to make one of these visits, undertaking to be back in time to prepare dinner. This would normally have meant an absence of about half an hour. But as the girl left a heavy shower came on, with the result that, after sheltering under a tree for a few minutes, she abandoned her purpose and returned to the house some fifteen minutes earlier than she had expected. Braeside is built on sloping ground, the hall door being level with the road in front while the basement kitchen has an independent entrance to the lower ground behind. Flora used this lower entrance, and as she passed through she heard Dr Philpot speaking in a loud and agitated voice. Something in the sound suggested disaster and she ran up the back stairs to the hall to see if anything was wrong. There she found Mrs Philpot lying on the floor at the foot of the stairs, motionless and the colour of death. As a matter of fact the lady was then dead, though Flora did not know this until later. Dr Philpot, with an appearance of extreme anguish and despair, was telephoning for help. His call made, he put down the receiver and then, noticing the girl, cried: 'She's dead, Flora! She's dead! She has fallen downstairs and been killed!' He was terribly upset and indeed seemed hardly sane for some hours. Presently Dr Ferguson, the senior medical officer of the Institute, arrived and a few minutes later Sergeant MacGregor of the local police.

Dr Philpot afterwards explained that he was writing letters in his study when he heard a sudden scream from his wife and a terrible noise like that of a body falling down the stairs. He rushed out to find Mrs Philpot lying in a heap at the bottom of the lower flight. She was unconscious and a large contusion on her temple showed that she had struck her head heavily on the floor. He laid her on her back and tried everything that his knowledge suggested to bring her round, but it was evident that she had been fatally injured and in a minute or two she was dead. The doctor had been so busy attending to her that he had not had a moment to summon aid, but directly he saw that all was over he telephoned for his chief and the police.

The lower flight consisted of sixteen steps. At the top was a small landing. On this the stair carpet was worn and there was a tiny hole. After the tragedy the edge of this hole next the lower flight was found to be raised and torn. That, coupled with the fact that the deceased lady was wearing very high-heeled shoes, suggested the theory that she had met her death by catching her heel in the carpet while descending the stairs.

Such was the gist of the story as understood by French. He thought it over in some doubt, considering it from various angles. The tale certainly hung together, and there was nothing impossible in it. Everything indeed might well have taken place exactly as described, and French felt that had he not known of the confession, no suspicion of foul play would have entered his mind. But in the light of the confession he saw that the events might bear another interpretation. Philpot was alone with his wife at the time of the occurrence; and he probably knew beforehand that he would be alone, that Flora had obtained half an hour's leave of absence. When Flora returned Mrs Philpot was dead. There was no witness of the accident. No one other than Philpot knew how the lady died. To have staged the accident would have been easy, and a blow on the temple with some heavy weapon such as a cricket bat would have produced a bruise similar to that caused by a fall. Moreover, a resourceful man could have produced the suggestion that she had tripped by deliberately raising the edge of the carpet at the hole. Yes, it could all have been done exactly as the confession suggested.

Were these the considerations, French wondered, which had caused the dissatisfaction in the mind of the local superintendent, or were there still further circumstances throwing suspicion on Philpot? Whether or not, he felt the case against the doctor was strong enough to justify a visit to Kintilloch.

But one point—a vital one—he could settle before starting, or so he believed. Walking down the Embankment to Charing Cross, he went to the writing room of the station hotel and wrote a letter on the hotel paper.

'*5th November.*

'DEAR SIR,—I should be grateful if you would kindly inform me if a man named Henry Fuller ever worked for you as gardener, and if so, whether you found him satisfactory. He has applied to me for a job, giving you as a reference.

'Apologising for troubling you,

'Yours faithfully,
'CHARLES MUSGRAVE.'

French addressed his letter to 'Herbert Philpot, Esq., M.D., Thirsby, Yorkshire, W.R.' and dropping it into the hotel letter box, returned to the Yard.

Two days later he called for the reply, explaining to the porter that he had intended to stay in the hotel but had had to change his plans. Dr Philpot wrote briefly that there must be some mistake, as no one of the name mentioned had ever worked for him.

But French was not interested in the career of the hypothetical Henry Fuller. Instead he laid the letter down on his desk beside the confession and with a powerful lens fell to comparing the two.

He was soon satisfied. The confession was a forgery. The lens revealed a shakiness in the writing due to slow and careful formation of the letters which would not have been there had it been written at an ordinary speed. French had no doubt on the matter, but to make assurance doubly sure he sent the two documents to the Yard experts for a considered opinion. Before long he had their reply. His conclusion was correct, an enlarged photograph proved it conclusively.

But even if the confession were forged, French felt that the circumstances were so extraordinary that he could not drop the matter. The whole affair smacked of blackmail, and if blackmail had been going on he thought it might in some way have a bearing on the Starvel tragedy. At all events, even though a forgery, the confession might state the truth. It seemed necessary, therefore, to learn all he could about the affair and he went in and laid the whole matter before his Chief for that officer's decision.

Chief Inspector Mitchell was surprised by the story.

'It's certainly puzzling,' he admitted. 'If the document were genuine one could understand it a bit. It's possible, though it's not easy, to imagine circumstances under which it might have been written. It might, for example, be that Roper had proof of the doctor's guilt, which he held back on getting the confession to enable him to extort continuous blackmail. Even in this case, however, it's difficult to see why he couldn't have blackmailed on the proof he already held. But none of these theories can be the truth because the document is not genuine. A forged confession is useless. Why then should Roper value it sufficiently to store it in a safe deposit? I confess it gets me, French, and I agree that you should go into it further. I don't see that it will help you in any way with the Starvel affair, but you never know. Something useful for that too may come out. Say nothing to Philpot in the meantime, but get away to this place in Scotland and make a few inquiries.'

That night French took the 11.40 sleeping car express from King's Cross. He changed at Edinburgh next morning and, having breakfasted, continued his journey into Fifeshire in a stopping train. Eleven o'clock saw him at Cupar, the head-quarters of the Kintilloch district, and fifteen minutes later he was seated in the office of the superintendent, explaining to that astonished officer the surprising development which had taken place.

'They told me from Headquarters that you were not satisfied about the affair when it occurred,' French concluded. 'I wondered if you would tell me why?'

'I will surely,' the other returned, leaning forward confi-dentially, 'but you'll understand that we hadn't what you'd call an actual suspicion. There was, first of all, the fact that it wasn't a very common kind of accident. I've heard of an occasional person falling downstairs, but I've never heard of anyone being killed by it. Then there was nobody there when it happened except Philpot: there was no one to check his statement. What's more, he knew the servant was going out. The girl's statement was that Mrs Philpot was with the doctor in the study when she asked permission to go. It all looked possible, you understand. But the thing that really started us wondering was that the Philpots were supposed to be on bad terms, and it was whispered that Philpot was seeing a good deal of one of the nurses up at the Institute. It's only fair to say that we couldn't prove either of these rumours. The only definite things we got hold of were that the Philpots never went anywhere together, Mrs Philpot being socially inclined and he not, and that he and the nurse were seen one day lunching in a small hotel in Edinburgh. But of course there was nothing really suspicious in these things and the rest may have been just gossip. In any case he didn't marry the nurse. The talk made us look into the affair, but we thought it was all right and we let it drop.'

French nodded. The superintendent's statement was comprehensive and he did not at first see what more there was to be learned. But he sat on, turning the thing over in his mind, in his competent, unhurried way, until he had thought out and put in order a number of points upon which further information might be available.

'I suppose that other doctor—Ferguson, you called him—was quite satisfied by the accident theory?'

'Sergeant MacGregor asked him that, as a routine question. Yes, there was no doubt the blow on the temple killed her and in his opinion she might have received it by falling down the stairs.'

'And the servant girl had no suspicion?'

'Well, we didn't exactly ask her that in so many words. But I'm satisfied she hadn't. Besides, her story was all right. There was nothing to cause her suspicion—if she was telling the truth.'

'Is she still in the town?'

'I don't know,' the superintendent returned. 'I have an idea that she married shortly afterwards and left. But Sergeant MacGregor will know. Would you have time to go down to Kintilloch and see him? I could go with you tomorrow, but I'm sorry I'm engaged for the rest of today.'

'Thank you, I'd like to see the sergeant, but I shouldn't think of troubling you to come. I think indeed I shall have to see all concerned. It's a matter of form really; I don't expect to get anything more than your people did. But I'm afraid I shall have to see them to satisfy the chief. You see, there may be some connection with this Starvel case that I'm on. You don't mind?'

'Of course not. I'll give you a note to MacGregor. These country bumpkins become jealous easily.'

'Thank you. I think there's only one other thing I should like to ask you, and that's about Roper. Do you know anything of him?'

'I don't, but he might have lived at Kintilloch all his life for all that. I don't know the local people very well. The sergeant will help you there. He is a useful man for his job—a shrewd gossip. There's not much happens in his district he doesn't know about.'

A short run in a local train brought French to Kintilloch and he was not long in finding the local police station and introducing himself to Sergeant MacGregor. That worthy at first displayed a canny reserve, but on seeing his superintendent's note became loquacious and informative. With the exception of two pieces of information, he had little to tell of which French was not already aware. Those two items, however, were important.

The first was that he had known John Roper well. Roper had been for six years an attendant at the Ransome Institute. He had been, the sergeant believed, directly under Dr Philpot. At all events he and the doctor knew each other intimately. As to the man's character; MacGregor knew nothing against him, but he had not liked him, nor indeed had many other people. Roper was an able man, clever and efficient, but he had a sneering, satirical manner and was unable to refrain from making caustic remarks which hurt people's feelings and made him enemies. He left his job and the town some three or four years after Dr Philpot as a result of trouble at the Institute, and so far as the sergeant could tell, no one was very sorry to see the last of him. The sergeant had supposed he had gone to Brazil, as he had applied for a passport for that country. He had informed the sergeant that he had a brother in Santos and was going out to him.

The second piece of news was that Flora Macfarlane, the Philpots' maid, had been married a month or so after Mrs Philpot's death, and to no less a person than John Roper. The girl who had all but witnessed her mistress' tragic death had herself five years later been a victim in that still more terrible tragedy at the old house in Starvel Hollow.

As French shortly afterwards walked up the long curving drive of the Ransome Institute, he felt that he was progressing. He was getting connections which were binding the isolated incidents of this strange episode into a single whole, and if that whole was not yet completely intelligible, he hoped and believed it soon would be. There was first of all the confession. He had started with the confession as a single fact, connected incomprehensibly with Roper through the medium of possession, but not connected with Philpot at all. Now the connection between Roper and Philpot had been demonstrated. Roper had first-hand information about the doctor from their respective positions on the staff of the Institute, and he had as good as first-hand information about the doctor's household from the girl he afterwards married. It all looked bad. Every further fact discovered increased the probability that Roper was blackmailing Philpot, and that the confession was a true statement of what had happened.

French's interview with Dr Ferguson was disappointing. He asked first about Roper and received very much the same information that Sergeant MacGregor had given him. Roper had been attendant to an invalid gentleman, a great traveller, with whom he had been over most of Europe and America. On the invalid's death he had applied for a job at the Ransome. He was a fully qualified nurse, very intelligent and efficient, but he had not been personally liked. He seemed rather inhuman and did not mind whom he offended with his sharp tongue. He was, however, good with the patients, except for one thing. On two occasions he had been found giving troublesome patients unauthorised drugs to keep them quiet. The first case was not a bad one, and on promising amendment, he was let off with a caution. When the second case was discovered he was immediately dismissed. He had not asked for, nor been given, a discharge.

Anxious to see whether Roper's handwriting contained any idiosyncrasies which had been reproduced in the forged documents, French with some difficulty obtained some old forms which he had filled up. These he put in his pocket for future study.

He then turned the conversation to Philpot. But he was here on difficult ground and had to be very wary and subtle in his questions. Between doctors, he knew, there is a considerable freemasonry, and he felt sure that if Ferguson imagined Philpot was suspected of murder, he would take steps to put him on his guard; not in any way to take the part of a murderer, but to see that a colleague in trouble had a fair chance. That Philpot should get any hint of his suspicions was the last thing French wanted, as he hoped the man's surprise at an unexpected question would force him into an involuntary admission of guilt.

At all events Ferguson told him nothing about Philpot that he had not known before. He asked and obtained permission to interrogate a number of the staff who remembered the two men, but from none of these did he learn anything new about either.

He could see nothing for it, therefore, but to interview Philpot forthwith, and returning to the station, he caught the last train to Edinburgh. There he stayed the night, and next day took a train which brought him through the Border country to Carlisle and thence in due course to Hellifield and Thirsby.

112

8

Dr Philpot's Story

Doctor Philpot lived in a small detached house at the end of the High Street of the little town, close enough to the centre of things to be convenient for patients, and far enough away to have a strip of garden round his house and to avoid being overlooked by his neighbours.

The reply to the letter he had written from 'Charles Musgrave' about the mythical gardener told French that the doctor's consulting hours were from six to eight o'clock in the evening, and at two minutes to eight on the day he had returned from Edinburgh French rang the doctor's bell. The door was opened by an elderly woman who led the way to the consulting room.

There seemed to French a vaguely unprosperous air about the place. The garden was untended, the railing wanted paint, and the house, while well enough furnished, looked neglected and dirty. French wondered if these were the outward and visible signs of the betting proclivities of their owner, of which the hotel landlord had taken so serious a view.

Dr Philpot was seated at a writing table, but he rose on

French's entry. His appearance was not exactly unprepossessing, but it suggested a lack of force or personality. Physically he was frail, neither tall nor short, and washed out as to colouring. His tired, dreamy-looking eyes were of light blue, his fair hair, thinning on the top, was flecked with grey, and his complexion had an almost unhealthy pallor. He had well-formed, rather aristocratic features, but his expression was bored and dissatisfied. He struck French as a dreamer rather than a practical man of affairs. But his manner was polite enough as he wished his visitor good-evening and pointed to a chair.

'My name is French, and I have called, not as a patient, but to consult you on a small matter of business.'

Dr Philpot glanced at the clock on the marble chimney piece.

'It is just eight,' he answered, 'I shall not have any more patients tonight. I am quite at your service.'

French sat down and made a remark or two about the weather, while he watched the man opposite to him keenly but unobtrusively. He was playing for time in which to ascertain what manner of man this doctor really was, so that he might handle the interview in the way most likely to achieve its end. Philpot replied politely but shortly, evidently at a loss to know why his visitor could not come to the point. But French presently did so with surprising suddenness.

'I am sorry, Dr Philpot, that I am here on very unpleasant business, and I must begin by telling you that I am a detective inspector from New Scotland Yard.'

As he spoke French made no secret of his keen scrutiny. His eyes never left the other's face, and he felt the thrill of the hunter when he noticed a sudden change come over its expression. From inattentive and bored it now became watchful and wary, and the man's figure seemed to stiffen as if he were bracing himself to meet a shock.

'I regret to say,' French proceeded, 'that information has recently been received by the Yard which, if true, would indicate that you are guilty of a very serious crime, and I have to warn you that if you are unable to offer me a satisfactory explanation I may have to arrest you, in which case anything which you may now say may be used in evidence against you.'

French was deeply interested by the other's reception of this speech. Dr Philpot's face was showing extreme apprehension, not to say actual fear. This was not altogether unexpected—French had seen apprehension stamped on many a face under similar circumstances. But what was unexpected was that the doctor should show no surprise. He seemed indeed to take French's statement for granted, as if a contingency which he had long expected had at last arisen. 'He knows what is coming,' French thought as he paused for the other to speak.

But Philpot did not speak. Instead he deliberately raised his eyebrows, and looking inquiringly at French, waited for him to continue. French remained silent for a moment or two, then leaning forward and staring into the other's eyes, he said in a low tone: 'Dr Philpot, you are accused of murdering your wife, Edna Philpot, at your home at Braeside, Kintilloch, about 5.30 on the afternoon of the 15th May, 1921.'

The doctor started and paled. For a moment panic seemed about to overtake him, then he pulled himself together.

'Ridiculous!' he declared coolly. 'Your information must be capable of some other explanation. What does it consist of?'

'It purports to be the statement of an eyewitness,' French

returned, continuing slowly: 'It mentions—among other things—it mentions—a cricket bat.'

Again Philpot's start indicated that the shot had told, but he answered steadily:

'A cricket bat? I don't follow. What has a cricket bat to do with it?'

'Everything,' French said grimly: 'if the information received is correct, of course.'

Philpot turned and faced him.

'Look here,' he said harshly, 'will you say right out what you mean and be done with it? Are you accusing me of murdering my wife with a cricket bat, or what are you trying to get at?'

'I'll tell you,' French rejoined. 'The statement is that you arranged the—"accident"—which befell your wife. The "accident," however, did not kill her as you hoped and intended, and you then struck her on the temple with a cricket bat, which did kill her. That, I say, is the statement. I have just been to Kintilloch and have been making inquiries. Now, Dr Philpot, when I mentioned the cricket bat you started. You therefore realised its significance. Do you care to give me an explanation or would you prefer to reserve your statement until you have consulted a solicitor?'

Dr Philpot grew still paler as he sat silent, lost in thought.

'Do you mean that you will arrest me if I don't answer your questions?'

'I shall have no alternative.'

Again the doctor considered while his eyes grew more sombre and his expression more hopeless. At last he seemed to come to a decision. He spoke in a low voice.

'Ask your questions and I'll answer them if I can.'

French nodded.

'Did you ever,' he said slowly, 'admit to anyone that you had committed this murder?'

Philpot looked at him in surprise.

'Never!' he declared emphatically.

'Then how,' French went on, slapping the confession down on the table, 'how did you come to write this?'

Philpot stared at the document as if his eyes would start out of his head. His face expressed incredulous amazement, but here again French, who was observing him keenly, felt his suspicions grow. Philpot was surprised at the production of the paper; it was impossible to doubt the reality of his emotion. But he did not read it. He evidently recognised it and knew its contents. For a moment he gazed breathlessly, then he burst out with a bitter oath.

'The infernal scoundrel!' he cried furiously. 'I knew he was bad, but this is more than I could have imagined! That Roper is at the bottom of this, I'll swear! It's another of his hellish tricks!'

'What do you mean?' French asked. 'Explain yourself.'

'You got that paper from Roper—somehow, didn't you?' The man was speaking eagerly now. 'Even after he's dead his evil genius remains.'

'If after my warning you care to make a statement, I will hear it attentively, and you will have every chance to clear yourself. As I told you I have learned about the case from various sources. I retain that knowledge to check your statement.'

Philpot made a gesture as if casting prudence to the winds.

'I'll tell you everything; I have no option,' he said, and his manner grew more eager. 'It means admitting actions which I hoped never to have to speak of again. But I can't help

117

myself. I don't know whether you'll believe my story, but I will tell you everything exactly as it happened.'

'I am all attention, Dr Philpot.'

The doctor paused for a moment as if to collect his thoughts, then still speaking eagerly though more calmly, he began:

'As you have inquired into this terrible affair, you probably know a good deal of what I am going, to tell you. However, lest you should not have heard all, I shall begin at the beginning.

'In the year 1913 I was appointed assistant on the medical staff of the Ransome Institute. One of the attendants there was called Roper, John Roper: the John Roper who lost his life at Starvel some weeks ago. He was a sneering, cynical man with an outwardly correct manner, but when he wished to be nasty, with a very offensive turn of phrase. He was under my immediate supervision and we fell foul of each other almost at once.

'One day, turning a corner in one of the corridors I came on Roper with his arms round one of the nurses. Whether she was encouraging him or not I could not tell, but when he saw me he let her go and she instantly vanished. I spoke to him sharply and said I would report him. I should have been warned by his look of hate, but he spoke civilly and quietly.

'"I have nothing to say about myself," he said, "but you'll admit that Nurse Williams is a good nurse, and well conducted. I happen to know she is supporting her mother, and if she gets the sack it will be ruin to both of them."

'I told him he should have considered that earlier, but when I thought over the affair I felt sorry for the girl. She was, as he had said, a thoroughly attentive, kindly girl, and a good nurse. Well, not to make too long a story, there I made my mistake. I showed weakness and I made no report.'

Philpot had by this time mastered his emotion and now he was speaking quietly and collectedly, though with an earnestness that carried conviction.

'But though I hadn't reported him, Roper from that moment hated me. He was outwardly polite, but I could see the hatred in his eyes. I, on my part, grew short with him. We never spoke except on business and as little as possible on that. But all the time he was watching for his revenge.

'In May, 1914, I married and set up house at Braeside. Then came the war and in '15 I joined up. After two years I was invalided out and went back to Kintilloch. Roper, I should say, was exempted from service owing to a weak heart.

'On my return after that two years I was a different man. I am not pleading neurasthenia, though I suffered from shell-shock, but I had no longer the self-control of my former days. Though I still dearly loved my wife, I confess I felt strongly attracted to other women when in their company. Thus it happened—I don't want to dwell on a painful subject—that I, in my turn became guilty of the very offence for which I had threatened to report Roper.' He spoke with an obvious effort. 'There was a nurse there—I need not tell you her name: she's not there now—but she was a pretty girl with a kindly manner. I met her accidentally in Edinburgh and on the spur of the moment asked her to lunch. From that our acquaintance ripened and at last, by fate's irony— well, Roper found her in my arms one evening in a deserted part of the Institute shrubbery. I can never forget his satanic smile as he stood there looking at us. I sent the girl away and then he disclosed his terms. The price of his silence was ten shillings a week. If I would pay him ten shillings a week he would forget what he had seen.

'Well, just consider my position. The incident was harmless in itself and yet its publication would have been my ruin. As you probably know, in such institutions that sort of thing is very severely dealt with. If Roper had reported me to the authorities my resignation would have followed as a matter of course. And it was not I alone who would have suffered. The nurse would probably have had to go. My wife also had to be considered. I needn't attempt to justify myself, but I took the coward's way and agreed to Roper's terms.

'Then there was triumph on his evil face and he saw that he had me. With outward civility and veiled insolence he said that while my word was as good to him as my bond, the matter was a business one, and should be settled in a business way. To ensure, continued payment he must have a guarantee. The guarantee was to take the form of a statement written and signed by myself, stating—but I can remember its exact words. It was to say:

'"I, Herbert Philpot, doctor of medicine and at present assistant on the staff of the Ransome Institute in this town, under compulsion and in the hope of avoiding exposure, hereby admit that I have been carrying on an intrigue with Nurse So-and-so of the same institution. I further admit unseemly conduct with her in the grounds of the Ransome Institute on the evening of this 2nd October, 1920, though I deny any serious impropriety."'

Philpot was now speaking in low tones with every appearance of shame and distress, as if the memory of these events and the putting of them into words was acutely painful to him. His manner was convincing, and French felt that the story, at least so far, might well be true.

'You can't think less of me than I do of myself, Inspector, when I tell you that at last after a protest and a long argument I submitted even in this humiliation. I am not trying to justify myself, but I just couldn't face the trouble. I wrote the statement. Roper took it, and thanking me civilly, said he would keep it hidden as long as the money was paid. But if there was a failure to pay he would send it anonymously to the Institute authorities.

'After that everything seemed to become normal again. Every Saturday. I secretly handed Roper a ten-shilling note and our relations otherwise went on as before. And then came that awful afternoon when my wife lost her life.

'I can never forget the horror of that time and I surely need not dwell on it? If you have made inquiries at Kintilloch you will know what took place. Every word I said then was the literal truth. I shall pass on to what happened afterwards, but if there is any question you want to ask I will try to answer it.'

'There is nothing so far.'

'One evening about a week after the funeral Roper called at my house and asked for an interview. I brought him into my study and then he referred to the ten shillings a week and said that he was sure I would see that his knowledge had now become vastly more valuable, and what was I going to do about it? I said that on the contrary it was now almost worthless. My wife was dead and I didn't care what became of myself. There was only the nurse to think of, and even about her I didn't now mind so much, as she had gone to America. At the same time for peace sake I would continue the payments. He need not, however, think he was going to get any more out of me.

'His answer dumbfounded me. It left me terribly shaken and upset. He said he expected I hadn't known it, but the police suspected me of murdering my wife, and were making all sorts of inquiries about me. He pointed out that it was generally believed my wife and I hated each other: that we were seldom seen together and that she had been overheard speaking disparagingly of me. Then he said I was alone in the house when she met her death; no one had seen the accident and there was only my word for what had taken place. He said it was known there was a cricket bat in the hall, and that it would be obvious to anyone that a blow on the temple from the flat side of the bat would look just like a bruise caused by striking the floor. All this, he said, the police had discovered, but what prevented them taking action was the fact that they didn't think they could show a strong enough motive to take the case into court. That—he said—and I shall never forget the devilish look in his eyes—that was where he came in. He had but to go forward and relate the incident in the shrubbery to complete their case. He explained that he could do it in a perfectly natural way. He would say that while the affair was only a mere intrigue he did not consider it his business to interfere, but when it came to murder it was a different thing. He did not wish to be virtually an accessory after the fact.

'His remarks came as a tremendous shock to me. The possibility of such a terrible suspicion had not occurred to me, but now I saw that there was indeed a good deal of circumstantial evidence against me. I need not labour the matter. The result of our long conversation is all you wish to hear. In the end I was guilty of the same weakness and folly that I had shown before; I asked him his price and agreed to pay it. Two pounds a week, he demanded, until further notice, and I gave way. But when he went on to say that as before he required a guarantee and must have a written confession of the crime, I felt he had passed the limit. I refused to avow a crime of which I was not guilty, and dared him to do his worst.

'But once again he proved himself one too many for me. With his cynical evil smile he took two photographs out of his pocket and handed me one. It was an extraordinarily clear copy of my confession of the intrigue with the nurse. Then he handed me the other photograph and at first I just couldn't believe my eyes. It was a copy of this,' and Dr Philpot picked up the note that French had found in Roper's safe deposit.

'I asked him, of course, for an explanation and he admitted brazenly that he had forged the letter. He had spent the week since the accident making copy after copy until he had got it perfect. When I stormed at him and threatened him with arrest he just laughed and said the boot was on the other foot. He said I needn't have the slightest uneasiness, that so long as the money was paid the letter would never see the light of day. Otherwise the document would be enclosed anonymously to the police. You may guess how it ended up. I promised to pay: and I paid.'

Dr Philpot's face looked more grey and weary than ever and his eyes took on a deeper sombreness as he said these words. He waited as if for French to speak, but French did not move and he resumed:

'After all that had happened, life at Kintilloch became inexpressibly painful for me and I began to look out for another job. Then I heard that the principal doctor of this little town was old and in failing health, and there was a possible opening for a newcomer. I resigned the Ransome job and set up my plate here. But every week I sent two treasury notes to Roper.

'Some fifteen or sixteen months ago, when I had been here

between three and four years, I had a letter from Roper saying that he had seen an advertisement for a man and wife to act as servants to a Mr Averill of Starvel in my neighbourhood. As he had shortly before left the Ransome he wished to apply. As a matter of fact, I found out later that he had been dismissed for drugging a patient. I forgot to say also that he had married my former servant. If, he went on, I would use my influence with Mr Averill to get him the job he would cease his demand for the two pounds a week and send me the note he had forged.

'Mr Averill was by this time my patient, and I mentioned Roper to him. I could do so with a clear conscience for with all his faults Roper was an excellent attendant. His wife, Flora, also was a good servant and I believed they would suit Mr Averill well. At the same time I told Mr Averill just why he had left the Ransome. But Mr Averill thought that for that very reason he could get them cheap and after some negotiations they were engaged.

'The very same week Roper called on me and said I had kept my word in the past and he would keep his now. He said he was tired of crooked going and wished to live straight. He would blackmail me no longer. He handed me the forged note and watched me put it in the fire. I ceased paying him the money. From then to the day of his death he was civil when we met, and no unpleasant subjects were touched on. I began to believe his reformation was genuine, but now since you show me this I see he was unchanged. It is evident he must have made a copy of his forgery and kept one while he let me destroy the other. I wish you would tell me how you got it. What his motive can have been you may be able to guess, but I cannot.

'That, Inspector, is the whole truth of this unhappy affair.

I had hoped never to have to speak of it again, and now that I have told you of it I trust that the whole miserable business may be decently buried and forgotten.'

French nodded gravely. He was puzzled by this long story of the doctor's. The tale was certainly possible. As he reviewed each point he had to admit that not only was it possible, but it was even reasonably probable. Given a man of weak character as this doctor appeared to be, and a clever and unscrupulous ruffian, as Roper had been painted, the whole affair could have happened quite naturally and logically. Moreover it adequately covered all the facts.

On the other hand, if Philpot *had* killed his wife he would tell just some such tale as this. There was no one to refute it. Roper and his wife were dead and the nurse had left the country. Of course, it might be possible to trace the nurse, but it certainly couldn't be done easily or rapidly.

As he turned the matter over in his mind it seemed to French that the crucial point was the authenticity of the confession. If Philpot had written it, he had done so because he was guilty and because he, therefore, could not help himself. However terrible the putting of such a statement in black and white would be to him, it would be the lesser of two evils, the alternative being immediate betrayal. But if the confession were a forgery all this would be reversed. It could only have come into being in some such way as the doctor had described. In fact, in his case it would amount to a powerful confirmation of his story.

Now, upon this point there was no doubt. The confession definitely *was* a forgery. The Yard experts were unanimous, and their opinion under such circumstances might be taken for gospel. French might therefore start with a strong bias in favour of Philpot.

125

This French realised, and then he found himself again weighed down by doubt. Was it credible that a man would really pay blackmail for fear of having an obviously forged confession produced? At first French did not think so—he would not have done it himself—but as he considered the special circumstances he saw that this question did not accurately describe the situation as it would appear to the doctor. In the first place, Philpot did not know how bad a forgery the document was. It seemed to him his own writing, and he had no guarantee that it would not be accepted as such. But he knew that if it were produced he would almost certainly have the misery of arrest and imprisonment and possibly of trial also. Moreover, the episode of the nurse would come out, and the result of the whole business would have been ruin to his career. If Philpot had been a strong man he would no doubt have faced the situation, but as it was, French felt sure that he would take the coward's way. No, there was nothing in this idea to make him doubt the man's story.

On the contrary, Philpot's admission that he had submitted to blackmail was actually in his favour. If he had intended to lie surely he would have invented a tale less damaging to himself. He had not hesitated to tell French about the nurse and so present him with the very motive for his wife's murder which was lacking in the case against himself.

On the whole it seemed to French that the probabilities were on Philpot's side and he himself inclined to the view that he was innocent. Whatever the truth, he saw that he had no case to bring into court. No jury would convict on such evidence.

And if there was no evidence to convict the man of the murder of his wife, there was still less to associate him with the Starvel affair. In fact there was here no case against him at all. Even leaving Philpot's illness out of the question, there was nothing to indicate any connection with the crime. It would be just as reasonable to suspect Emerson or Oxley or even Kent.

French had an uncomfortable feeling that he had been following will-o'-the-wisps both in this affair and in Whymper's. The circumstances in each had been suspicious and he did not see how he could have avoided following them up, but now that he had done so it looked as if he had been wasting his time. Ruefully he saw also that he had rather got away from his facts. He had forgotten that the motive of the Starvel crime had not to be sought in anything indirect or ingenious or fanciful. The motive was obvious enough and commonplace enough in all conscience; it was theft. And such a motive French could not see actuating either Philpot or Whymper.

No, he must get back to the facts. Who had stolen the money? That was what he had to find out. And he would not get it the way he was going. He must start again and work with more skill and vision. First, he must reassure this doctor, and then he must get away to some place where he could think without interruption.

'I am sorry, Dr Philpot, to have had to give you the pain of reopening matters which I can well understand you would have preferred to leave closed. It was necessary, however, that my doubts on these matters should either be confirmed or set at rest. I may say that I accept your story and am satisfied with the explanation you have given me. I hope it may be possible to let the affair drop and at the present time I see no reason to prevent it.' He rose. 'I wish you goodnight, doctor, and thank you for your confidence.'

9

The Value of Analysis

The next morning was fine and bright, with an invigorating autumn nip in the air. The kind of day for a good walk, thought French, as after breakfast he stood in the hotel coffee room, looking out on the placid life of the little town, exemplified at the moment in the dawdling passage of three tiny children with school satchels over their shoulders. He liked the place. He had taken a fancy to it on that first evening of his arrival, and what he had seen of it since had only confirmed his first impression. The surroundings also seemed attractive, and he hoped to explore them more fully before he left.

As he stood gazing into the main street it occurred to him that for his explorations no time more propitious than the present was likely to offer. For the moment he was at a dead-lock in his case. After he had finished writing out the doctor's statement on the previous evening he had thought over the affair and he had not seen his way clear. What he required was a detailed study of the whole position in the hope of lighting on some further clue or line of research.

And what better opportunity for such contemplation could there be than during a long tramp through lonely country? Surely for once duty and inclination coincided?

Whether this latter was strictly true or not, ten minutes later saw him starting out with a stick in his hand and a packet of sandwiches in his pocket. He turned in the Starvel direction, and climbing up the side of the valley, came out on the wide expanse of the moor. Ahead of him it lay, stretching away in irregular undulating waves into the grey-blue distance, with here and there a rounded hill rising above the general level. For miles he could see the ribbon of the road showing white against the browns and greens of the grass where it wound up over shoulders and ridges and mounted the far sides of hollows. Extraordinarily deserted was the country-side, a solitude quite astonishing in so densely populated a land as this of England.

For a time French tramped on, his mind occupied with his surroundings, but gradually it turned back to his case and he began reckoning up his progress, and considering how he could best attack what still remained to be done. And the more he thought of it, the less rosy the outlook seemed. Ruefully he had to admit that in point of fact he was practically no further on than when he started. He had done a good deal of work, no doubt, but unfortunately it had brought him only a negative result. His researches into the movements of Whymper and Philpot had been unavoidable, but these had proved side lines and he did not believe that either would help him with the main issue.

He let his mind rest once again on Philpot's statement. If it were true, Roper showed up very badly. From every point of view he seemed a thorough-paced blackguard. Though this had come out more particularly from the doctor's story

129

it was fairly well confirmed by what French had been told at Kintilloch. Neither Sergeant MacGregor nor Dr Ferguson had a good word to say about the man. No one appeared to like him, and in the end he had been dismissed from the Institute for a fault of a particularly serious nature.

But he was a clever rascal also. French was amazed when he considered how he had succeeded in worming himself into old Averill's confidence. Even making allowance for the old man's weak-minded senility, it was almost incredible that this shifty scoundrel should have been trusted with a secret which Whymper would risk a murder charge rather than reveal.

French tramped on, pondering over the matter in his careful, painstaking way. Yes, that was a point. Misers were proverbially suspicious, and Averill's knowledge of Roper's break at the Ransome would not tend to increase his trust in him. His confidence was certainly rather wonderful.

And then French suddenly stood stock still as an idea flashed into his mind. Was his confidence not too wonderful to be true? Had Roper really wormed his way thus far into old Averill's confidence? He had not hesitated to blackmail Philpot; had he played some similar trick on Whymper?

As French considered the suggestion, a point which had before seemed immaterial now took on a sinister significance. Though Averill was represented as the moving spirit of the affair, his connection with it had never been directly proved. Roper, and Roper alone, had appeared. It was true that a note purporting to come from Averill had been produced, but in the light of Philpot's revelation of Roper's skill as a forger, who had written it? Was there any reason why Roper should not have engineered the whole thing?

French reviewed the circumstances in detail. The first move was Roper's. He had met Whymper outside the church gate and told him that Mr Averill wished to see him, asking him to go out there that evening. Secretly, mind you; no one was to know of the visit. Whymper had accordingly gone out. But he had not seen Averill. He had seen Roper, and Roper only. It was true that he was presented with a note purporting to be from Averill, but had Averill written it? French remembered that the handwriting was extremely like Averill's, but in the absence of any reason for suspecting its authenticity he had not given it the careful scrutiny which he might have done. That was an error he must repair at once, and if the shadow of a doubt was aroused in his mind he must send the papers to the Yard for expert opinion.

Altogether it undoubtedly looked as if the whole of the Whymper episode might have been Roper's work. But if so, what about the £500? Surely in this case Roper must have stolen it? And if he had stolen it—French grew almost excited as step after step revealed itself—if Roper had stolen it, did it not follow that he had murdered Averill, rifled the safe, taken out the notes and replaced them with burnt newspapers?

And then French saw a step farther. If he were right so far, Roper's motive in the Whymper incident became clear as day. If Roper had stolen thousands of pounds worth of notes he must find out whether it was safe to pass them. Were the numbers of the notes known? This was a matter of vital importance, and it was one on which he could not possibly ask for information. If suspicion became aroused, to have made inquiries on the point would be fatal. He must therefore arrange for someone else to pass a number of the notes, and preferably a number of those most recently acquired by Averill. Moreover, this person must not, if suspected, be able to account satisfactorily for their possession.

Given the knowledge of Whymper's feeling for Ruth and some acquaintance with Averill's family affairs, a clever and unscrupulous man like Roper could, easily have invented a story to make Whymper his dupe.

All this, French recognised, was speculation. Indeed it was little more than guesswork. But it was at least a working theory which covered all the facts, and he believed it was worth while following it up.

He turned aside off the road, and sitting down in the thin, autumn sunshine with his back against an outcropping rock, slowly filled and lit his pipe as he pursued his cogitations.

If Roper had stolen the notes and put burnt newspapers in the safe, he must have intended to burn the house. And here again the motive was clear. In no other way could he so conveniently get rid of Averill's body and the traces of his crime. In fact, the plan had actually succeeded. It was not the doings at Starvel which aroused suspicion, but Whymper's passing of the note some three weeks later. The coroner's court had brought in a verdict of accidental death. If Tarkington had not kept the numbers of the notes sent out to Averill and advised his headquarters that those notes had been destroyed, no doubts would ever have arisen.

But just here was a snag. Could so able a man as Roper have bungled so hideously as to have allowed himself and his wife to be caught in the trap he had arranged for Averill? Or had he intended to murder Mrs Roper also? There was certainly no evidence for suspecting this. But whether or not, what terrible nemesis could have overtaken Roper? Had he really been drunk and paid for his indulgence with his life? French did not think so. He could not devise any convincing explanation of Roper's death, and he began to wonder if this objection were not so overwhelming as to upset the theory of the man's guilt which he had been so laboriously building up.

He gazed out over the wide expanse of the moor with unseeing eyes as he dreamily puffed at his pipe and wrestled with the problem. And then a further point occurred to him. Did not this theory of the guilt of Roper throw some light on Ruth Averill's visit to York? French had noted it as a curious coincidence that she should have left the house on the day before the tragedy. But now he wondered if it was a coincidence. Had her absence been arranged; arranged by Roper? He reconsidered the facts from this new angle.

First, it was significant that all the arrangements had been carried through by Roper. Just as in Whymper's case, Mr Averill was supposed to be the prime mover, but his power was manifested only through Roper. Roper it was who handed Ruth the note from Mrs Palmer-Gore; doubtless a forged note. Roper had produced the ten pounds. Roper had arranged about the journey, and Roper had used his influence to prevent Ruth from seeing her uncle. When she had persisted she had found the old man asleep, breathing heavily and looking queer and unlike himself. As to the cause of that appearance and that sleep French could now make a pretty shrewd guess. Roper had been faced with a difficulty. He could not keep Ruth from her uncle without arousing suspicion. Nor could he allow her to have a discussion with him or his plot would have been exposed. He had, therefore, taken the only way out. He had drugged the old man. Ruth could pay her visit, but she would learn nothing from it.

French was thrilled by his theory. It was working out so well. He was congratulating himself that at last he was on the right track, when another snag occurred to him and brought him up, as it were, all standing.

The Palmer-Gore invitation could not have been forged! Had Mrs Palmer-Gore not written it, the fact would have come out on Ruth's arrival at York.

Here was a rather staggering objection. But the more French thought over the case as a whole, the more disposed he became to believe in Roper's guilt. The man was a clever scoundrel. Perhaps he had been able to devise some way to meet this difficulty also.

On the whole French was so much impressed by his theory that he determined to go into it without loss of time in the hope that further research would lead to a definite conclusion.

He ate his sandwiches, then leaving his seat in the lee of the rock, walked back to Thirsby. Among his papers was the letter which Roper had given to Whymper, and this he once again compared with the samples of old Mr Averill's handwriting he had obtained from Tarkington.

Possibly because of the doubt now existing in his mind, this time he felt less certain of its authenticity. After some study he thought that some further samples of the genuine handwriting might be helpful, and walking down to Oxley's office, he asked if the solicitor could oblige him with them. Oxley handed him four letters, and when French had critically examined these he found his suspicions strengthened. While by no means positive, he was now inclined to believe Whymper's was a forgery. He therefore sent the lot to the Yard, asking for an expert opinion to be wired him.

In the meantime he decided that he would concentrate on a point which he felt would be even more conclusive than forged letters; the matter of Mrs Palmer-Gore's invitation to Ruth. If Roper had got rid of Ruth so that the coast might be clear for the robbery, he had provided the invitation. He had either written it himself or he had arranged the circumstances which caused Mrs Palmer-Gore to do so. If he had done either of these things he was pretty certain to be guilty.

The only way to learn the truth was to interview Mrs Palmer-Gore. French therefore took the evening train to York, and nine o'clock found him at Oakdene, Ashton Drive, asking if the lady of the house could see him.

Mrs Palmer-Gore was a big, rather untidy, kindly-looking woman of about fifty. French, rapidly sizing her up, introduced himself in his real character, apologised for his late call and begged her kind offices. If she wouldn't mind his not giving her the reason of his inquiry for the moment, he should like to ask a question. Would she tell him just why she had asked Miss Ruth Averill to York some eight weeks previously?

Mrs Palmer-Gore was naturally surprised at the inquiry, but when she understood that the matter was serious she answered readily.

'Why, I could scarcely have done anything else. Mr Averill's note was phrased in a way which would have made it difficult to refuse.'

'Mr Averill's note? I didn't know he had written.'

'Yes, he wrote to say that he hoped he was not presuming on an old friendship in asking me whether I would invite Ruth to spend a day or two. He explained that she had recently been rather run down and depressed, and that the one thing she wanted—a day or two of cheerful society—was just the thing he couldn't give her. If I would condone a liberty and take pity on her he did not think I would regret my action. He went on to say that Ruth was greatly interested in roses, and as he was sure I was going to the flower show, he wondered if I would add to my kindness by allowing her to accompany me. He said that Ruth was longing to see it, but that he had no way of arranging for her to go.'

'I'm quite interested to hear that,' French returned. 'It rather falls in with a theory I have formed. Had you often had Miss Ruth to stay with you?'

'Never before. In fact I had only seen her three or four times. Some twelve years ago I spent a day at Starvel and she was there. Besides that I met her with Mr Averill a couple of times in Leeds.'

'But you were pretty intimate with Mr Averill surely? I don't want to be personal, but I want to know whether your intimacy was such that you might reasonably expect him to ask you to put his niece up?'

Mrs Palmer-Gore seemed more and more surprised at the line the conversation was taking.

'It's a curious thing that you should have asked that,' she declared. 'As a matter of fact, I was amazed when I read Mr Averill's letter. He and I were friendly enough at one time, though I don't know that you could ever have called us intimate. But we had drifted apart. I suppose we hadn't met for five or six years and we never corresponded except perhaps for an exchange of greetings at Christmas. His letter was totally unexpected.'

'You thought his asking for the invitation peculiar?'

'I certainly did. I thought it decidedly cool. So much so, indeed, that I considered replying that I was sorry that my house was full. Then when I thought what a terrible life that poor girl must have led I relented and sent the invitation.'

'It was a kind thing to do.'

'Oh, I don't know. At all events I am glad I did it. Ruth is a sweet girl and it was a pleasure to have her here and to let my daughters meet her. I would have given her as good a time as I could if she had not been called away.'

'You haven't kept Mr Averill's letter?'

'I'm afraid not. I always destroy answered letters.'

'You recognised Mr Averill's handwriting, of course?'

'Oh yes. I knew it quite well.'

'Now, Mrs Palmer-Gore, I am going to ask you a strange question. Did you ever suspect that that letter might be a forgery?'

The lady looked at him with increasing interest.

'Never,' she answered promptly. 'And even now when you suggest it I don't see how it could have been. But, of course, it would explain a great deal. I confess I can hardly imagine Mr Averill writing the note. He was a proud man and the request was not in accordance with my estimate of his character.'

'That is just what I wanted to get at,' French answered as he rose to take his leave.

What he had learned was extraordinarily satisfactory. It looked very much as though his theory about Roper was correct. The great snag in that theory had been Mrs Palmer-Gore's invitation, and now it was evident that Roper could have arranged for it to be given. Some remark of Mr Averill's had probably given the man Mrs Palmer-Gore's name, and by skilful questions he could have learned enough about her to enable him to construct his plot.

As French sat in the smoking room of his hotel, not far from the great west front of the minster, he suddenly saw a way by which he could establish the point. The letter Mrs Palmer-Gore had received had stated that Ruth was longing to see the flower show. Was she? If she was, the letter might be genuine enough. If not, Averill could scarcely have written it, and if Averill had not written it no one but Roper could have done so.

It was with impatience at the slowness of the journey that French returned next morning to Thirsby to apply the final test. He was lucky enough to catch Ruth as she was going out and she took him into the drawing room.

'I was talking to a friend of yours a little while ago, Miss Averill,' French said when they had exchanged a few remarks: 'Mrs Palmer-Gore, of York.'

'Oh yes?' Ruth answered, her face brightening up. 'How is she? She was so kind to me, especially when the terrible news came. I can never forget her goodness.'

'I am sure of it. In the short time I was with her I thought she seemed most attractive. You went to York to see the flower show?'

Ruth smiled.

'That was the ostensible reason for her asking me. But, of course, show or no show, I should have been delighted to go.'

'I dare say; most people like to visit York. You hadn't then been looking forward to the show?'

'I never even heard of it until Mrs Palmer-Gore mentioned it in her letter. But naturally I was all the more pleased.'

'Naturally. You're a skilful gardener, aren't you, Miss Averill?'

She smiled again and shook her head.

'Oh, no! But I'm fond of it.'

French, in his turn, smiled his pleasant, kindly smile.

'Oh, come now, I'm sure you are not doing yourself justice. Mr Averill thought a lot of your gardening, didn't he?'

'My uncle? Oh, no. I don't think he knew anything about it. You remember he was an invalid. He hadn't been in the garden for years.'

'But do you mean that you never discussed gardening with him? I should have thought, for example, you would have talked to him of this York flower show.'

'But I thought I explained I didn't know about that until Mrs Palmer-Gore's letter came, and after it came my uncle was too ill to speak about anything.'

Here was the proof French had hoped for!

With some difficulty keeping the satisfaction out of his voice, he continued his inquiries.

'Of course I remember you told me that. But I must get on to business. I'm sorry to have to trouble you again, Miss Averill, but there are one or two other questions I have thought of since our last meeting. Do you mind if I ask them now?'

'Of course not.'

French leaned forward and looked grave.

'I want to know what kind of terms Roper was on with his wife. You have seen them together a good deal. Can you tell me?'

Ruth's face clouded.

'I hate to say anything when the two poor people are dead, but if I must tell the truth, I'm afraid they were not on good terms at all.'

'I can understand what you feel, but I assure you my questions are necessary. Now, please tell me what exactly was the trouble between those two?'

'Well,' Ruth said slowly, and an expression almost of pain showed on her face, 'they had, I think—what is the phrase?—incompatiblity of temperament. Mrs Roper had a very sharp tongue and she was always nagging at Roper. He used to answer her in a soft tone with the nastiest and most cutting remarks you ever heard. Oh, it was horrible!

Roper really was not a nice man, though he was always kind enough to me.'

This was really all that French wanted, but he still persisted.

'Can you by any chance tell me—I'm sorry for asking this question—but can you tell me whether Roper was attached to any other woman? Or if you don't know that, have you ever heard his wife mention another woman's name in anger? Just try to think.'

'No, I never heard that.'

'Have you ever heard them quarrelling?'

'Once I did,' Ruth answered reluctantly. 'It was dreadful! Roper said, "By—," he used a terrible curse—"I'll do you in some day if I swing for it!" And then Mrs Roper answered so mockingly and bitterly that I had to put my hands over my ears.'

'But she didn't make any definite accusation?'

'No, but wasn't it dreadful? The poor people to have felt like that to one another! It must have been a terrible existence for them.'

French agreed gravely as he thanked Ruth for her information, but inwardly he was chuckling with delight. He believed his theory was proved, and once it was established, his case was over. If the murderer lost his life in the fire Scotland Yard would no longer be interested in the affair and he, French, could go back to town with one more success added to the long list which already stood to his credit.

He returned to the Thirsdale Arms, and getting a fire lighted in his room, settled down to put on paper the data he had amassed.

10

Whymper Speaks at Last

By the time French had completed his notes the theory he
had formed had become cut and dry and detailed. He was
immensely delighted with it and with himself for having evolved
it. Except for the failure to explain Roper's death it seemed
to him flawless, and for that one weak point he felt sure that
a simple explanation existed. In the hope of lighting on some
such he decided before putting away his papers to go once
more in detail over the whole case as he now saw it.

First there was the character of Roper. Roper was a clever
and unscrupulous man with a cynical and discontented
outlook on life. He was, in fact, the sort of man who might
have planned and carried out the Starvel crime.

His anxiety to get the job at Averill's was an interesting
feature of the case. It must have been a poor job for a man
who had been male nurse in the Ransome Institute. It was
not only a hard and thankless job in itself, but it meant being
buried in one of the bleakest and most barren solitudes of
England. Moreover, such a job would lead to nothing, and
as Averill was paying, it was unlikely that the salary was

other than miserable. Of course after dismissal from the Institute Roper might have been glad of anything, but French did not feel satisfied that this really explained the matter. His thoughts took another line.

The belief in Averill's wealth was universal and Roper could scarcely have failed to hear of it when inquiring about the place. The feebleness of the old man and the isolation of the house were, of course, patent. Was it too much to conclude that the idea of robbery had been in Roper's mind from the first? If so, a reason why he had ceased to blackmail Philpot might be suggested. The doctor was the one person in the neighbourhood who knew his real character. If anything untoward happened at Starvel, the doctor would immediately become suspicious. It was, therefore, politic to suggest a reformation of character to Philpot, and the best way in which this could be done was undoubtedly the way Roper had chosen. But he was not going to spoil the affair by haste. This was the one great effort of his life and he was out to make a job of it. No time nor trouble nor inconvenience was too great to devote to it. So he waited for over a year. How many a wife murderer, thought French, has aroused suspicion by marrying the other woman within the twelve months. Roper was not going to make the mistake of acting too soon.

During this time of waiting the man had doubtless been perfecting his scheme. And then another factor had entered into it. He had come to hate his wife. Why not at one fell stroke achieve both wealth and freedom? The same machinery would accomplish both.

In the nature of the case French saw that all this must necessarily be speculative, but when he came to consider the details of the crime he felt himself on firmer ground.

The first move was to get Ruth Averill out of the way, and

here the *modus operandi* was clear. Roper had evidently either heard enough about Mrs Palmer-Gore from Mr Averill to give him his idea, or he had discovered her existence from old letters. He had forged the note to her from Averill, and intercepting its reply, had used its enclosure to induce Ruth to go to York. As he couldn't prevent the girl from visiting her uncle, he had drugged the old man so that the fraud would remain hidden.

His next care was to make sure that Averill's bank notes could be passed without arousing suspicion; in other words, that their numbers were unknown. To this end the fraud on Whymper was devised. Whymper was to be used to test the matter, and in the event of the theft being discovered, Whymper was to pay the penalty. So Whymper was brought out to the house on the night of the crime and there given the fateful money, being told some yarn which would make him spend it in a mysterious way for which he would be unable to account. That that yarn was connected with something discreditable about Ruth's parents French shrewdly suspected, and he determined to see Whymper again and try to extract the truth from him.

Whymper duped and sent away from Starvel, French thought he could picture the next sinister happenings in the lonely old house. Averill first! The frail old man would prove an easy victim. Any method of assassination would do which did not involve an injury to the skeleton. A further dose of the drug, smothering with a pillow, a whiff of choloroform: the thing would have been child's play to a determined man, particularly one with the training of a male nurse in a mental hospital.

Then Mrs Roper! How the unfortunate woman met her end would probably remain for ever a mystery. But that she died by her husband's hand French was growing more and more certain.

Witnesses to the theft removed, the safe must have claimed Roper's attention next. French in imagination could see him getting the keys from under their dead owner's pillow, opening the safe, and packing the notes in a suitcase. How it must have gone to Roper's heart to leave the gold! But obviously he had no other course. Gold wouldn't burn. It must therefore be found in the safe. Then came the substitution and burning of the newspapers. Here Roper made his first slip. Doubtless he was counting that the safe would fall to the ground level when the floor it stood on burned away and the churning of the sovereigns would reduce the paper ashes to dust. But there he had been wrong. Enough was left to reveal the fraud.

There was plenty of petrol and paraffin in the house and Roper's next step must have been to spill these about, so as to leave no doubt of the completeness of the holocaust. In that also he was only too successful.

So far, French felt he was on pretty firm ground. He was becoming convinced that all this had happened, substantially as he had imagined it. But now came the terrible snag. Or rather two snags, for the one did not entirely include the other. The first was: What had happened to Roper? The second; Where was the money?

The more French puzzled over the first of these problems the more he came to doubt his first idea that some quite simple explanation would account for it. That nearly every criminal makes some stupid and obvious blunder during the commission of his crime is a commonplace. Still French could not see so astute a man as Roper making a blunder so colossal as to cost him his life. What super-ghastliness had happened upon that night of horrors? Had Roper started the fire before killing his wife and been overcome by fumes while in the act of murder? Had he taken too much drink to steady his nerves and fallen asleep, to meet the fate he had prepared for others? French could think of no theory which seemed satisfactory.

Nor could he imagine where the money might be. Was it burned after all? Had the receptacle in which it had been packed been left in the house and had its contents been destroyed? Or had Roper hidden it outside? Here again the matter was purely speculative, but French inclined to the former theory. All the same he determined that before he left the district he would make a thorough search in the neighbourhood of the house.

There was still the matter of the Whymper episode to be fully cleared up, and French thought that with the help of his new theory he might now be able to get the truth out of the young man. Accordingly he left the hotel and walked up the picturesque old street to the church. Whymper was busily engaged with a steel tape in giving positions for a series of new steps which were to lead up to the altar and French, interested in the operation, stood watching until it was complete. Then the young fellow conducted him for the second time to the vestry room, and seating himself, pointed to a chair.

'As no doubt you can guess, I've come on the same business as before,' French explained in his pleasant, courteous tones. 'The fact is, I've learned a good deal more about this Starvel business since I last saw you, and I want to hear what you think of a theory I have evolved. But first, will you tell me everything that you can of your relations with Roper.'

'I really hadn't any relations with Roper except what I have already mentioned,' Whymper returned. 'Of course I had seen him on different occasions, but the first time I spoke to him was the first time I called on Miss Averill. He opened the door and showed me into the drawing-room. The next time I went we spoke about the weather and so on, but I had no actual relations with him until the night of the tragedy, when he gave me Mr Averill's message at the church gate.'

'It never occurred to you to doubt that the message did come from Mr Averill, I suppose?'

'Of course not,' Whymper answered promptly. 'You forget the note Mr Averill sent me when I got to Starvel.'

'I don't forget the note. But suppose I were to suggest that Roper had forged the note and that Mr Averill knew nothing whatever about it? I should tell you that it has been established that Roper was a very skilful forger.'

'Such an idea never occurred to me. Even if Roper was a skilful forger I don't see why you should think he forged this note. What possible motive could he have had?'

'Well, I think we might possibly find a motive. But let that pass for the moment. Go over the circumstances again in your mind and let me know if you see any reason why Roper should not have arranged the whole business himself.'

Whymper did not at once reply. French, anxious not to hurry him, remained silent also, idly admiring the pilasters and mouldings of the octagonal chamber and the groining of the old stone roof.

'I don't see how Roper could have done it,' Whymper said presently. 'There's the money to be considered. The £500 couldn't have been forged.'

'No. But it could have been stolen, and I have no doubt was.'

'Surely not! You don't really believe Roper was a thief?'

'At least he might have been. No, Mr Whymper, you haven't convinced me so far. Does anything further occur to you?'

'Yes,' said Whymper: 'the story he told me. No one could have known it but Mr Averill.'

French leaned forward and his face took on an expression of keener interest.

'Ah, now we're coming to it,' he exclaimed. 'I suggest that that whole story was a pure invention of Roper's and that it had no foundation in fact. Now tell me this.' He raised his hand as Whymper would have spoken. 'If the story were true would you not have expected to hear something of M. Prosper Giraud and Mme. Madeleine Blancquart at Talloires?'

Whymper seemed absolutely dumbfounded at the extent of the other's knowledge.

'Why,' he stammered with all the appearance of acute dismay, 'how do you know about that? I never mentioned it.'

'You did,' French declared. 'To the police at Talloires. I traced you there and found out about your inquiries. It was perfectly simple. If the story had been true would you not have had an answer to your inquiries?'

A sudden eagerness appeared in the young man's face. He leaned forward and cried excitedly:

'My Heavens, I never thought of that! I supposed Roper had made a mistake about the address. Oh, if it could only be so!' He paused for a moment, then burst out again: 'You may be right! You may be right! Tell me why you thought it might be Roper's invention. I must know!'

'In the strictest confidence I'll tell you everything,' French answered, and he began to recount, not indeed everything, but a good many of the reasons which had led him to believe in Roper's guilt. Whymper listened with painful intensity, and when the other had finished he seemed almost unable to contain his excitement.

'I must know if you are right,' he cried, springing from his chair and beginning to pace the room. 'I must know! How can I be sure, Inspector? You have found out so much; can't you find out a little more?'

'That's what I came down for, Mr Whymper,' French said gravely. 'I must know too. And there's only one way out of it. You've got to tell me the story. I'll not use it unless it's absolutely necessary. But I'll test it and get to know definitely whether it's fact or fiction.'

Whymper paused irresolutely.

'Suppose,' he said at length, 'suppose, telling you the story involved letting you know of a crime which had been committed—not recently; many, many years ago. Suppose the criminal had escaped, but my story told you where you could find him. Would you give me your word of honour not to move in the matter?'

French glanced at him sharply.

'Of course not, Mr Whymper. You know it is foolish of you to talk like that. Neither you nor I could have knowledge of that kind and remain silent. If you learn of a crime and shield the criminal, you become an accessory after the fact. You must know that.'

'In that case,' Whymper answered, 'I can't tell you.'

French became once more suave, even coaxing.

'Now, Mr Whymper, that is quite an impossible line for you to take up. Just consider your own position. I have ample evidence to justify me in arresting you for the theft of Mr Averill's money. If I do so, this story that you are trying to keep to yourself will come out: not privately to me, but in open court. Everyone will know of it then. By keeping silent now you will defeat the very object you are striving for. Attention will be forced on to the very person you are trying to shield. And when it comes out you will be charged as an accessory. On the other hand, if you tell me the whole thing here and in private you will ease your mind of a burden and may clear yourself of suspicion of the theft. And with regard to the other crime we may find that it is a pure invention and that no such thing ever took place. Now, Mr Whymper, you've got to take the lesser risk. You've got to tell me. As I say, I'll not use your evidence unless I must.'

Whymper made no reply and French, recalling his theory that the secret concerned Ruth's parentage, decided on a bluff.

'Well,' he said, quite sharply for him. 'If you won't speak I shall have to get the information from Miss Averill. I shall be sorry to have to force her confidence about her parents, but you leave me no option.'

The bluff worked better than French could have hoped. Whymper started forward with consternation on his face.

'What?' he cried. 'Then you know?' Then realising what he had said, he swore. 'Confound you, Inspector, that was a caddish trick! But you won't get any more out of me in spite of it.'

French tried his bluff again.

'Nonsense,' he answered. 'It would be far better for Miss Averill that you should tell me than that she should. But that's a matter for you. If you like to tell me, well; if not, I shall go straight to her. Look here,' he leaned forward and tapped the other's arm, 'do you imagine that you can keep the affair secret? I've only got to trace Mr Simon Averill's history and go into the matter of Miss Ruth's parentage and the whole thing will come out. It's silly of you.' He waited

149

for a moment then got up. 'Well, if you won't, you won't. You'll come along to the station first and then I'll go to Miss Averill.'

Whymper looked startled.

'Are you going to arrest me?'

'What else can I do?' French returned.

Whymper wrung his hands as if in despair, then motioned the inspector to sit down again.

'Wait a minute,' he said brokenly. 'I'll tell you. I see I can't help myself. It is not that I am afraid for myself, but I see from all you say that I have no alternative. But I trust your word not to use the information if you can avoid it.'

'I give you my word.'

'Well, I suppose that is as much as I can expect.' He paused to collect his thoughts, then went on: 'I have already explained to you about Roper meeting me when I reached Starvel and his saying that Mr Averill was too ill to see me, and you have seen the letter that I took to be from Mr Averill, stating that he did not wish to put the matter in question in writing, that Roper was his *confidential* attendant, that he understood the affair in question and had been authorised to explain it to me. Of course on receipt of that letter I was prepared to believe whatever I heard, and I did believe it.'

'Quite natural,' French admitted suavely.

'Roper began by saying that his part in the affair was very distasteful to him, that he felt he was intruding into a family and very private matter, but that he had no alternative but to carry it through as Mr Averill had given him definite instructions to do so. He added that he was particularly sorry about it, as the matter was bound to be very painful to me. It was about Miss Averill.'

150

Whymper was evidently very reluctant to proceed, but he overcame his distaste after a moment's hesitation and in a lower voice continued:

'He went on to ask me, again with apologies, whether Mr Averill was correct in believing I wished to marry Miss Averill. If I did not, he said the information would be of no interest to me and he need not proceed with the matter. But if I did wish to marry her there was something that I should know.

'As a matter of fact, I wanted the marriage more than anything else on earth, and when I said so to Roper he gave me the message. He told me that, a few days before, Mr Averill had received a letter which upset him very much and, Roper thought, had brought on his illness. But before I could appreciate the significance of the letter he would have to explain some family matters.

'Mr Simon Averill had a brother named Theodore—I shall call them Simon and Theodore to distinguish them. As a young man Theodore had all the promise of a brilliant career. He had gone into business in London and held a very good position as French representative of his firm. He had married a French lady of old family and great beauty. One child was born, a daughter, Ruth.

'But unfortunately he was not steady, and as time passed he grew wilder and wilder and his relations with his wife became more and more strained. At last when Ruth was four years old and they were living in London, there was some fearful trouble which finished him up.

'Roper did not know the details, but it was a scandal in some illicit gambling rooms in London. Theodore was caught cheating. They were all half drunk and in the row that followed a man was killed. It was never known who actually fired the shot, but Theodore was suspected. At all events he disappeared and was never heard of again. It was the last straw for his wife and she collapsed altogether. She brought Ruth, a child of four, to Simon, begged him to look after her, and then committed suicide.

Nothing more was heard of Theodore Averill and everyone concerned believed him dead. Simon's surprise may be imagined then, when during the last two or three days he received a letter from him. This was the letter which I told you had upset him so much.

'I didn't see the letter, but Roper told me it said that Theodore was living under the name of Prosper Giraud at Talloires in Savoy. He had escaped from London to Morocco and after wandering about for a year or two had entered the French Foreign Legion. After serving several years he left that and went to Talloires, where he supported himself by writing short stories for the magazines. He did fairly well, and was comfortable enough, but recently a disastrous thing had happened to him. He had been in poor health for some time and had begun to talk in his sleep. His old housekeeper, Mme. Madeleine Blancquart, must have listened and heard something which gave his secret away, for one morning she came to him and said she had discovered all, and asked what he was going to pay to have the matter kept from the English police. He was unable to give what she demanded and for the sake of his family he prayed his brother Simon to help him. If Simon wouldn't do so, nothing could save him. He would be brought to England and perhaps executed, and Simon and Ruth would have to bear the shame.'

The recital of these facts was evidently very painful to Whymper, but he went on doggedly with his statement.

'Simon in his delicate state of health was much upset by

the whole thing, so Roper said. If the story was true he was willing to make some allowance, both because he didn't wish to have his brother come to such an end and also for his own and Ruth's sake. He had, therefore, replied sending twenty pounds, and saying that he would either go over himself to Talloires or send a representative within a month to discuss the situation.

'He found he was too feeble to go himself and for the same reason he couldn't well spare Roper, so he cast round for someone who could do it for him, and he thought of me. He thought that if I wanted to marry Miss Averill the secret would be safe with me and also I should be just as anxious to have the matter settled as he was.

'Of course I agreed to go. You can understand that I really hadn't any option, though as far as I was concerned myself I didn't care two pins what Theodore had done or hadn't done. Roper said Simon would be extremely relieved to hear my decision. He said also that Simon did not wish me to go for about three weeks, lest it would look too eager and Mme. Blancquart would think she had frightened us.

'Roper went on to say that Simon was giving me £500. Out of this I was to take my expenses and the balance was to buy off Mme. Blancquart. He did not want me to give her a lump sum, but to arrange a monthly payment which she would know she would lose if she informed. I was to find someone in Talloires who would take the money and dole it out for a percentage. The *curé* possibly might do it, or I could employ a solicitor. He left the arrangements to my judgment. In any case I was to make the best bargain I could with the woman.

'That was all on the Wednesday night before the fire started. Then came the tragedy. With Simon dead I didn't know what on earth to do. Of course I saw that I must carry out my promise just the same, and go out to Talloires and try to arrange for Theodore's safety, but I thought that if Simon's money went to Ruth, Theodore might try to make trouble with her. However, I could do nothing until I saw him and Mme. Blancquart, and I arranged to go to Talloires at the end of the three weeks as Simon had asked me.

'You can guess the rest. I took the money and went to Talloires. But as you know, I could find no trace either of Prosper Giraud or Mme. Blancquart.

'I was in a difficulty then. I had no doubt that the message was really Simon's. It never occurred to me that Roper could invent the story or steal the money, and when I failed to find the people I simply thought he had made a mistake in the address. I was pretty bothered, I can tell you. I was expecting every day to read of Theodore's arrest, and I could do nothing to prevent it.' The young man was very earnest as he added: 'I swear to you that what I have told you is the literal truth. I don't know whether you will believe me, but whether or not, I am glad I've told you. It is a tremendous weight off my mind, and if you can prove that the story was only Roper's invention I'll be ten thousand times more relieved.'

French felt that he might very well believe the statement. Not only had Whymper's manner changed and borne the almost unmistakable impress of truth, but the story he told was just the kind of story French was expecting to hear. No tale that he could think of would have better suited Roper's purpose: to make this young fellow change stolen bank notes the possession of which he could not account for. The more French thought it over in detail, the more satisfied he felt with it. It was true that there were two minor points which he did not fully understand, but neither would invalidate the tale, even if unexplained. Of these, the first was: Why had Roper asked Whymper to wait for three weeks before going to France? And the second: If the young man was as enamoured of this girl as he pretended to be, why had he not proposed to her so as to be in a proper position to offer her his protection?

A little thought gave him the answer to the first of these problems. Evidently no suspicion must fall on Whymper other than through the notes. If he were to rush away directly the tragedy occurred, any general suspicion which might have been aroused might be directed towards him for that very reason. That would be no test of the safety of passing the notes. But if three weeks elapsed before he made a move, suspicion must depend on the notes alone.

With regard to the second point French thought he might ask for information.

'I don't want to be unnecessarily personal, Mr Whymper, but there is just one matter I should like further light on. You were, I understand you to say, anxious to marry this young lady and desired to protect her from trouble with Mme. Blancquart. If that were so, would it not have been natural for you to propose to her and so obtain the right to protect her?'

Whymper made a gesture of exasperation.

'By Heavens, I only wish I had! It might have come out all right. But, Inspector, I have been a coward. To be strictly truthful, I was afraid. I'll tell you just what happened. After the tragedy I was very much upset by this whole affair. And it made me awkward and self-conscious with Miss Averill to have to keep secret a thing which concerned her so closely. I tried not to show it in my manner, but I don't think I quite succeeded. I think my manner displeased her. At all events she grew cold and distant, and—well! there it is. I didn't dare to speak. I was afraid I would have no chance. I thought I would wait until I found something out about her father. Then when this began to seem impossible, I determined to risk all and speak, but then you came threatening me with arrest for theft. I couldn't propose until that was over. And the question is, is it over now? Are you going to arrest me or how do I stand?'

'I'm not going to arrest you, Mr Whymper. You have given me the explanations I asked for, and so far I see no reason to doubt your story. I am glad you have told me. But though I believe you, I may say at once that I believe also the whole thing was Roper's invention. Why did he not show the letter he alleged Theodore Averill had written?'

'I don't know. I assumed there was something further in it which Mr Averill wished to keep from Roper and me.'

French shook his head.

'Much more likely it didn't exist and he wanted to save the labour and risk of forging it. Now, Mr Whymper, there is only one thing to be done. You or I, or both of us together, must go to Miss Averill and ask her the truth. I do not mean that we must tell her this story. We shall simply ask her where her father lived, and where she was born. Records will be available there which will set the matter at rest.'

Whymper saw the common-sense of this proposal, but he said that nothing would induce him to ask such questions of Miss Averill. It was, therefore, agreed that French should call on her and make the inquiries.

Ruth was at home when French reached the Oxleys, and she saw him at once. French apologised for troubling her so soon again, and then asked some questions as to the possible amount of petrol and paraffin which had been at Starvel on the night of the fire. From this he switched the conversation on to herself, and with a dexterity born of long practice led her to talk of her relatives. So deftly did he question her, that when in a few minutes he had discovered all he wished to know, she had not realised that she had been pumped.

In answer to his veiled suggestions she told him that her father's name was Theodore Averill, that he had lived in Bayonne, where he had held a good appointment in the wine industry, and that he had married a French lady whom he had met at Biarritz. This lady, her mother, had died when she was born and her father had only survived her by about four years. On his death she had come to her Uncle Simon, he being her only other relative. She was born in Bayonne and baptised, she believed, by the Anglican clergyman at Biarritz. Her father was a member of the Church of England and her mother a Huguenot.

'This,' French said when, half an hour later, he was back in the vestry room of the old church, 'will lead us to certainty. I will send a wire to the Biarritz police and have the records looked up. Of course, I don't doubt Miss Averill's word for a moment, but it is just conceivable that she might have been misled as to her birth. However, we want to be absolutely sure.'

He wired that evening and it may be mentioned here that in the course of a couple of days he received the following information:

1. Mr Theodore Averill was a wine merchant and lived at Bayonne.
2. Mr Averill and Mlle. Anne de Condillac had been married in the English church at Biarritz on the 24th of June, 1905.

3. Mrs Averill had died on the 17th of July, 1906, while giving birth to a daughter.
4. This daughter, whose name was Ruth, was baptised at the Anglican church, Biarritz, on the 19th of August, 1906.
5. Mr Theodore Averill had died on the 8th of September, 1910, his little four-year old daughter then being sent to England.

So that was certainty at last. Roper was the evil genius behind all these involved happenings. He it was who had got Ruth away from the doomed house; he had sent Whymper off to pass the stolen notes so that he might learn if their numbers were known; he had murdered Simon Averill: he had stolen the notes from the safe; he had murdered his wife: he had burned the house. All was now clear—except the one point at which French, trembling with exasperation, was again brought up. What had happened to Roper? What blunder had he made? How had he died? And again: Where was the money? Was it hidden or was it destroyed?

As French went down to the police station to tell Sergeant Kent he might withdraw his observation on Whymper, he determined that next morning he would begin a meticulous and detailed search of the ground surrounding the ruins in the hope of finding the answer to his last question.

But next morning French instead found himself contemplating with a growing excitement a new idea which had leaped into his mind and which bade fair to change the whole future course of his investigation.

11

A Startling Theory

Inspector French's change of plans was due to a new idea which suddenly, like the conventional bolt from the blue, flashed across the horizon of his vision.

For some reason he had been unable to sleep on that night on which he had completed his proof that the Whymper incident had been engineered by Roper. French, as a rule, was a sound sleeper: he was usually too tired on getting to bed to be anything else. But on the rare occasions when he remained wakeful he nearly always turned the circumstance to advantage by concentrating on the difficulty of the moment. His brain at such times seemed more active than normally, and more than one of his toughest problems had been solved during the hours of darkness. It was true that he frequently reached conclusions which in the sober light of day appeared fantastic and had to be abandoned, but valuable ideas had come so often that when up against a really difficult case he had thankfully welcomed a sleepless night in the hope of what it might bring forth.

On this occasion, when he had employed all the conventional

aids to slumber without effect, he turned his attention to the one problem in the Starvel Hollow tragedy which up to now had baffled him: the cause of Roper's fate. How had the man come to lose his life? What terrible mistake had he made? How had Nemesis overtaken him? French felt he could see the whole ghastly business taking place, excepting always this one point. And the more he thought of it, the more difficult it appeared. It seemed almost incredible that so clever a man should have blundered so appallingly.

He had asked himself these questions for the hundredth time when there leaped into his mind an idea so startling that for a moment he could only lie still and let his mind gradually absorb it. Roper's death seemed the incredible feature of the case, but *was this a feature of the case at all? Had Roper died?* What if his death was a fake, arranged to free him from the attentions of the police so that he might enjoy without embarrassment the fruits of his crime?

French lay trying to recall the details of a paragraph he had read in the paper a year or two previously and wondering how he had failed up to the present to draw a parallel between it and the Starvel Hollow affair. It was the account of the burning of a house in New York. After the fire it was found that a lot of valuable property had disappeared and further search revealed the remains of two human bodies. Two servants were believed to have been in the house at the time, and these bodies were naturally assumed to have been theirs. Afterwards it was proved— French could not remember how—that the two left in the house had planned the whole affair so as to steal the valuables. They had visited a cemetery, robbed a grave of two bodies, conveyed these to the house, set the place on fire and made off with the swag. Had Roper seen this paragraph and determined to copy the Americans? Or had the same idea occurred to him independently?

How Roper might or might not have evolved his plan was however, a minor point. The question was—had he evolved and carried out such a plan? Was he now alive and in possession of the money?

It was evident there were two possible lines of inquiry, either of which might give him his information.

The first was the definite identification of the body which had been found in the position of Roper's bed. Was there any physical peculiarity about Roper which would enable a conclusion to be reached as to whether this body was or was not his? It was true that the remains had been examined by Dr Emerson and unhesitatingly accepted as Roper's, but the doctor had had no reason for doubt in the matter and might therefore have overlooked some small point which would have led to a contrary conclusion.

The second line of inquiry was more promising. If Roper had carried out such a fraud he must have provided a body to substitute for his own. Had he done so, and if he had, where had this body been obtained?

Here was an act which, French felt, could not have been done without leaving traces. Roper had proved himself a very skilful man, but the secret acquisition of a dead body in a country like England was an extraordinarily difficult undertaking, and of course the more difficult an action was to carry out, the greater were the chances of its discovery. Proof or disproof of his theory would be quickly forthcoming.

Hour after hour French lay pondering the matter, and when shortly before daylight he at last fell asleep, he had laid his plans for the prosecution of his new inquiry.

He began by calling on Dr Emerson. The doctor was writing

in his consulting room when French was shown in, and he rose to greet his visitor with old-fashioned courtesy.

'Sorry for troubling you again, doctor,' French began with his pleasant smile, 'but I wanted to ask you a question. It won't take five minutes.'

'My dear sir, there is no hurry. I'm quite at your disposal.'

'Very good of you, Dr Emerson, I'm sure. It's really a matter more of idle curiosity than a serious inquiry. I was thinking over that Starvel affair, and I wondered how you were able to identify the bodies. It was a phrase in the evidence that struck me. I gathered that you said that the bodies of each of the three occupants of the house were lying on the sites of their respective beds. I should like to ask if that was stated from definite identification of the remains, or if it was merely a reasonable and justifiable assumption?'

'If that is what you read, I am afraid I have not been correctly reported. I certainly never said that the body found at each bed was that of the owner of the bed. That they were so I have no doubt: from every point of view I think that is a reasonable and justifiable assumption, to use your own phrase. But actual identification was quite impossible. It is rather an unpleasant subject, but fire, especially such a furnace as must have raged at Starvel, destroys practically all physical characteristics.

'But you were able to tell the sex and age of the victims?'

'The sex and approximate age, yes. Given a skeleton or even certain bones, that can be stated with certainty. But that is a very different thing from identification.'

'I thought I was right,' French declared. 'I had always heard that was the result of fire, and therefore was puzzled. Identification of burnt remains has however been frequently established from rings or jewellery, has it not?'

'Certainly, though there was nothing of the kind in the instance in question. Indeed, such identification would have been almost impossible in any case. In that intense heat gold rings or settings would have melted and the stones themselves would have dropped out and would only be found by an extraordinarily lucky chance.'

French rose.

'Quite so. I agree. Well, I'm glad to know I was right. We Yard Inspectors are always on the look-out for first-hand information.'

So the first of the three lines of inquiry had petered out. The bodies were unidentifiable, and therefore so far as that was concerned, his theory might be true or it might not.

As he strolled slowly back to the hotel, French considered his second clue: the provision by Roper of a body to take the place of his own.

From the first the difficulty of such a feat had impressed French, and as he now thought of it in detail, this difficulty grew until it seemed almost insurmountable. Where could bodies be obtained? Only surely in one of three ways: from a medical institution, from a cemetery, and by means of murder.

With regard to the first of these three, it was true that bodies were used for medical purposes, for dissection, for the instruction of students. But they were not obtainable by outside individuals. French thought that it would be absolutely impossible for Roper to have secured what he wanted from such a source. So convinced of this was he that he felt he might dismiss the idea from his mind.

Could then the remains have been obtained from a cemetery?

Here again the difficulties, though not quite so overwhelming, were sufficiently great as almost to negative the suggestion. Of one thing French felt convinced; that neither Roper nor any other man in Roper's position could have carried out such an enterprise singlehanded. One or more confederates would have been absolutely necessary. To mention a single point only, no one person would have had the physical strength to perform such a task. No one person, furthermore, could have taken the requisite precautions against surprise or discovery, nor could one person have carried out the needful transport arrangements between the cemetery and Starvel.

The whole subject, as French thought out its details, was indescribably gruesome and revolting. But so interested was he in its purely intellectual side—as a problem for which a solution must be found—that he overlooked the horror of the actual operations. For him the matter was one of pure reason. He did not consider the human emotions involved except in so far as these might influence the conduct of the actors in the terrible drama.

Assuming then that the remains had not been procured from a cemetery, there remained but one alternative—murder! Some unknown person must have been inveigled into that sinister house and there done to death, so as to provide the needful third body! If Roper were guilty of the Starvel crime as French now understood it, it looked as if he must have been guilty of a third murder, hitherto unsuspected.

Here was food for thought and opportunity for inquiry. Who had disappeared about the time of the tragedy? Was anyone missing in the neighbourhood? Had anyone let it be known that he was leaving the district or going abroad about that date? Instead of being at the end of his researches, French was rather appalled by the magnitude of the investigation which was opening out in front of him. To obtain the necessary information might require the prolonged activities of a large staff.

He was anxious not to give away the lines on which he was working. He decided therefore not to make his inquiries from Sergeant Kent at the local station, but to go to Leeds and have an interview with the chief constable.

Accordingly, unconsciously following the example of Oxley and Tarkington several weeks earlier, he took the 3.30 p.m. train that afternoon and two hours later was seated in Chief Constable Valentine's room at police headquarters. The old gentleman received him very courteously, and for once French met someone who seemed likely to outdo him in suavity and charm of manner.

'I thought, sir, my case was over when I had cleared up the matter of the bank notes passed to Messrs Cook in London,' French declared as he accepted a cigarette from the other's case, 'but one or two rather strange points have made me form a tentative theory which seems sufficiently probable to need going into. In short—' and he explained with business-like brevity his ideas about Roper with the facts from which they had sprung.

The chief constable was profoundly impressed by the recital, much more so than French would have believed possible.

'It's a likely enough theory,' he admitted. 'Your arguments seem unanswerable and I certainly agree that the idea is sufficiently promising to warrant investigation.'

'I'm glad, sir, that you think so. In my job, as you know, there is always the danger of being carried away by some theory that appeals because of its ingenuity, while overlooking some more commonplace explanation that is much more likely to be true.'

'I know that, and this may of course be an instance. I am glad, however, that you mentioned your theory to me. It is an idea which should be kept secret, and I shall set inquiries on foot without giving away the Starvel connection.'

'Then, sir, you can't recall any disappearances about the time?'

'I can't. And I don't expect we shall find any. Do you?'

'Well, I was in hope that we might.'

Major Valentine shook his head.

'No, Inspector; there I think you're wrong,' he said with decision. 'If Roper really carried out these crimes, he's far too clever to leave an obvious trail of that kind. We may be sure that if he inveigled some third person to the house and murdered him, a satisfactory explanation of the victim's absence was provided. You suggested it yourself in your statement. The man will ostensibly have left his surroundings, never to return. If he was a native he will have gone to America or some other distant place. If he was a visitor he will have left to return home. Somehow matters will have been arranged so that he will disappear without raising suspicion. Don't you think so?'

'Yes, sir, I certainly do. But it's going to make it a hard job to trace him.'

'I know it is. If he lived in a large town it will be so hard that we probably shan't succeed, but if he came from the country or a village the local men should have the information.'

'That is so, sir. Then I may leave the matter in your hands?'

'Yes, I'll attend to it. By the way, where are you staying?'

French told him, and after some desultory discussion, took his leave and caught the last train back to Thirsby. He was partly pleased and partly disappointed by his interview. He had hoped for the co-operation of the chief constable, but

166

Major Valentine had gone much further than this. He had really taken the immediate further prosecution of the investigation out of French's hands. French was therefore temporarily out of a job. Moreover French had the contempt of the Londoner and the specialist for those whom he was pleased to think of as 'provincial amateurs.' And yet he could not have acted otherwise than as he had. The organisation of the police with all its ramifications was needed for the job, and the chief constable controlled the organisation.

Next morning after he had brought his notes of the case to date, French left the hotel, and walking in the leisurely, rather aimless fashion he affected in the little town, approached the church. It had occurred to him that he would spend his enforced leisure in an examination of the cemeteries in the immediate district, to see if any local conditions would favour the operations of a body-snatcher.

Owing to the renovation, the church gate was open and French, passing through, turned into the graveyard surrounding the picturesque old building. It also was old—old and completely filled with graves. As French leisurely strolled round the paths, he could not find a single vacant lot. Even on the wall of the church itself there were monuments, one of which bore the date 1573 and none of which were later than 1800. Though the place was carefully tended there were no signs of recent interments, and French was not therefore surprised to learn from one of the workmen that there was a new cemetery at the opposite end of the town.

He stood looking round, considering the possibilities of grave robbing. The church was almost in the centre of the town and the graveyard was surrounded on all sides by houses. In front was the old High Street, fenced off by a tall iron railing and with a continuous row of houses and shops opposite. The other three sides were bounded by a six-foot wall, the two ends abutting on the gables and yards of the High Street houses, and the back on a narrow street called Church Lane, again with houses all the way along its opposite side. There were heavy wrought iron gates leading to both Church Lane and High Street.

The longer French examined the place, the more certain he became that the robbery of a grave by less than three or four persons was an absolute impossibility. However, he saw the sexton and made sure that both gates were locked on the night in question.

He next paid a similar visit to the new cemetery. Here the difficulties were not quite so overwhelming as it was farther from the town and much less overlooked. At the same time even here they were so great as to make theft practically impossible.

In the afternoon he tramped to the only other cemetery in the district—that of a village some three miles north-east of Starvel. But again his investigations met with a negative result and he definitely put out of his mind the theory that Roper had robbed a grave.

For two days he kicked his heels in Thirsby, hoping against hope that he would hear something from Major Valentine and wondering whether he should not go back to London, and then he accidentally learned a fact which gave him a new idea and started him off on a fresh line of investigation.

As a forlorn hope it had occurred to him that he would call again on Ruth Averill to inquire whether she could think of anyone who might have visited Starvel after she left for York. He did not expect an affirmative reply, but he thought the inquiry would pass the time as profitably as anything else.

Ruth, however, had known of no one.

'We never had a visitor, Mr French,' she went on, 'rarely or ever. Except those three or four calls of Mr Whymper's of which I told you, I don't think a single person had come to the place for a year. Why should they?'

'It must have been lonely for you,' French said sympathetically.

'It was lonely. I didn't realise it at the time, except just after coming back from school, but now that I have plenty of people to speak to I see how very lonely it was.'

'You didn't feel able to make confidants of the Ropers? Of course,' French went on hastily, 'I know they were only servants, but still many servants are worthy of the fullest confidence.'

Ruth shook her head.

'No, I didn't feel that I could make friends with either. It was not in the least because they were servants. Some of the cottagers were even lower socially, and yet they were real friends. But there was something repellent about the Ropers, or at least I thought so. I was never happy with either of them. And yet both were kind and attentive and all that. Of course, there was Mr Giles. He was always friendly, and I enjoyed helping him with his insects. But I didn't really see a great deal of him.'

French felt sorry for the young girl, as he thought of the unhappy life she must have led.

'I think I understand how you feel,' he returned gently. 'Personality is a wonderful thing, is it not? It is quite intangible, but one recognises it and acts on it instinctively. And that Mr Giles whom you mentioned. Who is he, if it is not an impertinent question?'

'Oh, he is dead,' Ruth answered sadly and with some surprise in her tones. 'Did you not hear about him? He lived close to Starvel—at least, about half a mile away—but his cottage was the nearest house. He was dreadfully delicate and, I am afraid, rather badly off. He was wounded in the War and was never afterwards able to work. He was interested in insects and kept bees. He collected butterflies and beetles and wrote articles about them. Sometimes I used to help him to pin out his specimens. He taught me a lot about them.'

'And you say he died?'

'Yes, wasn't it tragic? The poor man died just at the time of the Starvel affair. It was too terrible. When I came back from York I found he had gone too.'

French almost leaped off his seat as he heard these words. Was it possible that in his careless, half-interested inquiries he had blundered on to the one outstanding fact that he needed? Could it be that Mr Giles' death represented Roper's search for a body? That he was his third victim?

Crushing down his eagerness French did his best to simulate a polite and sympathetic interest.

'How terrible for you, Miss Averill!' he said with as real feeling in his tones as he could compass. 'One shock added to another. Tell me about it, if it is not too painful a recollection.'

'Oh no, I'll tell you. He fell ill a few days before I went to York—influenza, Mrs Roper thought, but he must have been fairly bad as he had Dr Philpot out to see him. Both the Ropers were certainly very good to him. They went up and nursed him, for the woman who usually looked after him had not time to stay with him for more than an hour or so in the day. I went up and sat with him occasionally, too. On the morning I went to York he seemed much worse. I called on my way into Thirsby, and he was lying without moving and was terribly white and feeble looking. His voice also was very faint. He just said he was comfortable and had everything he wanted. Mrs Roper said that if he didn't soon get better she would send Roper in for Dr Emerson. Dr Philpot, I should explain, had just gone down with influenza.'

'And what was the next thing you heard?'

'Why,' Ruth made a little gesture of horror, 'the next thing I knew of it was that we met the funeral. It was awful. It was the second day after the fire. I wanted to go out and see Starvel, and Mrs Oxley drove me out in their car. When we were coming back, just as we reached the point where, the Starvel road branches off, we saw a funeral coming in along the main road. It was trotting and we waited to let it pass on. Mr Stackpool—that's the vicar—and Dr Emerson were there and they told us whose it was. Of course we joined them. *Poor* Mr Giles. I *was* sorry for him. But nothing could have been done. Dr Emerson said he became unconscious the same day that I saw him, and passed away, without suffering. That was something to be thankful for at least.'

'Indeed, yes,' French agreed with feeling. 'I wonder if I haven't heard about Mr Giles. He was a very tall old man, wasn't he, and walked with a stoop?'

'Oh no, he wasn't specially tall or old either. Just medium height and middle age, I should say. Nor did he walk with a stoop. You must be thinking of someone else.'

'I suppose I must,' French admitted, and as soon as he reasonably could he took his leave.

That he now held in his hand the solution of the mystery he no longer doubted. He would have wagered ten years of his life that this Giles' remains had been taken from the wreck of Starvel and interred under the name of John Roper. Such a supposition, moreover, was consistent with the medical evidence. Dr Emerson had stated at the inquest that the third body was that of a man of middle height and middle age. This, of course, had been taken as applying to Roper, but it might equally apply to Giles. It was certainly a lucky thing for Roper's scheme that a person so suitable for his diabolical purpose should happen to live so near to the scene of the crime. Or more probably, it was this very fact that had suggested the idea of the substitution to Roper.

But if Giles had been murdered, what about Dr Emerson's certificate? In this wretched case the solution of one problem only seemed to lead to another. French felt that he had still further work before him ere he could begin the second stage of his case—the search for Roper. Lost in thought he returned to the Thirsdale Arms for lunch.

12

A Somewhat Gruesome Chapter

To inquire of a fully fledged and responsible medical man whether he has or has not given a false death certificate, without at the same time ruffling his feelings, is an undertaking requiring a nice judgment and not a little tact. As French once again climbed the steps to Dr Emerson's hall door early that same afternoon, he felt that the coming interview would tax even his powers of suave inquiry. In a way, of course, it didn't matter whether the doctor's feelings were ruffled or not, but both on general principles and from a desire to prevent his witness becoming hostile, the detective was anxious to save the other's face.

'How are you, doctor? Here I am back to worry you again,' French began pleasantly as he was shown in to the consulting room. They chatted for a few moments and then French went on: 'I wanted to ask you in confidence about an acquaintance of Miss Averill's, a Mr Giles who died recently. You knew him?'

'I attended him. I attended him for some years until Dr Philpot came, then he took him over as well as most of my other country patients. I am not so young as I was and the arrangement suited us both. He died while Dr Philpot was ill, and I went out and gave the necessary certificate.'

'So I gathered, and that's why I came to you. What a curious coincidence it was that this man should pass away at the very time of the fire! That all four of Miss Averill's closest acquaintances should die at practically the same time is, you must admit, as strange as it is tragic.'

Emerson looked at his visitor curiously.

'Strange enough and tragic enough, I admit,' he answered, 'but such coincidences are not infrequent. It is my experience that coincidences which would be deemed too remarkable for a novel constantly occur in real life.'

'I quite agree with you. I have often said the same thing. Mr Giles was an invalid, was he not?'

'Yes, from what he told me the poor fellow had a rather miserable life. He was always delicate, and when he volunteered in 1914, he was rejected because of his heart. As the war dragged on the authorities became less particular and in 1917 he was re-examined and passed for foreign service, wrongly, as I think. However, that's what happened. He went to France and in less than a month he was in hospital, having been both gassed and wounded. As a result his heart became more seriously affected. Even five years ago he was in a state in which death might have occurred from a sudden shock, and myocarditis is a complaint which does not improve as the years pass.'

'Then it was myocarditis he died of?'

'Yes. He had an attack of influenza on the previous Thursday. When Dr Philpot got laid up and asked me to take his patients over he told me he had seen Mr Giles and that he was in a bad way. The influenza made an extra call on

174

the poor man's heart which no doubt hastened his end, but the actual cause of death was myocarditis.'

'Does this disease leave any infallible signs after death? I mean, can a doctor say definitely, from the mere inspection of the remains that death was due to it and to no other cause? Don't think me impertinent in asking. I told you we inspectors were always out after first-hand information.'

Dr Emerson raised his eyebrows as if to indicate delicately that the question was perhaps not in the best taste, but with only the slightest hint of stiffness he replied:

'In this case the question does not arise. This man was in a serious condition of health; his heart might have failed at any moment. Moreover, he was suffering from influenza, which puts an extra strain on the heart. Dr Philpot gave it as his opinion that he would not recover. When therefore I learned that he had died suddenly I was not surprised. It was only to be expected. Further, when I examined him he showed every sign of death from heart failure.'

'But that is just the point, doctor. Excuse my pressing it, but I really am interested. For my own information I should like to know whether these signs that you speak of were absolutely peculiar to a death from heart disease. I understood, please correct me if I am wrong, but I understood that only an autopsy could really establish the point beyond question.'

Dr Emerson hesitated.

'These are very peculiar questions,' he said presently. 'I think you should tell me what is in your mind. It seems to me that I am equally entitled to ask how the death of Mr Giles affects the cause of the Starvel fire?'

French nodded, and drawing forward his chair, spoke more confidentially.

'You are, doctor. I had not intended to mention my suspicion, but since you have asked me, I'll answer your question. I will ask you to keep what I am about to say very strictly to yourself, and on that understanding I must tell you that I'm not connected with an insurance company: I'm an inspector from Scotland Yard. Certain facts which I do not wish to go into at present have led me to suspect that Mr Giles may have been murdered. I want to make sure.'

Dr Emerson stared as if he couldn't believe his ears, and his jaw dropped.

'God bless my soul!' he cried. '*Murdered?* Did I hear you say murdered?'

'Yes,' said French, 'but I am not sure about it. It is only a suspicion.'

'A pretty nasty suspicion for me, after my certificate! But you couldn't be right. The very idea is absurd! Who could have murdered such a harmless man, and badly off at that!'

'Well, I think it might be possible to find a motive. But if you don't mind, I'd really rather not discuss what may prove to be a mare's nest. However, you see now the object of my questions. I want to know the possibilities from the medical point of view. Perhaps you will tell me about that autopsy?'

Dr Emerson was manifestly disturbed by French's suggestion. He moved uneasily in his chair and gave vent to exclamations of scepticism and concern. 'Of course,' he went on, 'I'll tell you everything I can, and I needn't say I most sincerely hope your suspicion is unfounded. You are perfectly correct on the other point. Only an autopsy can establish beyond question the fact of a death from myocarditis. If I had had the slightest doubt in Mr Giles' case I should have required one before giving a certificate. But I had no doubt, and with all due respect to you I have none now.'

'You may be right, doctor. I'll tell you as soon as I know myself. In the meantime thank you for your information and not a word to a soul.'

French left the house with a deep satisfaction filling his mind. Dr Emerson's admission was what he had hoped for and it very nearly banished his last remaining doubt. But he felt that he ought to get Dr Philpot's views also. Philpot had seen the man before death and his evidence would certainly be required if the matter went further.

Accordingly, he turned in the direction of the younger man's house, and a few minutes later was entering a consulting-room for the second time that day.

'Good afternoon, doctor,' he said, with his usual cheery smile. 'I've come on my old tack of looking for information. But it's a very simple matter this time: just one question on quite a different subject.'

Dr Philpot was looking changed: old and worn and despondent. French was rather shocked at his appearance. He was sitting forward in his chair, hunched over the fire, with his head resting in his hands and a look of brooding misery on his features. He looked like a man upon whom a long expected blow had at last fallen; a man at the end of his tether, who does not know which way to turn for relief. And then, somewhat to French's surprise, the cause came out.

'Of course, of course,' the other murmured, rousing himself as if from an evil dream. 'If you want to know anything from me ask it now, for I'm leaving the town almost at once.'

French was genuinely surprised.

'Leaving the town?' he repeated. 'You don't mean—? Do you mean for good?'

'For good, yes. And I don't want ever to see the cursed

place again. But it's my own fault. I may as well tell you, for you'll hear it soon enough. I have failed.'

'Financially, you mean?'

Philpot glanced at his visitor with sombre resentment.

'Financially, of course. How else?' he growled. 'It was never a land flowing with milk and honey, this place, but for the last few months my position has been getting more and more impossible. The only things I get plenty of are bills—bills everywhere, and no money to meet them. I've struggled and fought to keep my end up, but it has been no good. When I came, I couldn't afford to buy a practice, and though I've not done so badly owing to Dr Emerson's giving up his more distant patients, I haven't built up quickly enough and my little capital couldn't stand the strain. Another three or four years and I might have got my head above water.' He made a gesture of despair. 'But there it is and complaining won't help it.'

French's natural reaction was to show sympathy with anyone in trouble, and he could not help feeling sorry for this doctor who had made a mess of his life and who now, nearing middle age, was going to have to begin all over again. But when he remembered what the landlord of the Thirsdale Arms had told him of the man's gambling proclivities, his sympathy was somewhat checked. To continue gambling when you know that your indulgence is going to prevent your paying your just debts is but a short way removed from theft. Of course, French did not know how far the landlord's story was true, so it was with relief that he reminded himself that he was not Philpot's judge, and that his business was simply to get the information he required as easily and pleasantly as he could.

'I am exceedingly sorry to hear what you say,' he declared

gravely, and he was not altogether a hypocrite in making his manner and tone express genuine regret. 'It is a terrible position for anyone to find himself in and I can well understand how you feel. But, though bad, you must not consider it hopeless. Many a man has passed through a similar trouble and has come out on top in the end.'

Philpot smiled faintly.

'I appreciate your kindness,' he answered. 'But don't let us talk about it. I told you in order to explain my departure and because you would hear it in any case. But if you don't mind, I would rather not speak of it again. You said something about a question, I think?'

'Yes, but first I must ask just this. You say you are leaving here. Suppose through some unexpected development in this Starvel case you are wanted to give evidence. Can I find you?'

'Of course, I am going to a friend in Glasgow who says he can find me a job. I shall be staying with Mrs MacIntosh, of 47 Kilgore Street, Dumbarton Road.'

French noted the address.

'Thanks. I do not think I shall want you, but I should be remiss in my duty if I failed to keep in touch with you. The other question is about a friend of Miss Averill's, a man named Giles, who died about the time of the fire. I wish you would tell me what he died of.'

Dr Philpot looked at him in surprise. Then something approaching a twinkle appeared in his eye.

'Hullo! Another—er—unexpected development? Is it indiscreet to inquire?'

'It is,' French answered, 'but I'll tell you because I really want my information. It may be a very serious matter, Dr Philpot, and I am mentioning it in strict confidence only. I have certain reasons to suppose that Mr Giles may have been murdered and I want to get your views on the possibility.'

Dr Philpot's astonishment at the announcement was quite as marked as that of his *confrère,* but he made less effort to conceal his scepticism.

'My dear Inspector! You're surely not serious? Giles? Oh come now, you don't expect me to believe that? What possible motive could anyone have for doing such a thing?'

French did not explain the motive. He said he didn't claim infallibility and admitted he might be wrong in his theory. He was simply collecting facts and he wanted any the other could supply.

'Well,' Philpot declared, 'these are the facts so far as I know them.' He crossed over to an index, and rapidly looking through it, withdrew a card. 'This is the man's record. He was seriously ill to begin with: he had a heart affection which might have killed him at any moment. I have attended him for years and his disease was growing worse. His life in fact was precarious. That is your first fact.

'The second is that during the week before his death he developed influenza. I went out and saw him on the Friday. I believed that his days were numbered and I expected to hear of his death at any time. He did die, if I remember correctly, on the following Tuesday. I did not see him then as I was myself down with 'flu, but Dr Emerson saw him and he can tell you if his death was natural. I don't know, Inspector, what you are basing your opinion on, but I can say with certainty that I shall be surprised if you are right.'

'It is your outlook on the matter which most strongly supports my suspicion,' French rejoined: 'yours and Dr Emerson's, for I have seen him and his is the same. He was expecting that Mr Giles would die from his disease, consequently when he did die he assumed that the disease was the cause. Perfectly natural, mind you: I'm not criticising him. But my point is that his preconceived idea made him less critical than he might otherwise have been.'

'Ingenious no doubt, but to me unconvincing. However, it is not my affair, but yours. Is there any other question that you wish me to answer?'

French rapidly reflected. He thought that there was nothing more. Between these two men he had got what he wanted.

'I don't think there is, doctor,' he returned. 'I'm afraid your information hasn't helped me on much, but after all it was facts that I wanted. I'll not detain you any longer. Allow me just to say that I hope your present difficulties will be shortlived and that you may soon settle down satisfactorily again.'

So, as far as the medical testimony was concerned, his theory about Giles' murder might well be true. Dr Emerson had really been very lax and yet, French imagined, most medical men in similar circumstances would have acted as he had done. But whether that was so or not, Emerson had jumped to conclusions and had signed the death certificate without having really taken any trouble to ascertain the cause of death. And this, if necessary, he could be made to admit in the witness box.

French saw that only one thing would settle the matter. Giles' coffin must be opened and the contents examined.

To obtain the necessary powers from the Home Office was a simple matter in London, where the request could be put through direct from the Yard. But here in Yorkshire it must come from the local authorities. French decided therefore that his proper course would be to put the additional facts that he had learned before Major Valentine and let that officer see to the rest. It was not a matter upon which he cared to telephone or write, so having made an appointment by wire, he once again took the afternoon train for Leeds.

'I believe, sir, that I have found where that third body was obtained,' he began, as he took his seat for the second time in the chief constable's room. 'It is, of course, only theory, indeed, you might almost say guesswork, but I think it works in. The nearest inhabitant to Starvel, a man living alone, died on the night before the fire.' French went on to relate in detail what took place and to give his views thereon.

The chief constable heard him in silence, and then sat for some moments thinking the matter over.

'I'm afraid I don't feel so sanguine about it as you seem to,' he said at last. 'At the same time I agree that the matter must be settled by an examination of the coffin. But I shall be surprised if Giles' body is not found within it.'

'It may be, sir, of course,' French admitted. 'But I'm glad you agree that we should make sure. In that case there is no object in delay. Will you obtain the necessary exhumation order, or is there anything you wish me to do in the matter?'

'No, I'll see to it. You may arrange with Kent to get the work done. Let Kent arrange for a magistrate to be present. A representative will be required from the Home Office, of course?'

'I'm afraid so, sir.'

'Then you may expect the order in a day or two. I shall be very much interested to hear the result. It will be impossible to keep the affair quiet?'

'I'm afraid so. There will be too many concerned in it.'

'Quite. Well, you must get up some tale about it. What are you going to say?'

'I haven't thought yet, sir. I'll dish out something when the time comes.'

When French reached Hellifield on his return journey he found Oxley on the platform.

'You been travelling also, Inspector?' Oxley greeted him. 'I've just been to Penrith for the day. These connections always make me curse. They're all arranged to and from Leeds, but people going to or from the north have to kick their heels here for the best part of an hour each way.'

'Can't please everybody, Mr Oxley,' French remarked tritely.

'You think not?' Oxley smiled. 'Well, how's the case?'

'Nothing doing for the moment. I was in seeing Dr Philpot this morning. He seems in a bad way, poor fellow.'

Oxley looked grave.

'It's a bad case, I fear.' He glanced round and his voice sank. 'From what I've heard and by putting two and two together I shouldn't wonder if he'll only pay two or three shillings in the pound. All gone to the bookies, or nearly all. You know, Inspector, between ourselves, when a man's in debt all round, as he is, it's not just the game to go putting his last few pounds on horses.'

'It's a fact, Mr Oxley. Of course, one must remember that the gambler plunges in the hope of pulling something off. If he had had some bits of luck he might have put himself square.'

'That's true, and you can imagine anyone taking the risk. If he wins his whole trouble is over, while if he loses he is little the worse. He may as well be hanged for a sheep as a lamb. But you haven't told me how the case is getting on.'

It was natural enough that Oxley should be interested in his investigations, but French thought he pushed his curiosity a little too far. They met fairly often—sometimes, he thought, not entirely by accident—and every time Oxley made a dead set at him to learn what he was doing and if he had reached any conclusions. French did not like being pumped, and as a result he became closer than ever. On this occasion it taxed even his skill to put the solicitor off without unpleasantly plain speaking, but he managed it at last and the talk drifted into other channels. Oxley was in his usual state of rather boisterous good humour, and before the train stopped at Thirsby he regaled French with the gossip of the district and told a number of the highly flavoured stories in which his soul delighted.

Coincidence ordained that French should meet at the station the one person whose curiosity as to the progress of the investigation was even keener than Oxley's—Tarkington's clerk, Bloxham. Bloxham never lost an opportunity of fishing for information, and French had little doubt that their frequent 'unexpected' meetings were carefully pre-arranged. On the present occasion the man joined French with a 'Walking to the hotel, Mr French? I'm just going that way too,' and immediately began to ask leading questions. But French's feelings were still somewhat ruffled from his encounter with Oxley, and for once Bloxham received as direct and decisive a reply as his heart could wish.

'Sorry, Mr French,' he stammered, staring at French in considerable surprise. 'I'm afraid we outsiders must bother you a lot. I was interested because of the notes, you understand, but of course if the thing is confidential that's another matter.'

'That's all right,' French returned, recovering his temper. 'Come and have a drink.'

Two days later the exhumation order came, and that same night shortly after twelve o'clock a little party emerged from the local police station, and separating at the door, set off by various routes in the direction of the cemetery. Inspector French walked down the High Street with Dr Laming, the Home Office representative, Sergeant Kent with Colonel Followes, the local magistrate from whom French had obtained the warrant for Whymper's arrest, went via Cross Lane, while a sturdy policeman armed with tools disappeared down a parallel street.

The night was dark and cloudy, with a cold south-westerly wind which gave promise of early rain. There was a thin crescent moon, though its light penetrated but slightly through the pall of cloud. The men shivered and turned up their collars as they faced the raw damp air.

The five met within the gates of the cemetery, which were opened to them by the caretaker and relocked behind them. Two gravediggers were in attendance. In the darkness and silence the little company moved off, and led by the caretaker, crossed the ground towards its north-easterly corner.

The place was very secluded. It lay on the side of a gently sloping hill whose curving bulk screened it from the town. It was tastefully laid out and well kept, but to the little party, with their minds full of their gruesome mission, it seemed eerie and sinister. The shrubs and bushes which French had so much admired on his previous visit, now presented shadowy and menacing forms which moved and changed their positions as the men passed on. Presently a beam from an acetylene bicycle lamp flashed out and the caretaker called a halt.

'This is it,' he said in a low voice, pointing to the long narrow mound of a grave.

Silently the two gravediggers advanced, and stretching a tarpaulin on the grass alongside the mound, began to remove the sods. Then they dug, first through dark soil and then through yellow, which they heaped up in a pyramid on the tarpaulin. They worked steadily, but a whole hour had passed before with a dull thud a spade struck something hollow.

'We're down at last,' the caretaker said, while the diggers redoubled their efforts.

Gradually the top of the coffin became revealed and the men, undermining the walls of their excavation, worked the clay out from round the sides. Presently all was clear.

As the interment had taken place only some two months earlier the coffin was still perfectly sound. Raising it was therefore an easy matter. Ropes were lowered and passed through the handles, and with a steady pull, the sinister casket came away from the clay beneath and in a few seconds was lying on the grass beside the hole. French, holding his electric torch to the brass plate, could read the inscription: 'Markham Giles, died 14th September, 1926. Aged 36.'

Meanwhile the sturdy policeman had come forward with a screwdriver and was beginning to withdraw the screws holding down the lid. Everyone but the case-hardened Home Office official felt a thrill of excitement pass over him as the fateful moment approached. Only Dr Laming and French had before taken part in an exhumation, and the feelings of the others were stirred by the gruesome nature of the operations and thoughts of the ghastly sight which they expected would soon meet their eyes. With French it was different. He was moved because his reputation was at stake. So much depended for him on what that raised lid would reveal. If he had put all concerned to the trouble and expense of an unnecessary exhumation, it would count against him. He found it hard to stand still and to preserve a suitable attitude of aloofness while the constable slowly operated his screwdriver.

At last the screws were removed and the lid was carefully raised and lifted clear. And then the eyes which had been bulging with anticipated horror, bulged still more with incredulous amazement. There was no sign of Markham Giles' body or any other! Instead, the coffin was half-full of dark, peaty earth! And when this earth was sifted nothing was found embedded in it.

The sight produced varying emotions in the onlookers. The uninitiated broke into exclamations of wonder: French felt such a wave of satisfaction sweep through him that he could have shouted in his delight: Dr Laming contented himself with a quick glance and a murmur of 'One for you, French. Congratulations.' All felt that they had assisted in a unique experiment, the result of which had triumphantly vindicated the authorities.

This, then, was the end of the mystery. The conclusion which French had reached by analysis and deduction had been tested and had proved true, and that proof established at one and the same time the whole of the steps of his line of reasoning. Roper was guilty of one of the most diabolical plots ever conceived in the mind of a criminal. He had allowed nothing to stand in his way. He had sacrificed the lives of no less than three people in order that he might with the greater security steal his employer's money. Every part of his devilish scheme was made clear, except one—his present whereabouts. French determined that he would immediately begin to trace him and that nothing would induce him to stop until he had succeeded.

It was not long before the news of the discovery leaked out. When French came down to breakfast next morning he found three reporters waiting for him, and he had hardly begun to speak to them when a fourth arrived.

'That's all right, gentlemen,' he said pleasantly. 'I am from Scotland Yard after all, and I'll tell you as much as I can. I only wish I knew more! As to what may or may not lie behind it I cannot hazard a guess; we are about to go into that. But the fact is that we received secret information—I can't give away the source—you may say an anonymous letter if you like—but information was forthcoming which led us to believe that that poor gentleman, Mr Giles, had become the victim of a gang of criminals. The story was to the effect that he had been murdered by chloroform or poison, and that after he had been coffined, the gang returned and removed the body, disposing of it in some other way. That was all, but it obviously suggested that the gang in question was that of the burglars who, as you are aware, have been active in these parts for many months, and that they had emptied the coffin in order to find a temporary safe deposit for their booty. That, at all events, was a possible explanation. On going into the matter I thought it was worth while testing the story by exhuming the coffin, and sure enough, the body was gone. But the other suggestion about the burglars' swag wasn't so happy. When we opened the coffin we found it half-full of earth: about the weight of the deceased. Needless to say we searched it thoroughly, but there was nothing else in it. So, whatever the motive of the crime, it was not to find a safe hiding place for valuables.'

The reporters were voluble in their interest and in the joy they evidently felt in the scoop vouchsafed them.

'Some story that, Inspector,' they cried. 'Tell us more and we'll give you a good write up.'

But French smilingly shook his head.

'Sorry it's all I'm at liberty to give away,' he declared. 'Come now, gentlemen, I haven't done so badly for you.

Plenty of men in my position wouldn't have told you anything.'

'But do you not think,' said one, the least vociferous of the four, 'that your theory may have been right after all? Is it not possible that the stuff was hidden in the coffin as you suggested, but was dug up and removed by the gang before you made your exhumation?'

'I thought of that,' French declared brazenly, 'and you may be right, though there were no signs of it. However, that is one of the things to be gone into.'

When French had breakfasted he went to see the undertaker who had conducted Giles' funeral, and there he received some information which still more firmly established the theory he had evolved.

'The whole arrangements,' explained Mr Simkins, the proprietor, in the course of the conversation, 'were carried out to Mr Roper's orders. Mr Roper said that Mr Giles had had an idea he mightn't get over the attack, and he had handed him the money for his funeral, asking him to see to it as he had no relative to do it. There were twelve pounds over when the ground was bought, and Mr Roper handed the money to me and told me to do the best I could with it. He said he thought the best plan would be to get the body coffined that afternoon—it was a Wednesday—and have the funeral on the Friday. He said the doctor thought the coffining should be done as soon as possible, and while the day of the interment didn't really matter, Friday would suit as well as any. That was the reason he gave for the arrangement, for you know, sir, in inexpensive funerals at such a distance, we generally do the coffining just before the funeral and so make the one journey do. But that was the way it was done.'

'I understand,' French answered. 'Mr Giles died on the

Tuesday, the coffining was done on the Wednesday, and the funeral took place on the Friday. That right?'

'That's right, sir.'

It seemed to French that the undertaker's statement demonstrated the sole remaining steps of Roper's plan so completely that every detail of that hideous night now stood revealed in all its ghastliness. He had not only murdered Markham Giles, but he had arranged that the body should he coffined in the lonely house on the night of the major tragedy. On that night he and probably Mrs Roper must have opened the coffin, taken out the remains, replaced them with the proper weight of earth, and once more screwed down the lid. A small hand-cart such as French had noticed in the unburnt outhouse at Starvel would serve to convey the remains to the Hollow, where they were to be used in such a terrible way to bolster up the deception.

Truly, it was a well-thought-out scheme! And how nearly had it succeeded! But its success would be short-lived. With set teeth and frowning brow French vowed to himself that he would not rest until he had the monster who had done this deed safely under lock and key.

13

The Piece of Yellow Clay

All that day Inspector French's thoughts kept reverting to that tense moment in the cemetery when the lid of the coffin had been raised and his theory had been so dramatically established. The memory filled his mind with a deep satisfaction. He felt that he had achieved nothing less than a veritable triumph. Other cases he had handled well, indeed he thought he might say brilliantly. But in no previous case had he solved his problem by such a creative effort of the imagination. He had imagined what might have happened, he had tested his theory, and he had found it had happened. The highest kind of work, this! His superiors could not fail to be impressed.

But there was more than that in it. Seldom had he known of a case which contained such arresting and dramatic features. When the facts became known they would make something more than a nine days' wonder. The old miser, living meanly in his decaying house at the bottom of that sinister hollow on the lonely moor; the hoarded thousands in his safe; the terrible conflagration which wiped out in a night the whole building and everything it contained; the discovery that the tragedy was no accident, but that murder lurked behind it; the other murder, when Markham Giles was done to death for a purpose too dreadful and gruesome to contemplate without a thrill of horror; these things would make the Starvel Hollow crime re-echo round the world. It would be the crime of the century. No one could fail to be moved by it.

And all would react to his, French's, advantage. For a moment he allowed himself to dream. Chief Inspector Armstrong was getting old. He must soon retire . . . French ran over in his mind his possible successors. Yes, it was conceivable . . . With this brilliant case to his credit it was almost likely . . . A ravishing prospect!

But French was at heart too sound a man to waste time in day-dreaming while there was work to be done. He had pulled off a *coup* and had every reason to be pleased with himself, but he had not completed his case. He had solved his problem, but he had not found his criminal. Until Roper was under lock and key he could not relax his efforts or look for his reward.

As he went over, point by point, all that he knew of the missing man, he saw that there were two matters upon which he should obtain further information before starting his search. Roper's statement to the undertaker was capable of verification. Had Dr Emerson stated that Giles' body required to be coffined without delay? If Roper had lied on this point, it would still further confirm the case against him. The second matter was a search of Giles' cottage. It was not a hopeful line of inquiry certainly, but it could not be neglected. Some clue to the tragedy might be forthcoming.

First, then, it was necessary to see Dr Emerson, and a few minutes later French was seated once again in his consulting-room. The doctor greeted him anxiously.

'I'm glad you called, Inspector,' he exclaimed. 'I was going up to the hotel to look for you. This is a terrible development.'

'You've heard then, Dr Emerson?'

'Just this moment. I met Kent and he told me. It is an amazing affair, almost incredible. What does it all mean, Mr French? Can you understand it?'

'I am afraid, sir, it means what I said on my last call; that Mr Giles was murdered.'

Dr Emerson made an impatient gesture.

'But good gracious, man, that doesn't explain it! Suppose he was murdered: where is his body? Have you a theory?'

French hesitated. He felt tempted to disclose his suspicions to this old man, whose interest and good faith were so self-evident. But his habit of caution was too strong.

'I have a theory, Dr Emerson,' he answered, 'but so far it is only a theory and I don't like to discuss it until I am reasonably sure it is true. I shall know in a short time and then I will tell you. In the meantime perhaps you will excuse me. But I want to ask you one more question. Roper saw you about the funeral arrangements?'

'Yes. He said that Giles had given him some money for the purpose and that he would see that the best use was made of it.'

'You thought it necessary, I understand, to have the coffining done without delay?'

Dr Emerson looked up sharply.

'*I* thought it necessary? Certainly not. You're mistaken there.'

'Is that so?' French returned. 'I thought you had told Roper that it must be hurried on. You didn't?'

'Never. I never even discussed the matter with him. I never thought of it. As a matter of fact there was no need to depart in any way from the usual procedure.'

'That's all right, doctor. Now there is one other point. Let us assume that murder was committed. I want you to tell me from the appearance of the body how that murder might have been done. If you are able to do so it might lead me to a clue.'

Emerson sprang to his feet and began pacing the room.

'Merciful powers! That's a nice question to ask me, after my giving a certificate of death from myocarditis!' he exclaimed.

'I know, doctor.' French spoke soothingly. 'But none of us are infallible, and if you made a mistake it's only what everyone does at one time or another. Your reasons for giving the certificate were very convincing, and if they were not sound in this case it is only because this case is one in a million. Don't worry about the certificate. Instead, just sit down and recall the appearance of the body and see if you can think of another cause of death. If you're not able to give a definite opinion we can still get something by elimination. I take it, for example, the man's skull was not battered in nor his throat cut? That limits the affair. You see what I mean?'

'Oh, I see right enough, and naturally I'll give you all the help I can. But tell me first, have you found the body?'

'No, nor have I the faintest idea where to look. That will be my next job, I suppose. I don't even say it's murder. But it may be, and if you can answer my question it might be a considerable help.'

Dr Emerson thought for some moments.

'Well,' he said at last, 'I must admit that murder is *possible*, though I don't for a moment believe death occurred otherwise than as I said. As to possible methods, there were no obvious wounds on the body and violence in the literal sense is therefore unlikely. A sharp blow over the heart or on the stomach might have caused heart failure without leaving physical marks, but in such a case the features would have looked distressed. For the same reason death from the shock of a sudden fright or start may be ruled out. It is of course true that certain kinds of poison might have been administered. A whiff of hydrocyanic acid gas would cause almost instantaneous death and produce the same appearance as death from natural causes. An injection of cocaine would do the same where there was heart disease, and there are other similar agents. But in these cases the difficulty of the average man in obtaining the substances in question and also in knowing how to use them if obtained, is so great that I think they might all be ruled out. No, Inspector, amazing as your discovery seems, I cannot think you are right in assuming murder.'

'But,' thought French, though he did not put his thought into words, 'if the man you suspect spent the best years of his life as male nurse in a medical institution, these difficulties pretty well vanish.' But he concealed his satisfaction, and, instead, simulated disappointment.

'That seems very reasonable, doctor, I must admit. At the same time I shall have to put inquiries in hand as to whether anyone recently tried to obtain cocaine or those other things you have mentioned. Of course, I don't say that necessarily I am right in my ideas.'

'I don't think you are right, though I confess I'm absolutely lost in amazement about that coffin. Come now, Inspector, you must know more than you pretend. Are your ideas hopelessly confidential?'

French shook his head, then said, 'I can tell you, doctor, that I know nothing more than I have already mentioned. I may have a surmise, but you will, agree that I could not repeat mere surmises which might also be slanders against perfectly innocent persons. If I find that my theories seem to have a basis on fact I may ask for your further help, but at present I see no signs of that. You'll agree that I'm right?'

Emerson admitted it, and after some further conversation French took his leave. So far everything was going satisfactorily. Each new fact which he learned tended to strengthen his theory. And incidentally and unexpectedly he had come on another piece of evidence, circumstantial of course, but none the less strong. According to Dr Emerson, the murder was most likely to have been committed by methods which Roper alone, of all the people that French could think of, had the knowledge and the ability to employ. French's satisfaction was intense as he noted the cumulative effect of his discoveries. By this method of cumulative circumstantial evidence was he accustomed to find suspicion grow to certainty and certainty to proof.

So much for the first of the two inquiries French had set himself to make. There remained the investigation of the late Markham Giles' cottage, and after a snack of early lunch at the hotel, he started out along the Starvel road.

It was dull and rather cold, but a pleasant day for walking. French tramped along, enjoying the motion and the extended view offered by the wide, open spaces of the moor. Though, owing to the atmosphere, the colouring was neither so warm nor so rich as it had previously appeared, there was a fascination in the scenery which strongly appealed to him. He had found a similar though keener charm in Dartmoor, which he had once explored on the occasion of a visit to a cracksman doing time in the great prison at Princetown. Indeed Dartmoor and Exmoor both figured on his list of places to be visited when time and money should permit.

Diverging from the Starvel road at the point where Ruth

Averill and Mrs Oxley had joined the deceased man's funeral, French skirted the edge of the Hollow and in a few minutes reached the cottage. It was a tiny box of a place, but strongly built, with stone walls and slated roof. Its architecture was of the most rudimentary kind, a door and two windows in front and at the back being the only relieving features in the design. The house stood a short distance back from the road in the middle of a patch of cultivated ground. Behind was a row of wooden beehives.

French looked round him. As far as he could see he was the only living thing in all that stretch of country. The town, nestling in the valley up which he had come, was hidden from sight below the edge of the moor. The three or four houses standing at wide intervals apart seemed deserted. No one appeared on the road or on the moor.

He walked up the little path to the door and busied himself with the lock. It was too large for his skeleton keys, but a few moments' work with a bit of bent wire did the trick, and presently he was inside with the door closed behind him.

The house consisted of three rooms only, a sitting-room, a bedroom, and a kitchen. A narrow passage separated the last two of these, the front portion of which formed a porch and the back a pantry. The atmosphere was heavy and nauseating, and this was soon explained by the fact that everything seemed to have been left just where it was when Giles died. The clothes were still on the bed and there was mouldy and decaying food in the pantry. Dust was thick over everything; indeed it was a marvel to French where so much dust should have come from in the heart of the country.

He opened the doors to let the atmosphere clear and then began one of his meticulous examinations. He did not expect to find anything of interest, yet he searched as if the key to the whole mystery lay waiting to be discovered. But after an hour he had to admit failure. There was nothing in the place from which he could get the slightest help.

Reluctantly he locked the doors and started back to Thirsby. He walked slowly, scarcely conscious of his surroundings as he racked his brains in the hope of seeing some other clue which might bring him more result. At first he could think of nothing, then another line of investigation occurred to him which, though it seemed hopelessly unpromising, he thought he might pursue.

He had been thinking that if his main theory were correct Giles' body must have been conveyed from his cottage to Starvel, probably during the darkness of that tragic Wednesday night. How had this been done? He had noticed in the single outhouse of Starvel which remained unburnt a light handcart, and it had before occurred to him that this cart might have been used. He now thought he would go down to Starvel and have another look at the outhouse and this handcart. A miracle might have happened and some helpful clue been left.

He turned aside from the road, and crossing the lip of the Hollow, went down to the ruins in the centre. The outhouse was a small stone shed built up against the yard wall. Through the broken and cobweb-covered window he could see that it contained, the handcart, a few gardening tools and some old broken crates and other rubbish. The door was secured with a rusty chain and padlock of which the key had disappeared.

A few seconds' work with his bent wire unfastened the lock and he pushed open the door and entered. The place was unspeakably dirty and he moved gingerly about as he began to look over its contents. But he was just as meticulous and thorough in his examination as if it were the throne room of a palace.

He had completed his work and was about to retire disappointed when the presence of a small scrap of yellow clay which he had observed on entering, but to which he had given no attention, suddenly struck him as being slightly puzzling. It was shaped like a half-moon, the inner edge showing a definite curve. Evidently it had caked round a man's heel and had dropped off, possibly as the heel had become drier in the shed. French looked round and presently he saw two more pieces. One was stuck to the rim of the left wheel of the hand-cart as if the wheel had rolled over a clod and picked it up, the other was on the left leg as if the leg had been put down on a similar clod which had stuck in the same way.

It was, of course, evident that the handcart had been not only wheeled over a place where there was yellow clay, but had been set down there. At first French saw nothing remarkable in this, but now it occurred to him that he had not noticed any clay of the colour in the neighbourhood. Where then had the pieces been picked up?

He had seen similar clay on the previous night, but not close by. The heap of stuff removed in opening the grave down in Thirsby was just that kind of material. He had noticed it particularly in the light of the acetylene lamp. It was of a characteristic light yellow and very stiff and compact like puddle. But he had seen nothing like it up on the moor. The soil all about was dark coloured, almost peaty.

He cast his thoughts back to that scene in the graveyard and then he recalled another point. He had looked down into the grave when the coffin was being raised, and he now remembered that the sides of the opening had shown black soil over the clay. A layer of some three feet six or four feet of dark, peaty soil had covered the yellow. French whistled softly as the possible inference struck him.

A worn but still serviceable looking spade stood in the

corner of the shed. French picked it up, and going a few yards out on to the moor, began to dig. He was not particularly expert, and before he had worked for many minutes he was in a bath of perspiration. But he persevered and the hole grew until at a depth of nearly three feet he found what he wanted. The spade brought up a piece of hard, compact clay of a light yellow colour.

French had grown keenly interested as he filled in the hole and removed the traces of his work. With a feeling of suppressed excitement he returned to the shed and carefully packed the half-moon shaped cake of clay in a matchbox. Then locking the door, he went out again on the moor and stood looking round him as he pondered the facts he had just learned.

The handcart had been recently set down in and wheeled across a patch of yellow clay. This almost certainly had been done on the last occasion it had been used, otherwise the clay would have been knocked off on subsequent journeys. For the same reason the place must have been close to Starvel. There was no exposed clay near Starvel, but it was to be found at a depth of some three feet below ground level.

From this it surely followed that someone had dug a hole near Starvel and wheeled the handcart to the edge before it was filled in.

French went a step farther. If he was correct that the body of Markham Giles had been brought to Starvel on that tragic night it was almost certain that the handcart had been used, as there was no other way, so far as he could see, in which the terrible burden could have been carried. But so long a journey would have knocked the clay off the wheel; therefore the journey to the hole had been made *after* that with the body. Further, the handcart could scarcely have been used since the fire: the tragedy was then over and the surviving actor had left the district.

Did these considerations not suggest that Roper, having brought the man's body to Starvel, had loaded up his booty on the handcart—possibly there were old silver or valuable ornaments as well as the banknotes—wheeled it out on the moor and buried it so as to hide it safely until he could come back and remove it?

French recalled his reasons for thinking that the booty might have been so hidden. All those notes—assuming there was nothing else—would have had a certain bulk. Probably a suitcase would have been necessary to carry them. A man with a suitcase is a more noticeable figure than one without. Would it not have been wise for a criminal fleeing from justice to hide the stuff, provided he could find a safe place in which to do so? Moreover—and this was the strongest point—had Roper been arrested without the notes nothing could have been proved against him. He could say he had escaped from the fire by the merest piece of good fortune or he could simulate loss of memory from the shock. Or again he could explain that he had feared to come forward lest he should be suspected. No matter what might have been thought, he was safe. But let him be found with the notes in his possession and he was as good as hanged.

French, looking round him there in the centre of the great Hollow, felt his spirits rising as he wondered if he were about to make the greatest *coup* of the whole case.

His question now was: Where would Roper make his cache? Not near the road where the disturbed earth would be visible to a chance passer by. Not near the house in case some of the crowds attracted by the fire should make an unexpected find. But not too far away from either lest he himself might have difficulty in locating the place.

French began to walk round the house in circles of ever

increasing radius, scrutinising the ground for traces of yellow clay. And so he searched until the evening began to draw in and dusk approached.

And then, as he was coming to the conclusion that it was getting too dark to carry on, he found what he wanted. Out on the open moor at the back of the house and at the bottom of a tiny hollow were unmistakable traces of recent digging. The ground over a few square feet was marked with scraps of disintegrating yellow clay and the sods with which the hole was covered still showed cut edges.

French was overwhelmed with delight. That he had found something of value, most probably a cache containing the stolen money, he had no doubt. Scarcely could he restrain his desire to open the hole again then and there. But it was getting dark and he had no lamp. He thought two witnesses would be desirable, so he curbed his impatience, noted carefully the position of the marks, and regretting the necessity for leaving it unguarded, set off on his return journey.

He called to see Sergeant Kent and arranged that he and a constable should meet him at the outhouse at eight o'clock on the following morning. At the hotel he dined, and saying that he had to take the night train to Carlisle, asked for a packet of sandwiches. Then he left the town and walked out once more to Starvel.

His mind was not at rest until he had again visited the site of the hole and made sure it remained undisturbed. Then, determined to take no chances, he re-entered the outhouse, and seating himself at a window from which he could see the hollow in the light of the moon, lit his pipe and composed himself to watch.

14

The Secret of the Moor

That night in the lonely shed beside the gaunt, blackened walls of the old house, proved one of the longest French had ever spent. But there was no escape from the vigil. If Averill's hoard lay beneath the sods a few yards away, the place must be watched. Roper might come for the swag at any time, and French could not run the risk of its being snatched at the last moment from his own eager clutches.

He pulled a couple of old boxes to the window, and sitting down, made himself as comfortable as he could. But time dragged leadenly. He watched while the moon crept slowly across the sky, he smoked pipe after pipe of his own special mixture, he speculated over the tragic business on which he was engaged and indulged in waking dreams of the time when he should be Chief Inspector French of the C.I.D., but nothing that he could do seemed to shorten the endless hours. He was cold, too, in spite of his heavy coat. He longed to go out and warm himself by a brisk walk, but he dared not risk betraying his presence. In the small hours he ate his sandwiches, and then he had to fight an overwhelming desire for sleep, intensified by the fact that he had been up a good part of the previous night. But his vigilance was unrewarded. There was no sign of a marauder, and as the first faint glow of dawn began to show in the east, he saw that he had had all his trouble for nothing. Altogether he was not sorry when just before eight o'clock Sergeant Kent and the constable put in an appearance, and as he stepped out to meet them he heaved a sigh of heartfelt relief.

'You're here before us,' Kent greeted him in surprise.

'That's right, but I was too early. Now, Sergeant, I asked you to come out here for rather an unusual purpose: in fact, so that we might dig a hole. Here is a spade and we'll go and begin at once.'

The sergeant looked as if he wondered whether French hadn't gone off his head, but he controlled his feelings and with his satellite followed the other's lead.

'I want you,' went on French when they had reached the site of his discovery, 'to see just why I wish to dig this hole at this place,' and he showed him the traces of the yellow clay and the cut sods. 'You see, someone has buried something here, and I want to find out what it is.'

Kent in a non-committal silence seized the spade and began digging. The constable then tried his hand, and when he had had enough, French relieved him. So they took it in turns while the hole deepened and the heap of soil beside it grew.

Suddenly the spade encountered something soft and yielding which yet resisted its pressure. Kent, who was using it, stopped digging and began to clear away the surrounding soil, while the others watched, French breathlessly, the constable with the bovine impassiveness which he had exhibited throughout.

'It's a blanket, this is,' the sergeant announced presently. 'Something rolled up in a blanket.'

'Go on,' said French. 'Open it up.'

Kent resumed his digging. For some minutes he worked, and then he straightened himself and looked at French wonderingly.

'Lord save us!' he exclaimed in awed tones. 'It's uncommon like a human corp.'

'Nonsense!' French answered sharply. 'It couldn't be anything of the kind. Get on and open it up and then you'll know.'

The sergeant hesitated, then climbed heavily out of the hole.

'Well, look yourself, sir,' he invited.

French jumped down, and as he gazed on the outline of the blanket covered object, his eyes grew round and something like consternation filled his mind. The sergeant was right! There was no mistaking that shape! This was a grave that they were opening and the blanket was a shroud.

French swore, then controlled himself and turned to the sergeant.

'You're right, Kent. It's a body sure enough. Clear away the soil round it while, the constable and I get that shed door off its hinges.'

The task of raising the uncoffined and decaying remains on to the improvised stretcher was one which French could never afterwards think of without a qualm of sick loathing, but eventually it was done and the men slowly carried the shrouded horror to the shed. There the door was placed upon a couple of boxes and French, clenching his teeth, turned back the blanket from the face.

In spite of the terrible ravages of time both Kent and the constable immediately recognised the distorted features. The body was that of Markham Giles!

205

The discovery left French almost speechless. If Markham Giles' body was here, *whose was the third body at Starvel?* Was the whole of his case tumbling about his ears? Once again he swore bitterly and once again pulled himself together to deal with the next step.

'This means an inquest,' he said to Kent. 'You and I had better get back to Thirsby and notify the coroner and so forth, and this man of yours can stay here and keep watch.'

They walked down to the little town almost in silence, French too full of his new problem to indulge in conversation, and the sergeant not liking to break in upon his companion's thoughts. On arrival Kent got in touch with the coroner while French rang up Major Valentine.

'No, sir, I don't know what to make of it,' he admitted in answer to the major's sharp question. 'It certainly does look as if the man I suspected was dead after all. But I would rather not discuss it over the 'phone. Could I see you, sir, if I went down to Leeds?'

'No, I'll go to Thirsby. I'd like to look into the matter on the spot. There will be an inquest, of course?'

'Yes, sir. Sergeant Kent is arranging it with the coroner. We shall want an autopsy also. One of the things I wanted to know is whom you think I should have to make it. But you can tell me that when you come.'

Major Valentine replied that he would drive over in his car and would pick up French at the police station at two p.m. on his way out to Starvel.

It was now getting on towards midday, but French decided that he would have time to make an inquiry and get lunch before the chief constable's arrival. He therefore turned into the High Street and walked to Pullar's, the largest shoe shop of the town.

'Mr Pullar in?' he asked pleasantly. He had met the man in the bar of the Thirsdale Arms and there was a nodding acquaintance between the two.

'I suppose you haven't heard of our discovery, Mr Pullar?' French began when he was seated in the proprietor's office. The whole business was bound to come out at the inquest, so he might as well enlist the other's goodwill by telling him confidentially something about it.

Mr Pullar cautiously admitted he hadn't heard anything unusual.

'This is unusual enough for anyone,' French assured him, and he told of the finding of the grave on the moor, though making no mention of his doubts and fears about Roper.

Mr Pullar was duly impressed and repeatedly begged that his soul might be blessed. When he had absorbed the news French turned to the real object of his call.

'I thought that maybe you could give me a bit of help, Mr Pullar. You'd perhaps be interested to know how I got on to the thing. Well, it was in this way.' He took from the matchbox the piece of clay he had found on the floor of the shed.

'I picked this up in the shed, and as that sort of clay is covered everywhere here with three feet of dark soil, it followed that someone had dug a hole more than three feet deep.'

Mr Pullar expressed his admiration of the other's perspicacity with the same pious wish as before.

'Now you see,' French continued, 'this clay was sticking to a shoe. It probably got a bit dry in the shed and dropped or got knocked off. Now, Mr Pullar, can you tell me what kind of a shoe it was?'

Mr Pullar shook his head. With every wish to assist, he was doubtful if he could answer the question. He picked up the piece of clay and turned it over gingerly in his fingers.

'Well,' he said presently, pointing to the hollow curve, 'that's been sticking round the outside of a heel, that has. If it had been a toe it would have been squeezed flatter. But that's the square-edged mark of a heel.' He looked interrogatively at French, who hastened to interject: 'Just what I thought, Mr Pullar. A man's heel.'

'Yes, a man's heel I would think: though, mind you, it's not easy to tell the difference between a man's and some of these flat-heeled shoes women wear now.'

'I thought it was a man's from the size.'

'No: it might be either a big woman or a small man. Sevens, I should say.' He got up and put his head through the office door. 'Here, John! Bring me three pairs of gents' black Fitwells: a six and a half, a seven and an eight: medium weight.'

When the shoes came Mr Pullar attempted to fit the circle of clay to the curve of each heel. French was delighted with the thorough and systematic way he set about it. He tried with all three sizes, then roared out for a pair of sixes and a pair of nines.

'It's no good, Mr French,' he said when he, had tested these also. 'Look for yourself. It's smaller than a nine, but you can't tell any more than that. It might be a six or a seven or an eight. It isn't sharp enough to say.'

French looked for himself, but he had to admit the other's conclusion was correct. The prints presumably had been made by a man with rather small feet, and that was all that could be said.

French was disappointed. He had hoped for something more definite. Roper admittedly had rather small feet, but the same was true of numbers of other men.

He bade Mr Pullar good day and returned to the hotel for

lunch. But he soon learned that the worthy shoe merchant had made the most of his opportunities. Scarcely had he sat down when the reporter of the local paper hurried into the coffee room and excitedly demanded details of the great find. And behind him appeared the hotel proprietor and a number of clients who had been supporting British industries in the bar.

French saw there was nothing for it but capitulation. Good-humouredly he told his story, merely stipulating that after his statement to the reporter he should not be troubled further until he had finished his lunch. This was agreed to, but it is sad to relate that French did not entirely play the game. His repast ended, he slipped out through the yard, and by devious ways reached the police station unnoticed. Major Valentine drove up as he arrived and in a few seconds the two men were whirling out along the Starvel road, while French told his story in detail.

'It's really an extraordinary development,' the chief constable commented. 'You assumed that Giles had been murdered in order to obtain his body for the Starvel fraud. If you were correct it followed that his coffin would be empty. You opened his coffin and it was empty. A more complete vindication of your line of reasoning it would be hard to imagine. And now it turns out that the body was not used for the Starvel fraud; therefore the whole of your reasoning falls to the ground. If you had not made a mistake and acted on false premises you would not have discovered the truth. Peculiar, isn't it?'

'Peculiar enough, sir. But I wish I could agree with you that I had discovered the truth. It seems to me I am further away from it than ever.'

'No; the correction of an error is always progress. But I'm

not denying,' Major Valentine went on with a whimsical smile, 'that there is still something left to be cleared up.'

French laughed unhappily.

'I don't like to think of it,' he said. 'But the post-mortem may tell us something. According to my previous theory this man was murdered. Now this discovery raises a certain doubt, though personally I have very little. But in any case we have no proof. Therefore I thought we should want a post-mortem.'

'Undoubtedly. We'll get Dr Lingard of Hellifield. This the shed?'

'Yes, sir. The body's inside.'

A few minutes sufficed to put the chief constable in possession of all the available information and the two men returned to the car.

'You know,' the major declared as he restarted his engine, 'if this man was murdered it doesn't say a great deal for that Dr Emerson. He gave a certificate of death from natural causes, didn't he?'

'If you ask my opinion,' French answered gloomily, 'he didn't examine the body at all. I saw him about it. It seems the man had been suffering from heart disease for years. He also had a touch of influenza some days before his death which might have caused heart failure. Dr Emerson practically admitted he had assumed this had happened. He also admitted that anyhow only a post-mortem could have made sure.'

'Careless and reprehensible, no doubt. But, French, I wonder whether we shouldn't all have done the same in his circumstances. The idea of foul play in such a case would never enter anyone's head.'

'That's what he said, sir. Until I told him about the empty

coffin he scouted the suggestion. When I mentioned that he didn't know what to say.'

'He'll be required at the inquest?'

'Of course, sir. And the other doctor, Philpot. He attended the man during his illness.'

They ran rapidly into the town and pulled up at the police station. Kent, recognising his visitor, hurried obsequiously to meet them.

'Good evening, Kent,' the major greeted him. 'Inspector French has just been telling me of this affair. Have you heard from the coroner?'

'Yes, sir, I saw him about it. Tomorrow at eleven he's fixed for the inquest.'

'Where?'

'At the courthouse. He asked that the remains might be brought in before that.'

'It's not allowing much time for the post-mortem. Better see the coroner again, Kent, and get him to take evidence of identification and adjourn for a week. I'll arrange with Dr Lingard about the post-mortem at once, and will you, French, get in touch with the local doctors. Meanwhile as we're here let us settle about the evidence.'

Kent led the way to his room and there a discussion took place on the procedure to be adopted at the inquest. A list of the witnesses was drawn up with a note of the testimony which was to be expected from each. Certain facts, it was considered, should be kept in the background, and Kent was instructed to see the coroner and ask him to arrange this also. When the business was complete the major rose.

'Then I shall see you at the adjourned inquest, Kent. French, if you'll come along I'll give you a lift as far as your hotel. As a matter of fact I'd like to have a chat with you,' he went on when they had left the police station. 'This new development is certainly very puzzling and I'd like to discuss it in detail. Have you a private sitting room?'

'Not all the time. I've had one once or twice for an evening when I had work to do, but ordinary times I don't have it. We can get it all right now though.'

'Well, you arrange it while I see to the car. And order some tea. You'll join me in a cup, won't you?'

'Thank you, I should like to.'

In a few minutes a fire of logs was crackling in the rather dismal private sitting-room of the Thirsdale Arms. Until tea was over the major chatted of men and things apart from the case, but when the waiter had disappeared with the tray and the two men had settled themselves with cigars before the fire he came to business.

'I admit, French, that I am not only tremendously interested in this case, but also extremely puzzled. From what you say, that's your position also. Now just to run over two or three points. I take it there is no doubt, as to the motive?'

'No, sir, we may take it as gospel that Mr Averill's thirty thousand pounds were stolen and that that's the key of the whole affair.'

'You suspected Whymper at first?'

'Yes, at first sight things looked bad for him. I needn't go over the details: he had some of the stolen money in his possession and had been to the house on the night of the tragedy and so on. But I went into the thing thoroughly and I was satisfied that Roper had made him his dupe. Whymper's all right, sir. We shall get nothing there.'

'I hear he and Miss Averill are to be married.'

'So I heard, in fact he told me himself. He wanted to propose and then this affair made him hold back. But as soon as I told him I was not going to arrest him he went straight to the lady and told her the circumstances and asked her to marry him. She accepted him and the wedding is to take place soon.'

'I know his father in Leeds and I'm glad to hear that he's definitely out of trouble. Then you suspected Philpot?'

'I suspected Philpot because of his connection with Roper, though there was nothing directly connecting him with the Starvel crime. But I soon saw that I was on the wrong track there too. He accounted for everything that seemed suspicious, and what was more, any points of his statement which in the nature of the case could be corroborated, were corroborated by other witnesses. Besides, he was ill at the time: there was the evidence of his housekeeper and others as well as Dr Emerson's testimony that he was unable to leave his bed. And there was his failure. If he had just obtained £30,000 he wouldn't have allowed the bailiff in.'

'Might not that have been a trick to put people off the scent?'

'No, sir, I don't think so. If he had been guilty he wouldn't have shown sudden evidence of wealth, but he wouldn't have gone bankrupt either—just for fear it might be taken as a trick. Of course, sir, I'm aware that none of this is absolutely conclusive. There was absence of evidence of guilt, but not proof of innocence, and, of course, illness can be faked and so on. But the thing that really cleared Philpot in my mind was the conduct of Roper. It's impossible to consider this case without considering Roper's conduct.'

'I know, and I really agree with you. Still let us exhaust the possibilities. You thought of other people, I suppose?'

'I thought of everyone else in the place almost. Oxley, Tarkington, Emerson and several others; even Kent I considered.

But there wasn't a shred of evidence against any of them. The only other real alternative to Roper is the burglars—the gang who have been operating for some months past. But here again Roper's conduct comes in. If Roper wasn't guilty he wouldn't have acted as he did.'

The chief constable smoked in silence for some moments.

'I think all you say is very sound. Now just run over the case against Roper and I shall try to pick holes.'

'First, sir, there was the man's character; vindictive, unscrupulous, a blackmailer, and as well as that a skilful forger. Admittedly this description came from Philpot, but all that could be known to outsiders was confirmed by the sergeant and many others at Kintilloch. Roper was the only person we know of, other than the burglar gang, who had the character and the ability to commit the crime.'

'Not convincing, but go on.'

'Not convincing alone, no doubt; but it does not stand alone. Secondly, there was the getting of Miss Averill out of the way; thirdly, there was the Whymper episode, and fourthly, the matter of Giles' funeral.'

'That's all right except that when we find Giles' body was not burned the whole case falls to the ground.'

French threw the stub of his cigar into the fire.

'Don't you believe it, sir. None of what I have been saying falls to the ground. Though I admit the motive of this Giles business is not clear, the facts remain and their significance remains. I don't now follow all Roper's scheme, but I still believe he is our man.'

Major Valentine nodded decisively.

'So do I, French, and we shall get him all right. Then you've no theory of where the third body came from?'

'I believe Roper enticed some other poor devil to the house

214

and murdered him also. I think, sir, we'll have to try again to find out if anyone disappeared about that time.'

'I'll see to it, but I'm not hopeful of doing better than before.'

Major Valentine showed signs of breaking up the conference, but French raised his hand.

'A moment, sir, if you please. I was thinking that this inquest gives us a chance that perhaps we should take advantage of. No more of those notes have come through. What, sir, would you say was the reason for that?'

'Well, if we're right about Roper being alive, I suppose because he's afraid.'

'That's what I think. And this business will make him still more afraid. Now I wonder if we couldn't set his mind at ease for him.'

'I don't quite follow.'

'Why, this way. Suppose that I was very frank in my evidence—very frank and open and comprehensive. Suppose that I should tell about the notes; about their numbers having been taken, and about the one turning up in London, and robbery being thereby suspected and my being sent down to investigate. Suppose I explained that I had succeeded in tracing that note and had found that it had been given by Mr Averill himself to a friend, and that the whole transaction was perfectly in order. But suppose I conveyed that only the numbers of the last batch of notes—say, twenty twenties— were known. Wouldn't that do the trick?'

'You mean that if the numbers of only twenty notes were known, Roper would feel safe in changing the others?'

'Quite so. Furthermore, if nothing was said about the ashes being newspaper he would think that the suspicion of robbery had been dispelled by the discovery that the note passed in London was all right.'

'It's worth trying. If he rises to it you'll get him.'

'Right, sir. Then I'll advise the coroner beforehand. Or perhaps you would do so?'

'I'll do it. Well, I must be getting home. I'm glad to have had this talk and I hope your scheme will meet with success.'

Next morning the inquest opened and formal evidence of identification of the remains of the late Markham Giles was taken. The proceedings were then adjourned for seven days to enable the police to prosecute inquiries.

15

French Baits his Trap

That day week was a red letter day in the history of Thirsby. The story of French's discoveries, by this time common property, had created an absolute furore in the little town. Never had such a series of tragedies and thrills disturbed its placid existence. Never had interest risen to such fever heat. It was therefore not surprising that every available seat in the court-house was occupied long before the hour of the adjourned inquest, and that a queue of eager, pushing people, unable to gain admittance, stretched away in a long column from its door. But the police had seen to it that all who were particularly interested in the tragedy had obtained places. In the row usually reserved for barristers sat Oxley with Ruth Averill, who had been summoned to attend as a witness, and Mrs Oxley, who looked on the girl as her charge and insisted on accompanying her. Whymper, now an accepted lover, sat next Ruth, and behind were Tarkington, Bloxham, Emerson, Philpot and the police doctor, Lingard. Major Valentine and French were together in the seat usually occupied by the clerk of the Crown, while Kent, looking harrassed and anxious, was standing in the body of the court, fumbling with a sheaf of papers and whispering to his subordinates.

The coroner was that same Dr Lonsdale who had acted in a similar capacity some nine weeks earlier when the inquiry into the death of the three victims of the Starvel fire had taken place. He also seemed worried, as if he feared the elucidation of these mysterious happenings might try his powers beyond their capacity.

The preliminaries having been gone through already, the coroner began to take evidence immediately, and Dr Emerson was called.

'You attended the late Mr Markham Giles?' the coroner asked when he had obtained the other's name and qualifications.

'I attended him up until five years ago, when Dr Philpot took the case over. Owing to Dr Philpot's being ill at the time of his death I was again called in.'

'For what complaint did you formerly attend the deceased?'

'Myocarditis. It was a disease of some years' standing.'

'Myocarditis is heart disease, isn't it? Was the deceased badly affected?'

'Five years ago, fairly badly. I have no doubt that at the time of his death he was much worse, as the disease is incurable and progressive.'

'We can no doubt get that from Dr Philpot. When did you hear of Mr Giles' death, Dr Emerson?'

'On Wednesday morning, 15th September.'

'Who told you of it?'

'John Roper, the Starvel manservant.'

'Did you go out to Starvel and examine the body?'

'Yes, I did, after first consulting Dr Philpot on the case.'

'Oh, you saw Dr Philpot. And what was the result of your consultation?'

'Dr Philpot told me that Mr Giles had developed influenza, and that he had seen him on Thursday. He was very weak and Dr Philpot did not expect him to get over it.'

'Then you examined the body?'

'Yes, I went out to Starvel immediately.'

'And what opinion did you then form as to the cause of death?'

'I believed it to be myocarditis.'

'And you gave a certificate to that effect?'

'I did.'

'Did you make any specific examination of the remains on which you based your opinion?'

'Yes, so far as it was possible without a post-mortem.'

'And you were quite satisfied that you had made no mistake?'

'I was quite satisfied.'

'That will do in the meantime. Please do not go away, Dr Emerson, as I may have some further questions to put to you later.'

Dr Philpot was then called. He corroborated the evidence of the last witness in so far as it concerned himself. He had attended Mr Giles during the past five years. Deceased was suffering from myocarditis, which had become worse and of which he might have died at any moment. On the Thursday prior to his death witness had been informed by Roper, Mr Averill's manservant, that deceased seemed rather seriously ill, and he went out to see him. Deceased was feeble and witness believed that he was very near his end. Witness did not think he could live more than three or four days. When he heard of his death it was only what he had expected.

Ruth Averill was the next witness. She was nervous, but the sergeant was deferential to her and the coroner fatherly and kind. Her evidence was soon over. In answer to a number of questions she deposed that she had known Mr Giles fairly well and had been to sit with him on different occasions during his illness. On the Tuesday of that tragic week she had left Starvel to pay a short visit to York, and on her way into Thirsby she had called to see him. He had seemed very weak and frail. He could scarcely speak. Ruth had spent about ten minutes with him and had then driven on to Thirsby. She had never seen him again.

A number of persons were then called relative to the funeral. The clerk from the Town Hall who dealt with interments, the caretaker of the new cemetery, the undertaker and such of his men as had assisted, gave evidence in turn. The coroner was extremely detailed in his questions, and when he had finished the whole history of the sad affair stood revealed, with the exception of one point.

This was Roper's false statement to the undertaker that the body required to be coffined without delay. It had been decided that nothing must leak out connecting the death of Giles with Starvel, and it spoke volumes for the coroner's skill that he was able to obtain the other details of the interment while keeping Roper's duplicity secret.

From the united testimony given it seemed that Markham Giles had died at some time during the Tuesday night. Roper had stated to more than one witness that Mrs Roper had gone out to see him about eight o'clock on that evening, when she found him weak, but fairly easy and showing no sign of any early collapse. About nine the next moring, Wednesday, she went over again, to find that the man had been dead for some hours. Mr Giles was lying in the same position as he had occupied on the previous evening, and from the peaceful expression on his face it looked as if he had passed away painlessly. Mrs Roper had gone back for her husband, who had returned with her to the cottage. There they had done what they could, and Roper had then gone into Thirsby and made arrangements for the funeral. First he had reported the death to Dr Emerson. Then he had called at the Town Hall and purchased a grave, going on to the new cemetery to see the site. Lastly, he had visited the undertaker, arranging the details of the funeral.

The undertaker had known Mr Giles, and later on that day, the Wednesday, he had sent out two men with a coffin which he believed would be of the right size. His estimate had proved correct and the men had placed the remains in the coffin, screwing down the lid and leaving all ready for the funeral.

On the second day, the Friday, the interment took place. The same men who had coffined the remains lifted the coffin into the hearse, and they declared that they saw no signs of the screws having been tampered with or of the presence of any person in the house during their absence. The funeral was conducted in the customary manner, and when the grave had been filled none of those who had been present imagined that anything out of the common had taken place. Roper had paid all the bills in advance, saying that the deceased had had a premonition of his death and had handed him the sum of fifteen pounds to meet the expenses.

French was the next witness. The coroner had been carefully primed as to his evidence also, and asked only general questions.

'Now, Mr French, you made some unexpected discoveries about this matter?'

'I did, sir.'

'Will you please tell the jury in your own words the nature of these discoveries and how you came to make them.'

This was French's opportunity. Speaking respectfully and with an air of the utmost candour, he told very nearly the truth. Deliberately he slightly coloured the facts, coloured them with the object and in the hope that somewhere Roper would read what he had said—and be deceived into coming into the open.

'I was sent here,' he explained, 'on a matter arising out of the fire at Starvel. I made certain inquiries and received certain information. As to the truth of the information I cannot of course bear testimony, but I cannot explain the steps I took unless I mention it. With the object of accounting for my actions, sir, is it your wish that I do so?'

'If you please, Mr French. We quite understand that your actual evidence is confined to matters which came under your own observation. That does not prevent you introducing explanatory matter as to how you got your results.'

'Very good, sir. According to my information the following was the state of affairs which had obtained prior to my being sent down here. The late Mr Averill had a sum of money amounting to several thousand pounds stored in a safe in his bedroom. This was given in evidence at the inquest on the victims of the Starvel tragedy. It was not then mentioned, but it was the fact—always according to my information—that that money had consisted largely of twenty-pound notes. Mr Averill was in the habit of sending to the bank the various cheques, dividends and so forth by which he received his income. By his instructions these were cashed and the money was returned to Starvel in the form of twenty-pound notes, which the old gentleman placed with the others in his safe. All these notes were believed to have been destroyed in the fire. But it so happened that the numbers of the last consignment—ten notes, for £200—were taken by the bank teller before the notes were sent out to Starvel, and these notes were reported to the bank's headquarters as being destroyed. When, therefore, some three weeks after the tragedy one of them turned up in London, questions were asked. Reasons were given for believing that this particular note had been in Mr Averill's safe at Starvel on the night of the fire, so the suggestion at once arose that the fire was not an accident, but a deliberate attempt to hide a crime of murder and burglary. I was sent down to investigate the affair, and I may say that I found out who had passed the note and satisfied myself beyond question that he had received it in a legitimate manner, and that all his actions were perfectly correct and in order. It followed, therefore, that the finding of the note did not in reality support any theory of crime such as had been put forward.'

While French was speaking the proverbial pin could have been heard, had anyone tried the experiment of dropping it in the court-house. He had, to put it mildly, the ear of his audience. Everyone listened, literally, with bated breath. Though it was vaguely known that he was a detective working on the Starvel case, the story that he himself had circulated had been generally accepted; that he was employed on behalf of certain insurance companies to ascertain the cause of the outbreak. To find that the pleasant-spoken, easy-going stranger whom the townspeople had almost begun to accept as one of themselves, was none other than a full-fledged inspector from Scotland Yard, investigating what had been at first suspected to be a triple murder of an unusually terrible and sinister kind, was a discovery so thrilling as completely to absorb the attention of all.

'While engaged in clearing up the Starvel affair,' French went on, 'a hint was conveyed to me that I was working on the wrong case: that if I wanted a real mystery I should drop what I was at and turn my attention to the death and burial, particularly the burial, of Mr Giles. With your permission, sir, I do not feel at liberty to mention the source from which this hint came. It was very vague, but we men from the Yard are taught to pick up vague hints. I thought over the matter for some days before I guessed what might be meant. Could Mr Giles' coffin have been used as a hiding place for stolen goods? I knew, of course, of the many burglaries which had taken place in the surrounding country during the last six months. I knew also that if burglars wished to hide their swag, no better place could be devised than a coffin. There it would be safe until the hue and cry had died down, and from there it could be recovered when desired. If this theory were true, the gang of burglars would either have heard of Mr Giles' death and used the circumstances to their advantage, or they would have arranged the circumstance by murdering him. In either case they would have taken the remains from the coffin, buried them somewhere close by, and replaced them with the stolen articles.'

French paused and a wave of movement swept over the crowded assembly as its members changed their cramped positions. Seldom had the public had such a treat and they were not going to miss any of it. There was an instantaneous stiffening to concentrated attention as French resumed:

'After careful consideration I thought the matter serious enough to warrant action. I therefore obtained an order to open the grave, and there I found that my suspicions were well founded. There was no body in the coffin, but on the other hand there was no swag. The coffin was half-full of earth. But this did not of course invalidate the theory I have outlined. It only meant that if that theory were true we were late; that at some time within the past nine weeks the burglars had visited the churchyard and removed the stuff. This might or might not have happened.'

Again French paused and this time the coroner remarked quietly:

'And then, Mr French?'

'Then, sir, I returned to the gentleman's cottage and made a further investigation. Eventually I found traces of yellow clay lying about. All the soil in the district is dark, but at the grave I had noticed that a layer of dark soil covered a bed of similar yellow clay. So I dug a hole and found, as I expected, that this bed of clay extended under the moor also. It therefore seemed certain that someone had dug a hole in the vicinity, and on searching the moor I found the place. I took Sergeant Kent and a constable out, and the three of us re-opened the hole and found the body just as these gentlemen'—indicating the jury with a gesture—'have seen it.'

The police made no attempt to subdue the buzz of repressed though excited conversation which arose as French ceased speaking. The coroner was still laboriously writing down French's statement, but he soon laid his pen down and spoke.

'You have made such a complete statement, Mr French, that I have but little to ask you. There are just one or two small points upon which I should like further information,' and he went on to put his questions.

The coroner was a clever man and he played up well to the request of the police. To the public he continued to give the impression of a careful, painstaking official, laboriously trying to obtain all the facts in a difficult and complicated matter; in reality his questions were futile in every respect except that they directed attention away from the features of the case which the authorities wished kept secret.

The result was that when he had finished and asked if anyone else desired to put a question, all were convinced that there was no more to be learnt and embarrassing topics were avoided.

'Dr Reginald Lingard!'

The tall, thin, ascetic looking man seated beside Philpot rose and went into the box. He deposed that he practised at Hellifield and was the police surgeon for the district.

'Now, Dr Lingard,' began the coroner, 'at the request of the authorities did you make a post-mortem examination of the remains of the late Mr Markham Giles, upon which this inquest is being held?'

'That is so.'

'And did you ascertain the cause of death?'

'I did.'

'Will you tell the jury what that was.'

'The man died from shock following a large injection of cocaine.'

'But an injection of cocaine is surely not fatal?'

'Not under ordinary circumstances. But to a person suffering from myocarditis a large injection is inevitably so.'

Though the evidence of French ought to have prepared everyone for such a *dénouement*, there was a gasp of surprise at this cold, precise statement. It was only a few minutes since Dr Emerson had been heard to testify that he had given a certificate of death from heart disease without mention of cocaine, and that he had no doubt as to the correctness of his diagnosis. What, everyone wondered, would Emerson say to this?

'I suppose, doctor, you have no doubt as to your conclusion?'

'None whatever.'

'Could this cocaine have been self-administered?'

226

'Undoubtedly it could.'

'With what object?'

Dr Lingard gave a slight shrug.

'It is universal knowledge that many persons are addicted to the drug. They take it because of its enjoyable temporary effects. It might have been taken with that motive in this instance, or it might have been taken with the knowledge that it would cause death.'

'You mean that Mr Giles might have committed suicide?'

'From the medical point of view, yes.'

'Might it also have been administered by some other person?'

'Unquestionably.'

'With what object, Dr Lingard?'

'It is not easy to say. Possibly in ignorance or through error or with a mistaken desire to give the patient ease, or possibly with the object of causing his death.'

'You mean that the action might have been wilful murder?'

'Yes, that is what I mean.'

Again a movement ran through the tense audience. The coroner frowned and paused for a moment, then resumed:

'Do you know of any legitimate object—any legitimate object whatever—for which the cocaine might have been administered? Could it, for example, have been intended as a medicine or restorative?'

'I do not think so. In my opinion the drug could only have been administered in error, or with intent to kill.'

'Do you consider that the deadly nature of cocaine is known to the public? I mean, is that knowledge not confined to those with some medical training?'

'I think the danger to a weak or diseased heart is pretty generally known. Most people are aware that deaths have

227

occurred by its use, for example, by dentists, and that for this reason it is now seldom employed as an anæsthetic.'

The coroner slowly blotted his manuscript.

'Now, Dr Lingard, injections are administered with a hypodermic syringe, are they not?'

'That is so.'

'Is there any other way in which they can be given?'

'No.'

'Was such a syringe found in the present instance?' Dr Lingard did not know. He had examined the body only, not the house in which the death had occurred. The coroner turned to another point.

'Did the body show any sign of the injection having been forcibly administered?'

'No, but force sufficient to leave traces would not have been necessary.'

'Would death from this cause leave traces other than those ascertainable from a post-mortem?' Dr Lingard hesitated very slightly.

'I do not think so,' he answered. 'If it did they would be very faint and it would be easy to overlook them.'

'Was Dr Emerson at the post-mortem?'

'He was.'

'Have you anything else to tell us, anything which you think might throw further light on this extra-ordinary affair?'

No, Dr Lingard had nothing, and Dr Emerson was recalled. He declared emphatically that he had never had any suspicion that the deceased might have been addicted to the cocaine habit.

'You have heard the evidence the previous witness gave as to the cause of the deceased's death. Do you from your present knowledge agree with his conclusions?'

'Completely,' Dr Emerson answered. The man looked harassed and careworn, but his bearing remained dignified.

'Then how do you account for your certificate that death occurred from natural causes?'

Dr Emerson made a gesture of helplessness.

'How can I account for it except in the one way?' he replied. 'I was misled by the facts. I admit being in error, but I do not think that under the circumstances any doctor in the world would have acted otherwise than as I did.'

'Now, Dr Emerson,' the coroner leaned forward and looked keenly at his witness, 'tell me this. Did you really examine the body at all after death?'

'I certainly examined it. And I examined it with reasonable care, and neither then nor at any time since until I heard of this extraordinary development had I the slightest doubt that my certificate was incorrect.' He paused, then, as the coroner did not speak, went on again. 'You will admit that under the circumstances the idea of murder was the last that would occur to anyone. Five days earlier Dr Philpot had seen the man: he was then at the point of death. He told me he expected to hear of his death at any moment. When I heard of it I went out and examined the body. It had all the appearance of death from myocarditis. Only a post-mortem could have told the difference: only a post-mortem did tell the difference. As you know a post-mortem is seldom held unless there is suspicion of foul play. In this case there was none. I deeply regret that I was misled, but I believe in all honesty that there is no one who would not have acted as I did under similar circumstances.'

The coroner bowed and turned to the jury.

'As Dr Emerson has spoken so fully and frankly on this matter, I do not think that I am called upon to refer to it further. He no doubt realises how regrettable it was, for if suspicion had been aroused at the time instead of nine weeks later it might have made all the difference in capturing the criminal. In saying this I am not suggesting that blame attaches to him. Would anyone like to ask Dr Emerson any further question before he stands down?'

No one responded to the invitation, and Dr Philpot was recalled. He deposed that he had never seen any indications of the cocaine habit about deceased, and he did not believe that considering the state of his heart he could have used it.

Sergeant Kent was then sworn. He said that on learning the result of the post-mortem he had proceeded to the deceased's cottage and had there made a detailed search for cocaine or a hypodermic syringe, but without finding traces of either. The undertaker's men, recalled, also declared that they had seen nothing of the kind while attending to the body.

There being no further witnesses the coroner made a short businesslike statement summing up the evidence. As to the cause of death, he said, there could be no doubt. The medical evidence was complete and undisputed. Deceased had died as the result of an injection of cocaine, which his diseased heart was unable to stand. That injection might or might not have been self-administered. The evidence of both doctors was that in their opinion the deceased was not a victim of the cocaine habit, and it was for the jury to consider the probability of his having used it in this instance. He would direct their attention to another point. Had the fatal dose been self-administered, the syringe must have remained on or beside, the bed. It had not been found. Who then had removed it and why? On the other hand if the jury considered the dose had been given by some other person or persons, they must consider with what motive this had been done. If they believed a genuine error had been made they would return a verdict of death from misadventure, but if upon weighing all the circumstances they rejected the possibility of error they would return a verdict of wilful murder.

For nearly an hour the jury deliberated, and then they brought in the expected verdict of wilful murder against some person or persons unknown.

'You did that quite well,' Major Valentine assured French as the two men walked to the former's car after the inquiry. 'If Roper is alive and reads your evidence—and he is certain to do that if he is in the country—he will think he is safe and may start changing the notes. By the way, are you sure that Tarkington and that clerk of his won't give you away about the numbers of the notes? Your evidence must have sounded peculiar to them.'

'I thought of that,' French answered, 'and I saw them both and warned them. They'll hold their tongues.'

'I suppose no one has been trying to get just that information out of them?'

'No, sir. I, asked them that first thing, but no one had.'

Before Major Valentine left he discussed with French the steps that he would take to try to find out whether anyone had disappeared at the time of the fire. The inquiry had already been made, but this time it was to be pressed much more energetically. At the same time the watch for the stolen notes was to be redoubled, and French undertook to arrange that a general memorandum on the subject would be sent to all the banks in the country.

A third line of research was suggested by the medical evidence, and this French and the major agreed to work jointly. The most searching inquiries were to be made for anyone who had obtained or tried to obtain cocaine or a hypodermic syringe during a period of several weeks prior to the tragedy.

In addition to these three there was, of course, the most important and hopeful line of all, a direct search for Roper. French undertook to organise this with as little delay as possible.

After discussing the situation for nearly two hours the two men parted, hopeful that their several efforts would before long place the key of the mystery in their hands.

16

A Double Recall

When French settled down to consider how the search for
Roper could best be carried out he saw that he was up against
a very much steeper proposition than had appeared at first
sight.

There were two ways in which he could attack the problem.
He could attempt to trace the man's movements from the night
of the fire and go on step by step until he found him, or he
could try to discover his present whereabouts, irrespective of
how he had arrived there.

The first method was not very hopeful. Not only was there
little to go on, but such trail as the man must have left was
cold. It was now over two months since the tragedy, and
while the passage of a wanted man during the week previous
to an inquiry might be remembered by porters, taxi-men or
others who come in contact with the public, few would recall
having seen a stranger two months earlier.

Direct search, French thought, was much more promising.
For this he had behind him the whole of the amazingly
complete and far-reaching organisation of the police. If Roper

had not left the country he would find it hard to evade recognition by someone of the thousands of constables and detectives who would be looking out for him.

French remembered that the Kintilloch sergeant had mentioned that Roper had applied for a passport to Brazil, and he began operations by writing to the Yard to send a man to the Passport Office to obtain a copy of the photograph lodged. Then he set to work to compile a description of Roper. He saw Oxley, Whymper, Ruth and one or two others and got down from them details of the man's appearance. From these he synthesised the following:

'Wanted for murder. John Roper. Age 34; height about 5 ft. 9 inches; slight build; thick, dark hair; dark eyes with a decided squint; heavy dark eyebrows; clean shaven; sallow complexion; small nose and mouth; pointed chin; small hands and feet; walks with a slight stoop and a quick step; speaks in a rather high-pitched voice with a slight Lowland Scotch accent.'

On the whole French was pleased with the description. It was more complete than was usually obtainable from unofficial sources. It had not, of course, been volunteered by any of his informants, but had been gradually reached by persistent questions on each feature in turn. He sent it to the Yard, asking that it be published in the next issue of the Police Gazette along with a copy of the photograph obtained from the Passport Office. This meant that within three or four days every police officer in the land would be applying it to newcomers of less than ten weeks standing. If Roper had not escaped abroad or was not lying hidden in the most populous district of some great town there was a very good chance that he might be found.

In his letter to the Yard French had also asked that systematic inquiries should be made at the various seaports and from

234

steamship lines to try to find out if the man had left the country. He suggested concentrating on lines running to Brazil or calling at places from which other lines ran to Brazil. Airlines to the Continent he included as well as the ordinary cross-channel services, though from these he scarcely expected a result.

Next he determined to make, so far as he could, lists of the attendant's friends, places where he had spent his holidays, and any other details of his life that could be ascertained. Frequently he had found that such vague inquiries produced valuable results. It was a speculative move, of course, but he thought it would be worth a couple of days' work.

As Kintilloch was the most likely place to pick up such information, he travelled for the second time to the little Fifeshire town. There he interviewed everyone who, he thought, might help him, but entirely without result. Even when he visited the home of the late Flora Roper and discussed the affair with the unfortunate woman's mother he learned nothing valuable.

As he was leaving Kintilloch it occurred to him as a last forlorn hope that possibly Dr Philpot might be able to assist. The address the doctor had given him was in Glasgow, and to return *via* Glasgow was but little out of his way. He decided he would pay the call on chance.

About five o'clock that afternoon, therefore, he turned from Dumbarton Road into Kilgore Street and looked up No. 47. It was a rather decayed looking apartment house of a shabby-genteel type, and the landlady who answered his ring gave him the same impression of having fallen on evil days. Rather a comedown, French thought, for a man who had occupied a comfortable villa standing in its own grounds, to be reduced to this semi-slum lodging house. With a momentary feeling of pity he inquired if Dr Philpot was at home.

'There's no Dr Philpot lives here,' the woman answered in complaining tones. 'There's a *Mr* Philpot, if that's who you mean.'

'He may not be a doctor; I'm not sure,' French returned. 'The man I mean is fair-haired with a thin face, and could only have come to you within the last week.'

'Yes, that's him all right. But he isn't in.'

'When do you expect him?'

'He generally comes in about six or half past.'

'Then I'll call back.'

French strolled about the parks around Kelvinside until his watch warned him to return to Kilgore Street. Philpot had just arrived. He seemed glad to see French and told of his new life with an eagerness that the latter thought rather pathetic.

'I hated that place, Inspector,' he went on. 'I didn't realise it while I was there, but now that I have left I am surprised how much I hated it. But I believe I'm going to like my new work. I've got a job, you know.'

'Glad to hear it,' French returned cheerily. 'I hope it's a good one.'

'It's too soon to say that. I'm now a commission agent. It is by the kindness of an old friend. He has let me have one of his side lines to see how I get on. It doesn't sound a promising proposition, but I confess I've been surprised at its possibilities since I started. It concerns the marketing of inventions. My friend keeps in touch with the patent agents and approaches all the smaller patentees, then if the thing looks good I try to find a manufacturer or a market. I am to pay him a percentage of all my takings and already I've been in touch with five inventions, all of which are doing very well. If my luck holds I hope some day to be able to square all those people I now owe money to in Thirsby. Then my idea is to get across to the States and start afresh.'

French offered his congratulations and as soon as he reasonably could switched the conversation over to Roper. Philpot seemed considerably surprised, but he willingly discussed the attendant and obviously did his best to satisfy his visitor. He gave a good deal of information, but only one piece seemed to French at all useful.

Roper had occasionally visited Peebles. What he had gone for Philpot did not know, but he believed his family lived there. Roper had once referred to his widowed mother and had spoken of going to Peebles to see her.

'I'm sorry not to be able to give you more help,' Philpot apologised when French at last showed signs of coming to an end. 'I suppose it would be indiscreet to inquire what you're after?'

French hesitated. He had avoided mentioning his theory to anyone except Chief Inspector Mitchell and Major Valentine, and his working principle in such cases was reticence. For a moment he was tempted to confide in Philpot, then habit triumphed and he prevaricated.

'My dossier of the case is not complete without all the information I can put into it. It is academic, of course, but I like to do things thoroughly. Gets you a reputation for efficiency, you know. One can't afford to sneeze at it. Well, doctor, I'm glad to have seen you and I hope your good luck will continue.'

It was evident that Philpot realised that he had been put off, but he made no further reference to the subject, and his good-bye was cordial enough. French in his kindly way was pleased to see that the man had a chance of making good, and his congratulations and good wishes were really sincere.

After some thought he determined to follow up the doctor's

237

clue and next morning he went to Peebles. There he had little difficulty in finding Roper's mother. She kept a huckster's shop in the poorer part of the town, but it was evident that she was getting too old for the work, and that business was not flourishing. She was suspicious at first, but under the genial influence of French's manner she thawed and, presently became garrulous. French was soon satisfied that she had no idea that her son might be alive. He pumped her with his usual skill, pretending he was a former acquaintance of Roper's, but in the end also he was unable to learn anything helpful.

He returned to Thirsby and began a series of inquiries at the nearby railway stations, posting establishments, inns and villages, in the hope of coming on some trace of the quarry. But the trail was too old. For three days he worked early and late, but nowhere did he learn of any mysterious stranger who might prove to be the missing man. He was indeed about to give up in despair, when his labours were brought to an unexpected conclusion. Chief Inspector Mitchell wired an urgent recall to the Yard.

It was by no means the first of such recalls that French had received, though it was riot usual to interrupt an officer who was actually engaged in investigating a case. The incident always bred a slight uneasiness. The possibility of having made some serious blunder was ever present. And French was aware that his most unhappy experiences had almost invariably followed periods of exaltation and self-satisfaction. Chief Inspector Mitchell was an exceedingly shrewd man and he had a perfectly uncanny way of delving to the bottom of problems and of seeing clues that other people missed. French earnestly hoped that it was not so in the present instance.

He travelled up by the night train and early next morning reported at the Yard. There he found his fears were groundless.

238

The chief inspector, so far from grumbling, was in a very good mood and almost complimented him on what he had done.

'Well, French, you're up against it again, are you? What were you busy at when you got my wire?'

French explained.

'You can do something better. Read that.'

It was the typewritten note of a telephone conversation. It appeared that at four o'clock on the previous evening the manager of the Northern Shires Bank in Throgmorton Avenue had rung up to say that two twenty-pound notes bearing numbers on the list supplied in connection with the Starvel Hollow crime had been passed into the bank that afternoon. The cashier had just at that moment made the discovery, but unfortunately he was unable to remember from whom he had received them.

'By Jove, sir!' French exclaimed. 'Then Roper is in town!'

'It looks like it if your theory is right,' the chief inspector admitted. 'I sent Willis across at once and he saw the cashier. But the man couldn't say where the notes had come from. Willis got him to prepare a list of all the lodgments he had received that day, intending, if you didn't turn up, to go round the people today with Roper's description. You had better see him and find out what he has done. I want you to take over from him at once as he is really on that Colchester burglary.'

'Very good, sir. Do you know if the notes were together: if they seemed to have come in from the same party?'

'Willis asked that. They were not near each other in the pile. Of course, the argument is not conclusive, but the suggestion is that they came in separately.'

'If that is so it looks as if Roper was changing them systematically.'

'Possibly. In that case we may expect more notes to come in. That'll do, French. Go and see Willis and start right in.'

Inspector Willis was seated at the desk in his room, apparently trying to reduce to some sort of order the chaotic heap of papers which covered it.

'Hullo, French! Come in and take a pew,' he greeted his visitor. 'I don't know anyone I'd be better pleased to see. If you hadn't turned up within another ten minutes I was going out about those blessed notes, but now I shall be able to get down to Colchester on the next train. I'm on that burglary at Brodrick's, the jewellers. You heard about it?'

'The chief mentioned it, but I have heard no details. Interesting case?'

'Nothing out of the way. The place was broken into from a lane at the back and the safe cut with an oxyacetylene jet. They got about six thousand pounds worth. It happened that Brodrick had just sent a lot of stuff to town, else they'd have cleared twice that.'

'Any line on the men?'

'It was Hot Alf and the Mummer, I believe. It was their style, and Alf was seen in the town two days before. But I've not got anything definite yet. There's a fearful muck of stuff about it: look at all this.' He indicated the litter on the table.

'No finger-prints?'

'Nope. But I'll get them through the fences. I've only to sit tight and they'll give themselves away. But what about your do? I've got it finished, thank the Lord! There it is.' He pointed to a little heap of papers apart from the others. 'There's more in it, the chief hinted, than stolen notes, but he didn't say what it was.'

'There's pretty well everything in it so far as I can see,'

French rejoined. 'Murder—quadruple murder—theft, arson and body-snatching.'

Willis whistled.

'Body-snatching? Good Lord!' he exclaimed 'You don't often hear of that nowadays.'

'You don't,' French admitted, 'but this was not ordinary body-snatching. You remember the case a fire at Starvel in which the three occupants of the house were supposed to be burned? Well, one wasn't. He burgled the place and escaped with the swag: those notes that you were on to today. But he had to have a body to represent himself, so he murdered a neighbour and burned his in the house.'

'Lord, French! That's quite a tale. It would make a novel, that would. How did you get on to it?'

French gave a somewhat sketchy resumé of his activities and so led the conversation back to the notes. 'The chief said you would give me the details so as I could get ahead with it today.'

'Right-o. The chief called me in about four yesterday afternoon and said he'd just had a 'phone from the Northern Shires Bank that two of the Starvel notes had been paid in, and as you weren't there, I'd better take over. So I went and saw the teller. He couldn't say who had given him the notes, as it was only when he was balancing his cash after the bank closed that he recognised the numbers. I got him to make me a list of the lodgments during the day. That took a bit of time, but he had it at last. Then I went through it with him and we eliminated all the entries at which he was sure that no twenty-pound note was handled. That left just under two hundred possibles. Then I brought the list home and went over it again, ticking off people or firms who do not usually take in cash from the public, like shipowners, manufacturers and wholesale dealers. Of course, these are possibles, but not so likely as the others. It was rough and ready, but I wanted to tackle the most probable first. You follow me?'

'Of course. I should have done the same.'

'I waited up until I had put the probables in location order, and here is the list ready for you.'

'Jolly good, Willis. I'm sorry you had so much trouble. I'll carry on and hope for the best.'

'You'll get it all right,' Willis opined as he settled down again to his work.

All that day and the next French, armed with the list and with Roper's photograph and description, went from place to place interviewing managers and assistants in shops and business firms. But all to no purpose. Nowhere could he obtain any trace of the elusive twenty-pound notes, nor had any man answering to the description been seen. And then to his amazement he was taken off the inquiry.

Like other officers of the C.I.D., it was his habit to keep in as close touch with headquarters as possible while pursuing his investigations. At intervals therefore during these two days he called up the Yard and reported his whereabouts. It was during one of these communications that for the second time in two days he received an urgent recall.

In this case it was a summons which he could obey promptly, and twenty minutes after receiving the message he was knocking at the door of Chief Inspector Mitchell's room.

One glance at the chief's face showed him that at least there was no trouble brewing, Mitchell greeting him with a half smile.

'Sit down, French,' he said, 'and listen to me. I want to tell you a story.'

After glancing at a few papers which he took from a drawer, he began to speak.

17

Concerning Wedding Rings

'This morning about 10.30,' said the chief inspector, 'we had a 'phone from Inspector Marshall of the Whitechapel District. He wanted to know whether we had had any recent reports of thefts of small jewellery, as he had come across some in connection with a scrap between two lightermen. It seems that about ten o'clock last night a constable on patrol heard cries coming from an entry off Cable Street, as if someone was being murdered. He ran down and found a man on the ground with another belabouring him furiously with his fists. The constable pulled the victor off, to find his opponent was little the worse. The fellow was really more frightened than hurt. The constable would have dismissed the affair with a good-humoured caution to both, had it not been that in the heat of the explanations the cause of the quarrel came out. The men had obtained some jewellery, which both claimed, and when the constable saw the stuff he didn't wait for further discussion, but marched them both off to Divisional Headquarters. Marshall questioned them and reported their statements with his inquiry.

'The whole thing so far was purely commonplace, and if the jewellery had consisted of ordinary trinkets I should have thought no more about it. But the nature of the stuff tickled my fancy and I grew interested. You would hardly guess what they had. Wedding rings!'

'I certainly shouldn't have guessed that, sir.'

'I don't suppose you would. Well, that's what they had. Thirty-nine wedding rings on a cord. They were all much of the same size and value. And there was not another thing. They were searched, but nothing else was found on them.'

'Marshall, of course, asked them where they got them, and their answer was more interesting still. It appeared that the victor, James Grey, was the skipper of a Thames lighter and the vanquished, William Fuller, was his "crew." A third man was on board who looked after the engine, but he didn't come into the affair. Grey stated that about 8.30 that same evening they were working empty down the river. They had left a cargo of Belgian coal at an up-river works and were running down to their moorings for the night. They usually stopped about six, but trouble with their engine had delayed them on this occasion. It was rather a dirty night, raining and very dark and blowing a little. Grey, the skipper, was at the helm and Fuller was forward acting as look-out. The third man was below at the engines. Just as they began to emerge from beneath the Tower Bridge Fuller heard a smack on the deck beside him. He looked down and in the light of some of the shore lamps saw some bright objects rolling about on the planks. On picking one up he was astonished to find it was a wedding ring. He began to search and found several others, but the skipper swore at him for not minding his job, and he had to let the remainder lie. When they reached their moorings he tried again, but Grey was curious and came forward and found a ring himself. Then they had a proper look with lanterns and recovered the thirty-nine. Immediately, as might be expected, a row broke out. Both men wanted the rings. Fuller said they had fallen beside him and he had found all but one or two, but Grey held that he was skipper and that anything that came on the ship was his. They had to bury the hatchet temporarily so as not to give away the secret to their engineer, but the quarrel broke out again ashore, Fuller's cries attracting our man. What do you think of that, French? A good story, isn't it?'

'Like a book, sir. Just a bit humorous, too, if you don't mind my saying so.'

There was a twinkle in Chief Inspector Mitchell's eye as he continued:

'Oh, you think so, do you? Well, anyhow, as I say, I was interested. The men's mentality I found quite intriguing. I wondered how much imagination they had between them. Marshall described them as slow, unintelligent, bovine fellows. Now, such men could never have invented a tale like that. If they had been making it up they would have said they found a bag of rings in the street. The idea of wedding rings having been thrown over the parapet of the Tower Bridge just as they were passing beneath would only occur to men of imagination, and to have got all the details right would have involved, a very considerable gift of invention as well. Do you see what I'm getting at, French? Their story shows too much imagination for their intelligences as described by Marshall, and therefore I am disposed to accept it.'

Chief Inspector Mitchell paused and looked at French as if expecting a comment.

'I follow you all right, sir, and what you say sounds reasonable to me. And yet it's not very likely that anyone would throw thirty-nine wedding rings into the Thames off the Tower Bridge, for I take it it was into the river and not on to the boat they were intended to go.'

'I should say undoubtedly.' Mitchell sat for a moment drumming with his fingers on his desk and looking thoughtfully out of the window. 'You think the whole thing's unlikely, do you? Perhaps you are right. And yet I don't know. I think I can imagine circumstances in which a man might be very anxious to get rid of thirty-nine wedding rings. And what's more, to throw them over the parapet of the Tower Bridge at 8.30 in the evening seems to me a jolly good way of getting rid of them. How would you have done it, French?'

French glanced at his superior in some surprise. He could not understand the other's interest in this commonplace story of stolen rings. Still less could he understand why he had been interrupted in his useful and important work to come and listen to it. However, he realised that it would be tactless to say so.

'I don't know, sir,' he answered slowly. 'I suppose to throw 'em in the river would be the best way. But he should have seen there was nothing passing underneath.'

'Ah, now that is an interesting point also. But first, does anything else strike you?'

French looked wary.

'Just in what way, sir?'

'This. Suppose you want to throw a package into the river and you want to do it absolutely unobserved. Where will you do it?'

'I see what you mean, sir. That bridge at that time of night is about as deserted as any of the London bridges.'

'Exactly, that's what I mean. There is evidence there of selection which would never strike a man like these bargees. But you say he ought to have seen the boat. Why should our unknown not have looked out for passing boats? I'll tell you, I think. Though the bridge is *comparatively* deserted, it is *not* deserted. To look over the parapet far enough to see the water below would have attracted attention. A suicide might have been feared. Some officious person might have come forward. No, the unknown would simply chuck his parcel over without even turning his head, secure in the belief that even if by some miracle it was found, the contents would never be traced to him. Do you agree?'

'Seems quite sound, sir.'

'It may be sound or it may not,' Mitchell returned. 'All that I have been saying to you may be the merest nonsense. But it shows, I think, that the story these men told *may* be true. The chances of its being true are sufficiently great to warrant investigation before they are charged with theft. You agree with that?' This time French felt no doubt.

'Oh, yes, sir, I agree with that certainly. The men could not be convicted without going into their story.'

The chief inspector nodded as if he had at last reached the goal for which he had so long been aiming.

'That's it, French. Now will you start in and do it?'

French stared.

'Me, sir?' he exclaimed as if unable to believe his ears. 'Do you wish me to take it up?' The other smiled satirically.

'I don't know anyone who could do it better.'

'And drop my present case?'

'Only temporarily,' the chief assured him. 'A day or so will make little difference to your own affair, and I have no one else to send on this one. Look into it and try and find out if anyone dropped those rings off the bridge, and if so, who he was and why he did it. When you have done that you can go ahead again with the Starvel affair.'

French was completely puzzled. This was very unlike the line the chief usually took.

'Of course, sir, it's what you say; but do you not think it is very urgent that this bank-note business be followed up while the trail is warm? Every day that passes will make it more difficult to get the truth.'

'That applies even more strongly to this other affair. But it has the advantage of probably being a shorter inquiry. With luck you can finish it off tomorrow, and if so, that will delay the larger case only very slightly.'

French saw that whatever might be the chief's motive, he had made up his mind.

'Very good, sir,' he returned. 'I'll go down to Whitechapel at once and get started.'

'Right, I wish you would.'

French was conscious of not a little exasperation as he walked to Charing Cross and there took an eastward bound train. A few hours might make all the difference between success and failure in the Starvel case, and here he was turned on to this other business during the very period when it was most important he should be on his own job. He could not understand what was at the back of the chief inspector's mind. Apparently he suspected a crime, though what crime he had in view French could not imagine. Marshall could have dealt with ordinary petty theft. But if Mr Mitchell suspected a serious crime and if, as he said, no other officer was available to investigate the affair, his attitude would be explained.

But whether it were explained or not orders were orders, and French with an effort switched his mind off John Roper and on to lightermen and wedding rings. On arrival at Divisional Headquarters he saw Inspector Marshall and heard his account of the affair, which was almost word for word that of the chief inspector's.

'I don't know what the chief's got in his mind,' French grumbled. 'Here was I on that Starvel case and on a hot scent too, and why he should switch me off on to this affair I can't see. He's got some bee in his bonnet about it. He believes these fellows' yarn and he wants me to find the man who threw the rings over.'

Marshal made noises indicative of surprise and sympathy. 'I shouldn't have thought the chief inspector would have stood for that dope,' he remarked. 'What are you going to do about it?'

French didn't exactly know. He supposed he had better hear the men's story for himself, though, of course, after his colleague had examined them his doing so would be only a matter of form to satisfy the chief. Then he would think over the affair and try to plan his next move.

But rather to his own surprise, French found himself considerably impressed by the two men's personalities and the way they told their story. Both were heavy and slow-witted and, French judged, without any imagination at all, and both seemed reasonably honest. After he had questioned them he felt very much inclined to accept his Chief's view and to believe the tale.

'You say you found the rings by the light of a hand lamp,' he went on presently. 'Very good. Come along down with me to this boat of yours and we'll have another look by daylight. Perhaps you missed a few.'

The men didn't think so, but they were very willing to do anything which got them out of the police station. They led the two inspectors to the dirtiest wharf that French had ever seen, and there hailing a man in a wherry, the four were put aboard the Thames lighter *Fickle Jane.*

249

She was a long low craft more like a canal boat than a lighter. Nine-tenths of her was hold, but at one end there was a tiny fo'c'sle and at the other an equally diminutive engine-room. She was steered by a small wheel aft.

'Now,' French said to the 'crew,' 'go and stand just where you were when the rings came down.'

Fuller moved to the fo'c'sle and took up a position on the port side of the companion.

'And where did the rings strike?'

'Couldn't just say to a foot, guv'nor,' the man answered, 'but abaht that there bolt 'ead or maybe a bit forra'd.'

The point he indicated was starboard of the companion and midway between it and the side of the boat. French saw that objects falling at that point might scatter in any direction, and he began a careful search for further rings.

In less than a minute he found one. It had rolled down along the strip of deck at the side of the hold and jammed itself in a crack of the coaming timbers.

This discovery seemed to French to prove the men's story completely. He took their addresses and told them they were free and that if the owner of the rings could not be found they would be returned to them. He wanted them, however, to come up with him to the Tower Bridge and show him the exact point at which the incident had occurred, but for this they would be paid.

He was frankly puzzled as he stood looking over the parapet of the bridge after Grey and Fuller had gone. As far as he could see there was absolutely nothing in the nature of a clue to the person he sought. The rings were probably stolen, but not, he imagined, from a jeweller. Rather, he pictured some street row in which a hawker had been relieved of his stock-in-trade. Though, if this had been done, he could not imagine why the stock should have been thrown away.

There were, of course, some obvious steps to be taken, but French hesitated over them because he did not think any of them could bring in useful information. However, he couldn't stand there all day, and he might as well get on with all the lines of inquiry that suggested themselves.

First, he called at the Yard and arranged that any constables who had been on patrol duty on or near the Tower Bridge at 8.30 the previous evening should be found and sent to him for interrogation. Then with the rings in his pocket he went to a small jeweller's shop in the Strand, of which he knew the proprietor.

'I want your help, Mr Alderdice,' he said as they shook hands in the little private room at the back of the shop. 'I'm trying to find someone who amuses himself by throwing wedding rings into the Thames,' and he told his story, concluding: 'Now I wondered if you could tell me anything about these rings which would help me. Have you heard of any thefts of rings? Is there any way of identifying or tracing these? Might they be sold by a hawker, or would they be more probably from a jeweller's shop? Any information that you could give me would be most gratefully received.'

Mr Alderdice, a precise, dried-up little man, rubbed his chin thoughtfully.

'Well, you know, Mr French,' he said, 'I don't believe that I can think of anything in my trade about which I could give you less help. There are, as you know, millions of wedding rings in this city alone, and they are all more or less alike. In fact, sir, you might as well try to identify a given nail in an ironmonger's bin. I don't think it's possible. Needless to say though, I'll do what I can. Let me see the rings.'

He took the bunch, nattily untied the knot on the cord which held them, and taking the rings one by one, examined each carefully.

'They are all of eighteen carat gold,' he said in the manner of an expert pronouncing a deliberate judgment. 'They are fairly well the same size and thickness and would sell from – thirty to thirty-five shillings each, according to weight. I do not know much about the hawkers you refer to, but I should imagine that they would content themselves with a rather inferior article, and that these rings were sold by reputable jewellers. I have not heard of any cases of robbery of such rings. I do not see how you or anyone else could trace their sales, but of course that is speaking from my point of view: you gentlemen from the Yard have a wonderful way of finding out things.'

French made a grimace. 'I'm afraid my job's not very hopeful,' he bewailed as he thanked his friend and took his leave.

He walked slowly back to the Yard, thinking intently. This was one of those hateful jobs in which you had to work from the general; to deal with the whole of the possible sources of information concerned. He would now have to apply to all the jewellers' shops in London—a tremendous job. How much he preferred working from the particular! In that case, to complete the parallel, he would get a clue which would lead to the one shop or group of shops he required. But here the situation was reversed. He would have to deal with all jewellers, and he did not know exactly what he was to ask them.

He made several drafts and at last produced a circular which he considered satisfactory. In it he said that the Yard desired to trace a person who had got rid of forty wedding rings on the night of Monday, 6th December, of which the particulars were as followed, and that he would be obliged for any information which might help. In particular he wished to know whether any wedding rings had disappeared or been stolen recently. Failing that he would be grateful for the description as far as it could be ascertained, of all persons who had bought wedding rings within the previous four days, with the date and approximate hour of the purchase. Replies, which would be treated as entirely confidential, were to be sent to Inspector French at New Scotland Yard.

He set some men to work with directories to find out the addresses of jewellers in London and made arrangements to have the necessary copies of his circular prepared and delivered. Then he organised a staff to deal with the replies when they came in. Finally, having cleared his conscience with regard to the rings episode, he returned to his work on the bank-note case, picking up the thread at the point at which he had left off.

By next morning several hundred answers to his circular had been received and others were arriving continuously. Reluctantly he gave up the bank-note question and went to his office to have a look over them.

In accordance with his instructions, his staff had prepared a statement to which they added the information given in each reply. One column they had headed 'Robberies and Disappearance of rings,' and a glance down this showed French that none such had occurred. In a number of other columns they had put information about purchasers. These columns were headed with certain details of appearance, such as estimated age—over or under thirty, forty-five and sixty; tall, medium and short, dark and fair, with and without glasses, and so on. By this means it became possible to

253

determine whether the same person might have dealt in more than one shop.

There were a great many columns and comparatively few entries in each, and of those in the same column nearly all were distinguished by differences in other columns. Of course the vast number of the descriptions were vague and incomplete and most of the shops recorded purchases in connection with which the assistants could recall nothing of the purchaser. But this was only to be expected, and French worked with such results as he could get.

Of the 631 replies entered up, French gradually eliminated 625. The remaining six he examined more carefully, whistling gently as he did so. They were all under the general divisions, 'Homburg hat,' 'fawn coat,' 'dark,' 'with moustache,' and 'with glasses.' But this in itself conveyed little. It merely indicated a possibility. But when he found that four of the six shops were in the same street and that the purchases in all four had been made on the same day and at almost the same hour, his interest suddenly quickened. French considered that the matter was worth a personal call, and leaving the Yard, he drove to the first of the six and asked to see the manager.

'We're very sorry to have given you all this trouble,' he began as he produced the reply they had sent in, 'but the matter is really important. This may be possibly the man we want. Could I see the assistant who attended to him?'

In a few seconds a Mr Stanley was produced and French asked him to repeat his description of his customer.

'I remember the man quite clearly, sir,' Stanley answered: 'He had very dark hair and a thick, dark moustache and dark glasses. He wore a soft, grey Homburg hat and a fawn-coloured coat.'

'It is a pleasure to deal with you, Mr Stanley,' French smiled. 'You are certainly very observant. Now tell me, how do you come to remember the man so clearly?'

'I don't think there was any special reason, sir. Unless it was that I happened to look out of the window and saw him get out of a taxi, and that sort of fixed my attention on him. The taxi waited while he was in the shop and he got into it again and drove off when he had bought the ring.'

This was very satisfactory. If the customer was really the man French wanted, here was a clue and a valuable one. To find the taxi which had stopped at the shop at a given time on the previous day should not be difficult. He continued his questions.

'At what hour was that?'

'About half past eleven,' the salesman said after some thought. 'I couldn't say for sure, but it was about an hour before I went for dinner and that was at half past twelve.'

'He didn't seem at all agitated, I suppose?'

'No, sir. Not more than most of them.' Stanley smiled knowingly, and French felt that only for the sobering presence of the manager a wink would have conveyed the man's thought. 'Most of them are a bit, shall we say, nervous. But this man was just the same as the rest. He gave a size and said he wanted a medium weight, and that was all that passed.'

French nodded, and reverting to the description, tried for some further details with which to augment it. Though he had complimented Stanley on it, he realised that as it stood it was of little use. But the young man was unable to improve on his former effort and French was about to thank the two men and leave the shop when Stanley chanced to drop a phrase which sent the detective into a white heat of excitement and made him marvel at Chief Inspector Mitchell's perspicacity and his own obtuseness.

'And there was nothing in the slightest degree out of the ordinary in the whole transaction, no matter how trivial?' he had asked as a sort of general finalé to his catechism, more as a matter of form than because he hoped to gain any information, and it was in reply that the assistant, after saying: 'No, sir, I don't think so,' had pronounced the priceless words: 'Unless you would call changing a large note out of the ordinary. The man hadn't enough loose change to make up the thirty-five shillings and he asked me to change a twenty-pound note.'

'What!' roared French with a delighted oath, springing to his feet in his excitement. So that was it! He saw it all now! Like a flash this whole mysterious business of the wedding rings became clear as day. And the chief had guessed! Moreover the chief had given him a broad hint and he, like the *ass* that he was, had missed its meaning! He sat down and wiped his forehead.

Who was this mysterious individual, this dark-haired man with moustache and glasses, but Roper! Roper it was who had been going about buying wedding rings, and Roper it was who naturally found that he must get rid of such incriminating purchases at the earliest possible moment. The whole thing was clear! For every ring a £20 note, a tainted £20 note, a £20 note from Mr Averill's wrecked safe up at Starvel. And for every £20 note got rid of over £18 of good, clean, untraceable money brought in. It was a scheme, a great scheme, worthy of the man who had devised the crime as a whole.

As these thoughts passed through his mind French saw that the fact that the elusive purchaser had a moustache and glasses while Roper wore neither by no means invalidated his conclusion, but rather strengthened it. To a person of Roper's mental calibre a moustache would appear one of the best of disguises, while a man with a squint had practically no option but to wear tinted glasses if he wished to preserve his incognito. From disgust at his job French had suddenly swung round to enthusiasm. He had not now the faintest doubt that some forty-eight hours earlier, Roper, alive and in the flesh, had been in that very shop, having dealings with the salesman, Stanley. And then came the delightful thought that with so fresh a trail and with such a multiplicity of clues, the man's capture was a question of a very short time only. The steps to be taken were obvious, and the first was to find the taximan who had driven him round. This must be put in hand without delay.

He crushed down his impatience and turned once more to his companions, who had been regarding him with not a little surprise.

'That is important information you have just given me, Mr Stanley,' he declared. 'Now can you tell me if this is the man?' He handed over one of Roper's photographs.

And then his enthusiasm received a check. The salesman looked doubtfully at the card and shook his head.

'I don't know,' he said slowly. 'I couldn't just be sure. It's like him and it's not like him, if you understand what I mean. The man who came here had a moustache.'

'A false one,' French suggested.

The other brightened up.

'My word, but it might have been,' he exclaimed. 'I noticed it looked queer, now I come to think of it. It was very thick and long; thicker and longer than you generally see. And what you might call fuzzy round the top. Not like a real moustache. Yes, sir, I believe you're right. It looked just like a wad of hair set on.'

French laid a scrap of paper over the mouth.

'Now look again.'

Once more Stanley shook his head.

'No, sir, it's no good. I couldn't say for sure. You see that photograph shows his hair and his forehead and his eyes. Well, I didn't see any of those. He had tinted glasses and he wore his hat low down near his eyebrows. I couldn't tell. It might have been him and it might not.'

'Well, if you can't you can't, and that's all there is to it. Now another point. Have you the twenty-pound note?'

The manager disappeared, returning in a moment with a handful of money.

'Here are seven twenty-pound notes: all of that value we hold,' he explained. 'I cannot tell you certainly whether that paid in by your friend is among them, but it probably is, as the cashier thinks she did not give such a note in change and no lodgment was made at the bank since the sale.'

Eagerly French compared the numbers of the seven with those on his list, but this time he had no luck. If one of these had come from Starvel it was one of which Tarkington had not retained the number.

In spite of this French was certain that he had discovered the truth. But he felt that before acting on his theory he must put it to the proof. Fortunately there was a very obvious way of doing so. If he traced another sale and found that another £20 note had been tendered, no further doubt could possibly remain.

Pausing only to ascertain from the salesman that his customer had spoken with a Scotch accent, French hurried down the street to the next address on his list. There he had a somewhat different question to put to the manager. He was looking for a man who had within the last three or four days bought a wedding ring and who had paid for it with a £20 note. No, the manager need not be apprehensive. The note was good and the whole business in order: it was simply a question of tracing the man.

Inquiries speedily produced the desired information. A Mr Russell was sent for who had sold the ring in question. He remembered the purchaser, a slightish man of medium height with a heavy black moustache, a sallow complexion and tinted glasses. Owing to the latter he had not noted the colour of the man's eyes, but he had observed that his hair was long and very dark and that his hands were small. He thought the man might be the original of the photograph, but he could not be sure. When the bill had been made out the man had searched his pockets and had been unable to produce sufficient change. He had said: 'I'm afraid I'm short: I thought I had another ten-shilling note. Can you change twenty pounds?' The salesman had replied, 'Certainly, sir,' and the man had handed over a £20 note. Both the salesman and the cashier had examined it carefully and both were satisfied it was genuine. Unfortunately it had since been paid away and they could not therefore produce it.

This information resolved French's last doubt and he hailed a taxi and ordered the man to hurry to the Yard. He was more than delighted with his day. At long last he was on a hot trail. With the vast resources of the C.I.D. at his disposal it could not now be long before he had his hands on the criminal of Starvel and had accomplished that triumph which was to be another milestone on the road which led to promotion.

18

Cumulative Evidence

Inspector French's satisfaction in this new development was but slightly marred by his knowledge that a certain amount of the credit for it must be allotted to his Chief. Mr Mitchell had certainly spotted the true significance of the discarding of the wedding rings, but French now saw that this was a comparatively unimportant achievement. In the first place it was not due to superior ability, but to the lucky accident that the rings had fallen on the lighter instead of going overboard. In the second—and this French thought fundamental—the episode at the best had only hastened matters. If he had been left alone he would certainly have traced one of the notes. Perhaps indeed this would have proved quicker in the end.

But what, French asked himself, had led to the whole denouement? Was it not his, French's, foresight and ingenuity at the inquest? He had devised and skilfully baited a trap for his victim, and lo! the victim had walked into it with the most commendable promptness. He had fallen for the dope, as French's former acquaintance, Mrs Chauncey S. Root of

Pittsburg, would have put it. And now a little energetic action and the man would pay the price of his folly.

For some time after reaching his room French busied himself in putting in motion against the ingenious purchaser of rings the great machine of which he was a part. A telephone warning was sent to all stations that the man whose description had already been circulated in connection with the Starvel murders had disguised himself with a moustache and tinted glasses and had recently been in London occupied in certain businesses involving taxis and wedding rings. A number of men were put on to trace the taxi or taxis employed, others to try to obtain further information at the jewellers', while still others were sent round the hotels in the hope of picking up a scent. It was not indeed until the late afternoon that French had time to settle down really to consider where he now stood.

In the first place it was clear not only that Roper had remained in the country, but that he had kept himself in touch with events in Thirsby. Of course this latter did not mean much, for the circumstances of the Starvel case had created widespread interest and the details which came out at the inquest were fully reported in the papers. But Roper had evidently been uncertain as to how much the police knew, and French's evidence had had the desired reassuring effect.

It might, of course, have happened that Roper's hand had been forced. He might have run out of cash to live on or he might have required a lump sum, say, to leave the country. But whatever the reason, he had determined on a *coup*. And very cleverly he had arranged it. He must have made over £18 a purchase, and if he bought forty rings in a day his profits would amount to over £700. £700 a day was not bad.

The following day was Sunday, but by Monday evening reports had begun to come in from French's little army of workers. Sixteen more shops had been found at which Roper had bought rings and changed £20 notes, and one of these notes bore a Starvel number. Moreover it had been established that his activities had extended over at least three days. Inquiries at the fashionable restaurants had revealed the fact that on the Tuesday a man answering Roper's description had paid for his lunch at the Carlton with a similar note. French received these items thankfully, and having made a skeleton timetable of the three days in question, fitted each item into its appropriate place.

But none of those who had come in contact with Roper had been able to add to his knowledge of the man or to give a clue to his present whereabouts. It was not indeed until the middle of the following forenoon that information came in which promised more satisfactory results.

Within ten minutes of each other two telephone messages were received stating that taximen who drove Roper had been found. These men on discovery had been ordered to report themselves at the Yard, and they arrived almost simultaneously. French had them up to his room in turn.

The first driver said he had been hailed by a man of the description in question about 10.00 a.m. on Tuesday of last week. The fare had explained that he wished to engage his vehicle up till one o'clock. He was a traveller in precious stones and he wished to be taken to certain jewellers' of which he had a list. The taximan had done as he was asked. Starting near the Marble Arch, he had visited one jeweller's after another during the whole morning. Shortly after one the fare had instructed him to drive to Marylebone Station, which was then close by. There the taxi had been paid off, the fare disappearing into the station.

Asked if he could remember all the shops he called at, the man said he thought he could, and French at once despatched

Sergeant Carter with him to drive over the same ground and make inquiries *en route*.

The second taximan had a very similar story to tell. About three o'clock on the Thursday afternoon he was driving slowly down Aldwych, when he was hailed by a man of the description the sergeant had given him. The man had engaged him by the hour and had told him of his business in precious stones and they had driven to a number of jewellers, ending up about five-thirty at Malseed's, in the Strand. There the man had paid him off and he had seen him entering the shop as he drove away.

This driver also said he could remember the places at which he had called, and French sent another of his satellites round with him to amass information.

As far as it went, this was satisfactory enough. If the other taximen could be found, every minute of Roper's three days would soon be accounted for. And it would be a strange thing if amongst all those with whom he had come in contact, someone person had not learnt or noticed anything which would help to find him. French could recall many instances where a chance recollection of some physical peculiarity, of some word or phrase uttered, of some paper or small article dropped, had led to the identification of a criminal and he thought the chances of similar good fortune in the present instance were not too remote.

All through the afternoon information continued to come in, and when he had added the items to his skeleton timetable he found that he had learnt where thirty-one rings had been bought and where Roper had lunched on each of the three days in question. Of course, this information did not directly help with his present problem, but there were two other items of news which seemed more promising.

The first was that seven of the thirty-one shop assistants

who had been interviewed had noticed a fresh cut on Roper's thumb, small, but peculiarly shaped. This was an additional identification which might be useful in dealing with waiters, dining-car attendants, hotel porters and others who would be likely to observe a customer's hand.

The second item French received with deep satisfaction. Roper had spent the Tuesday night at the Strand Palace Hotel. This seemed to negative the suggestion that the man was living in London, and French therefore became much more hopeful of the prospects of finding his whereabouts on the Thursday night, the point at which he must start if he was to succeed in tracing him.

But it was not until the next afternoon that his hopes were fulfilled. When he reached the Yard after lunch he found that a telephone message had just been received from Sergeant Elliott, who was working the hotels in the Bloomsbury area. Roper, the man reported, had spent the Thursday night at the Peveril Hotel in Russell Square.

Within twenty minutes French had reached the building. Sergeant Elliott was waiting for him in the lounge.

'How did you get on to him?' French asked, after they had greeted each other heartily and withdrawn into a quiet corner.

'Just pegging away, sir; no special clue. This is the sixteenth hotel I've been to. But I think there's no doubt it's him. He turned up here about 7.15 on Thursday evening and asked for a room. On the plea of having a chill he had a fire in his room and dined there. Next morning he paid his bill to the waiter and left about 9.45.'

'Did he take a taxi?'

'Not from the hotel, sir. He just walked out, carrying a small suitcase in his hand.'

'Wasn't taking any risks. Confound him for giving us all

this trouble. See, Elliott, you look round and get hold of the men who were on point duty hereabouts on Friday morning. Some of them may have noticed him. Then go round to the nearby Tube stations. I'll go back to the Yard and get the taxis and the terminal stations worked. You follow me?'

'Right, sir. I'll go now.'

French turned to the manager's office to check his subordinate's information. There his inquiries speedily convinced him that Roper had indeed stayed in the hotel. It was true that he had registered under the name 'Jas. Fulton, Manchester,' but the handwriting set the matter at rest. That it was Roper's, French had no doubt whatever.

Except that one of the waiters had noticed the cut on the man's right thumb, this unfortunately was the only result of his inquiries. Though he was as thorough and painstaking as ever, he could find no clue to the man's present whereabouts.

Returning to the Yard, he recalled the men who were engaged on the hotels and jewellers' shops and set them new tasks. Some of them were to look for a taximan who had taken up a fare of the suspect's description in the neighbourhood of Russell Square about 9.45 on the morning of the previous Friday, the remainder were to visit the great stations in the hope of learning that the same man had left by train.

French was accustomed to prompt and efficient service, but when within an hour the wanted taximan had been found, he could not but admit pleasurable surprise. He therefore paid a somewhat unusual compliment to his subordinate on his prowess, and told him to fetch the man along.

The driver proved to be a big brawny Irishman. He stated he had picked up a fare like the man described at the Russell Square end of Southampton Row about the hour named. The man had carried a small suitcase and had been walking away from the Square. The driver had not seen his face clearly, as he had his collar turned up and his hat pulled low, but when French heard that he spoke with a Scotch accent, he felt that things were going as they should. It was therefore with keen interest that he waited for a reply to the question, Where had he driven him?

'To Gracechurch Street, sorr,' the man answered, 'to a block o' buildings half-way down the street on the left-hand side.'

'Could you find it again?'

'I could, sorr, surely.'

'Then drive there.'

An inspection of the plates at each side of the entrance door showed that the 'block o' buildings' contained eleven suites of offices. French stood contemplating the names and wondering in which of the firms Roper had been interested.

None of them seemed very promising at first sight. There were two coal merchants, a chemical analyst, a stockbroker, an engineer and architect, three shipping firms and three commission agents. Of these the shipping firms seemed the most hopeful and French decided to start with them.

Obtaining no information at the shipping offices, he went on to the remaining firms, and at the seventh he struck oil. The office boy at Messrs Dashwood and Munce's, stockbrokers, remembered such a man calling at the hour in question. He had, he believed, seen Mr Dashwood, and it was not long before French was seated in the senior partner's room.

Mr Dashwood, a tall, thin man with a shrewd expression and keen eyes, listened attentively while French stated his business.

'I admit,' he said, 'that the description you give resembles that of our client. But you must be aware, Inspector, that a client's dealings are confidential, and unless you can prove to me that this is really the man you want and that it is my duty to discuss his business, I do not think I feel called on to say any more.'

'I thoroughly appreciate your position,' French returned suavely, 'and under ordinary circumstances agree that you would be absolutely right. But these circumstances are not ordinary. Firstly, here are my credentials, so that you will see that I really am an officer of Scotland Yard. Secondly, I must take you into my confidence to the extent of telling you that the man is wanted for a very serious crime indeed—a triple murder, in fact. You will see, therefore, that you cannot keep back any information about him which you may possess.'

Mr Dashwood shrugged.

'What you say alters the matter. Tell me what you wish to know.'

'First, your client's name and address.'

Mr Dashwood consulted a small ledger.

'Mr Arthur Lisle Whitman, c/o Mr Andrew Macdonald, 18 Moray Street, Pentland Avenue, Edinburgh.'

'Was he an old client?'

'No, I had never seen him before.'

'And what was his business?'

'He wished us to purchase some stock for him.'

'Oh,' said French. 'Did he pay for it?'

'Yes, he paid in advance.'

'In notes of £10 and less in value, I suppose?'

Mr Dashwood shot a keen glance at the other.

'That's right,' he admitted. 'It seemed a peculiar way of doing things, but he explained that he was a bookmaker and had been doing some big business lately.'

'What was the amount?'

'Roughly two thousand pounds.'

'No twenty-pound notes, I suppose?'

'None. He counted it out here, and ten was the highest value.'

French was delighted. There was no doubt he was on the right track. Further, three days at £700 just made the required sum.

'In what stock were you to invest?'

'Brazilian. A thousand in Government five per cents and the rest in rails.'

This was satisfactory too. French remembered Roper's Brazilian passport. At the same time he was slightly puzzled. Surely the man was not mad enough to imagine he could get out of the country? Still, if he thought he was not suspected he might try to do so.

'Where was the interest to be paid? Did he say he was going out?'

'Yes. He said he was sailing in a few weeks and that he already had an account in the Beira Bank at Rio, to which the dividends were to be paid.'

French laid his photograph and description on the other's desk.

'That the man?'

Mr Dashwood examined the photograph and slowly read and re-read the description.

'I don't know,' he said at last. 'At first glance I should say not, but on consideration I'm not so sure. If it was he, he was disguised.'

'I have reason to believe he was disguised.'

'Then probably it was he. The features which he couldn't alter, such as his height and build, correspond all right.'

'Have you got a specimen of his handwriting?'

Yes, Mr Dashwood had his signature to certain forms. French gazed at the four specimens of 'Arthur Lisle Whitman' which were produced. And then he felt himself up against the same

268

difficulty which had confronted Mr Dashwood. At first sight the signatures were not so obviously Roper's as those in the Peveril register, but as French examined them he felt more and more satisfied that the man had indeed written them, though he had obviously made some attempt at disguise.

French was more than pleased with his interview when, after warning Mr Dashwood to keep the affair secret, he took his departure. In the first place the whole of Roper's scheme of escape was at last revealed. The man had evidently set himself two problems, first, to change his possibly incriminating twenty-pound notes in such a way that any which might afterwards be identified should not be traceable to him, and secondly, to get this money into Brazilian securities, payable in Brazil, with a similar immunity from risk. And very, cleverly he had solved both these problems.

But he had made an error, and French smiled grimly as he thought of it. He had given an address to Dashwood and Munce. A bad, a fatal error! A trip to Edinburgh for French, and Master John Roper's career would meet with a sudden check. And with that the Starvel Hollow crime would be avenged and French—he hoped against hope—would come in for his reward.

Could he not, French wondered, find out something about that address without leaving London? He turned into a telegraph office and sent a wire to the Edinburgh police. Early next morning there was a reply.

It seemed that Mr Andrew Macdonald of 18 Moray Street, Pentland Avenue, through whom 'Mr Arthur Lisle Whitman' was to be approached, was a small tobacconist with a rather shady reputation. It was evident therefore that Roper had adopted a time-honoured expedient to obtain his correspondence secretly. Letters could be addressed to Macdonald, and for a consideration they would either be re-addressed to Roper or be kept till called for. In either case Macdonald would not know who his client really was or where he was to be found, in the event of questions from inquisitive seekers.

French saw that Macdonald, at least if he was a man of strong character, could give a lot of trouble. He would admit that he kept letters for Whitman, but would state that Whitman always called for these and that he did not know where his client was to be found. And the closest watch kept by the police might be quite unavailing. French remembered a case in point in the East End. Here a small newsagent had been chosen as the intermediary, and though the place was kept under observation for several weeks, the criminal was never seen. It was only when he was captured through an entirely different line of research that the reason came out. The newsagent had guessed his establishment was being shadowed and he had exhibited a prearranged sign. He had placed a certain article in a certain place in his window. The criminal, riding past in a bus, had seen the danger signal and had kept away.

In the present instance French wished if possible to avoid the chance of a similar expensive and irritating delay. If he could devise some other method of attack, this clue of the tobacconist could be kept as a last resource.

He took his problem home with him that night, and after he had dined he drew an arm-chair up to the fire and settled down comfortably with his pipe to think the thing out. For a considerable time he pondered, then at last he thought he saw his way. He worked at the details of his plan until he was satisfied with them, then with a smile of triumph on his lips and deep satisfaction in his heart he knocked the ashes out of his pipe, switched off the lights and went up to bed.

19

The Last Lap

Next morning Inspector French was early occupied in making the necessary preparations for his great *coup*. The first of these involved a visit to Messrs Dashwood and Munce, and the business day had scarcely begun when he presented himself once more at their office.

'I am sorry, Mr Dashwood, for troubling you so soon again,' he apologised, 'but I want to ask you one other question. Can you tell me whether Mr Whitman saw your partner during his call? In other words, if Mr Whitman were to meet Mr Munce, would he recognise him?'

Mr Dashwood raised his eyebrows, but he answered without hesitation.

'Mr Whitman was shown in to me, and so far as I know, he did not meet my partner. But Mr Munce is in his room. We can ask him.'

The junior partner was a more good-natured looking man than Mr Dashwood, and French was sorry he had not had to deal with him throughout.

'No, I didn't see him,' he said with a pleasant smile. 'As a matter of fact I was out at the time you mention. I went over—' he looked at Dashwood—'to see Troughton about eleven and I did not get back till after lunch.'

French nodded.

'Now, gentlemen,' he went on, 'I am obliged for what you have told me and I am going to ask for your further help in this matter. What I want is very simple. If any letter or wire or telephone call comes to you from Whitman will you please advise me before replying. That is all.' He repeated to Mr Munce what he had already told Mr Dashwood as to his suspicion of Whitman's criminality, stating that under the circumstances he felt sure he could count on the assistance of both gentlemen.

Mr Dashwood hemmed and hawed and was inclined to demur. He was, he pointed out, a stockbroker, not a detective, and he didn't see why he should be involved in Inspector French's machinations. If the inspector wished to make an arrest it was up to him to do it himself. But fortunately for French, Mr Munce took the opposite view.

'Oh, come now, Dashwood, hang it all,' he protested, 'we'll have to do what the inspector wants. If this Whitman is a murderer we're pretty well bound to. Besides, Mr French doesn't want us to make any move, only to sit tight and not spoil his plans. What do you say, now?'

Mr Dashwood made a gesture as if washing his hands of the whole affair, and announced stiffly that if his partner considered such action in accordance with the traditional relations between stockbroker and client he would not press his own views. Mr Munce thereupon smiled genially at French and assured him that he could count on his wishes being carried out.

This was all right so far as it went, and it paved the way for French's next proceeding. Going to the nearest telegraph office, he saw the postmaster, showed him his credentials, and explained that he wished to send a reply prepaid telegram, the answer to which was not to be delivered at its address, but was to be sent to him at Scotland Yard. Then drawing a form towards him he wrote:

'To Whitman, care of Macdonald, 18 Moray Street, Pentland Avenue, Edinburgh.

'Serious fall in Brazilian stocks impending. Advise modification of plans. Would like an interview. Munce travels to Aberdeen by 10.00 a.m. from King's Cross, Tuesday. Could you see him at Waverley where train waits from 6.15 to 6.33?

'DASHWOOD & MUNCE.'

This, French thought, should draw Roper. Unless the man was extraordinary well up in Brazilian politics, of which the chances were negligible, he would suspect nothing amiss. And if he did not suspect a trap he would almost certainly turn up. Not only would he really be anxious about his money, but he would see that it would be suspicious not to show such anxiety.

All the same. French believed that the telegram should be confirmed by a letter. In the ordinary course of business such a letter would necessarily follow, and Roper might notice the omission.

To ascertain the form of Messrs Dashwood and Munce's correspondence French adopted a simple expedient. He wrote confidentially to the firm saying he had just learnt that the man in whom he was interested had particularly small ears, and asking whether Mr Dashwood had noticed Whitman's. This letter he sent by hand and in an hour back came an answer. It took a comparatively short time to print a similar letter form, and on this French typed the following with the same coloured ribbon and spacing:

'DEAR SIR,—Confirming wire sent you today. We beg to state that we have just had confidential advices from our agents in Brazil, warning us that unsettled conditions are imminent which are likely to depress Government securities considerably. Under these circumstances we feel that we would like to discuss the question of your investments, as we think you would be wiser to modify your original proposals. In such matters a personal interview is more satisfactory than correspondence, and as Mr Munce happens to be passing through Edinburgh next Tuesday, we thought perhaps it might be convenient to you to see him at the station. The train waits long enough to enable him to explain the situation fully.

'Yours faithfully,'

French copied the 'Dashwood and Munce' signature and despatched the letter by the evening mail. He was in hopes that it would allay any suspicion the telegram might have raised in Roper's mind, while at the same time involving no reply to the stockbrokers other than that of the prepaid wire which would be delivered at the Yard.

The next point to be considered was the matter of Roper's identification. French did not believe he could manage this himself. He had never seen the man. He had, of course, a copy of the photograph on the passport, but he did not consider this sufficient. In a matter of such importance he dared not leave a loophole for mistake. He felt he must have someone who knew Roper there to assist him.

He thought at once of Ruth Averill. Of all the persons he had come across she probably knew Roper's appearance best. But he felt the job was not one for a young girl and he cast round for someone else.

No one at Thirsby seemed suitable. Several people there had been acquainted with Roper, but he did not think any had known him sufficiently intimately to penetrate a disguise, should the man still be wearing one. Nor did he believe anyone at Kintilloch would be much better, though for a while he considered getting Sergeant McGregor.

Finally, he decided that he would ask Philpot. Philpot had known Roper intimately at the Ransome and had seen him at intervals up till the tragedy. He was now in Glasgow: nearer than anyone else that French could get. Moreover, Philpot hated Roper and would no doubt be glad to put the final spoke in his wheel. French was sure he would come for the asking.

Accordingly he drew a sheet of paper to him and wrote:

'*Strictly private and confidential.*

'New Scotland Yard.

'DEAR DR PHILPOT,—You will be surprised to hear from me, and particularly to learn that I believe I have got my hands on the man wanted for the affair I have been working on. I do not wish to give details in a letter, but it is a man whom you know well and whom we all thought to be dead. You can probably guess from this.

'We have found that under an alias he has been transferring his money abroad, and in the name of the stockbrokers concerned I have asked him to meet their junior partner at Waverley Station, Edinburgh, on

Tuesday next at 6.15 p.m. on the arrival of the 10.00 a.m. from King's Cross. The junior partner will not be there, but I shall, and I hope to make the arrest.

'My difficulty is that I cannot myself identify the wanted man. In this I want your kind help. Will you please meet me under Scott's Monument at 5.00 p.m.? I shall then ask you to accompany me to the station and from some inconspicuous place keep a look-out for him. When you see him you will tell me and I shall do the rest.

'I ask you to assist me in this, and feel sure that when you consider all the circumstances of the case you will agree to do so.

'Will you please wire your decision on receipt of this letter.

'Yours faithfully,

'JOSEPH FRENCH.'

For the next few hours French was like the proverbial hen on the hot girdle. Every time his telephone bell rang he snatched up the receiver hoping that the caller was the post office from which he had sent his message. Every time the door opened he looked up eagerly to see if it was not an orange coloured telegraph message that was being brought in. He found it hard to settle to work, so much depended on his plans succeeding.

When, therefore, about four in the afternoon a wire was brought to him, he had to exercise real self-control not to snatch the paper from the messenger. And then he could have laughed with delight. The message had been handed in at the General Post Office in Edinburgh, and read:

'To Dashwood and Munce,

'Dover House,

'Gracechurch Street,

'Your wire. Will meet Munce as suggested.

'Whitman.'

So far, so very excellent! Here was the major difficulty overcome! On Tuesday evening the public career of John Roper would come to a sudden stop. The end of the case was at last in sight.

Early the next morning a second telegram was handed to French, which gave him almost equally great satisfaction. It was from Philpot and read:

'Will meet you place and time stated.'

There was now just one other point to be settled. Roper was coming to the station to meet Munce. But Munce was not going to Edinburgh. Someone must therefore take his place.

It would be better to have someone as like Munce in appearance as possible. In spite of the statement of the partners, Roper might have got a glimpse of Munce or at least have had his description. In view of this very summons he might make it his business to learn what the man was like. French considered his brother officers and he soon saw that Inspector Tanner, with a slight make-up, could present himself as a very passable imitation of the junior partner. The men were about the same build and colouring, and an alteration in the cut of Tanner's hair, a pair of spectacles, different clothes and a change of manner would do all that was necessary.

French went to Tanner's room and arranged the matter. Tanner was to call and see Munce on some matter of a prospective investment which would afterwards fall through, and while there observe his model. He would then make himself up and travel to Edinburgh by the 10.00 a.m. from King's Cross. On reaching Waverley he would co-operate with French as circumstances demanded.

To enable him to keep his appointment with Philpot, French found he must leave London on the Monday night. He therefore took the 11.35 p.m. from Euston, and about eight o'clock the next morning reached Princes Street Station. He had not been to Edinburgh for years, and emerging from the station, he was struck afresh with the beauty of the gardens and the splendour of the Castle Rock. But Princes Street itself, which he had once thought so magnificent, seemed to have shrunk, and its buildings to have grown smaller and plainer. 'Too much foreign travel,' he thought, vaguely regretful of his change of outlook; 'the towns abroad certainly spoil one for ours.'

He spent most of the day in exploring the historic buildings of the old town, then as five o'clock approached he entered the Princes Street Gardens, and strolling towards Scott's Monument, took his stand in an inconspicuous place and looked around him.

Almost immediately he saw Philpot. The doctor was muffled in a heavy coat, a thick scarf high about his ears, and fur-lined gloves—a get-up, French shrewdly suspected, intended more as a disguise from Roper than a protection from the cold. He was approaching from the Waverley Station direction, walking slowly, as if conscious that he was early. French moved to meet him.

'Well, doctor, this is very good of you. A surprising development, isn't it?'

Philpot shook hands, and glancing round, said eagerly:

'Look here, I want to understand about it. I was quite thrilled by your letter. You tell me you know the Starvel murderer, and you seem to hint that it is Roper—at least, I don't know whom else you can refer to. But surely, Inspector, you couldn't mean that?'

'Why not?'

'Why not? Why, because—I don't know, but the idea seems absolutely absurd. Roper's dead. If he is not dead, whose was the third body found? Are you really serious?'

'Yes,' French said in a low tone. 'I am quite satisfied that Roper escaped from that house and that some poor devil was murdered and buried in his place. And what's more, I'll have him in an hour's time. Come. Let us walk to the station and take up a position before he arrives.'

They moved off, while Philpot clamoured for further details. French, true to his traditions of caution, was not over communicative, but he explained some of the reasons which had led him to believe in Roper's guilt, and told of the purchases of rings which the man had made to get rid of his tainted money. Philpot evinced the keenest interest and plied the other with questions.

French told him as much as his training would allow, which was as little as he conveniently could, and then he switched the conversation on to the coming scene. Did Philpot know the station? If so, where had they best hide so as to see the train arrive while remaining themselves unobserved?

On reaching the platform French introduced himself to the stationmaster and explained his business. He had arranged for Tanner to travel in the last first-class compartment in the train, and he now found out from the stationmaster where this coach would stop. Opposite was the window of one of the offices, and on French asking whether they might use it for reconnoitring purposes, the stationmaster at once gave them the unrestricted use of the room. There, hidden from view by a screen, the two men took up their positions and began to scrutinise those who were assembling on the platform to meet the train.

Philpot was fidgety and nervous, and from one or two remarks that he made, French saw the direction in which his thoughts were running. Evidently he was afraid that if he assisted in Roper's capture, the man would round on him and try to make trouble for him about Mrs Philpot's death. In vain French attempted to reassure him. He was clearly uneasy in his mind, but presently he seemed to master his fears and concentrated his attention on the platform outside.

Time passed slowly until the train was almost due. A large number of persons had collected and were strolling slowly up and down or standing talking in little groups. French and his companion watched the moving throng from behind their screen, but no one resembling Roper put in an appearance. This, however, was not disconcerting. It was not unlikely that the man had also taken cover and was waiting until he saw someone who might be Munce before coming out into the open.

French, as the time dragged slowly away, was conscious of the thrill of the hunter who waits before a clump of jungle for a hidden man-eater. The crisis that was approaching was almost as important to him as the tiger's exit to the sportsman. This was the last lap of his case, the climax of the work of many weeks. If he carried off his *coup* all would be well; it would bring the affair to a triumphant conclusion, and to himself possibly the reward he coveted. But if any slip took place it would be a bad lookout for him. There was his and

Tanner's time besides the expense of these journeys to Scotland, not to speak of his own loss of prestige. No, French felt he could not afford to miss this chance, and insensibly his brows contracted and his lips tightened as he stood waiting for what was coming.

Presently a movement amongst the passengers on the platform and a heavy rumble announced the advent of the express. The huge engine with its high-pitched boiler and stumpy funnel rolled slowly past, followed by coach after coach, brightly lighted, luxurious, gliding smoothly by. A first-class coach stopped opposite the window and French, gazing eagerly out, presently saw Tanner descend and glance up and down the platform.

Now was the moment! Roper could not be far away.

But Tanner continued to look searchingly about him. The additional bustle of the arrival waxed and waned and the platform began to clear, people drifting away towards the exit or clustering round carriage doors close to the train. And still no sign of Roper.

The express was timed to wait for eighteen minutes, and of these at least fifteen had slipped away. Porters were already slamming doors, and the guard was coming forward, lamp in hand, ready to give the right away signal. Tanner stepped forward clear of the train and once again gazed up and down the platform, then as the hands of the clock reached the starting time he turned back and retrieved his suitcase from the compartment. The guard whistled and waved his green lamp, the coaches began to glide slowly away, the dull rumble swelled up and died away, and in a second or two some rapidly dwindling red lights were all that were left of the train.

French was almost speechless from chagrin. Had his plan

failed? Was it possible that Roper had been one too many for him? Had the man suspected a plant and kept away from the station? Or was he even now in some hidden nook on the platform doubtful of Tanner's identity and waiting to see what would materialise?

As the minutes slipped away French, unspeakably disappointed, found himself forced to the conclusion that the affair had miscarried. Roper must have become alive to his danger. Perhaps he had suspected French's wire and had replied as he did merely in order to gain time to disappear. Perhaps by this time the clue of the tobacconist's shop itself was a washout. French swore bitterly.

But they could not remain in the office for ever, nor could Tanner be left to pace the platform indefinitely. With a word of explanation to Philpot, French passed out, and the two men strolled in the direction of Tanner. French greeted him quietly and introduced Philpot, and the three stood talking.

'Washout?' Tanner said laconically, glancing at his colleague.

'Looks like it,' French admitted, and turning to Philpot, began to apologise for having brought him from Glasgow on a wild goose chase. 'I'm sorry that I can't stay and offer you hospitality either,' he went on. 'I must get round to police headquarters and start some further inquiries. But let us go and have a parting drink to our mutual good luck in the future.'

They passed into the refreshment room, French preoccupied and, for him, somewhat brusque, Tanner frankly bored, and Philpot showing evidences of mixed feelings of disappointment and relief.

'I wish you people weren't so infernally close about your business,' the doctor complained as they stood at the bar waiting for the three small Scotches and sodas French had ordered. 'Here am I, vastly interested in the affair and anxious to know what your further chances are, and you're as close as a pair of limpets. Surely I know so much that a little more won't hurt. Do you think you'll get him soon?'

French laughed disagreeably.

'I don't say exactly how soon,' he answered grimly, 'but you may take it from me that we'll get him all right. We have a hot scent. We'll have the man before any of us are much older. Well, doctor, here's yours.'

He tossed off his whisky, while Philpot, picking up his glass, murmured his toast. And then suddenly French stiffened and stood motionless, staring at the other's hand. There in the flesh at the right-hand side of his right thumb and projecting slightly on to the nail was an almost healed cut of a peculiar shape: a shape which French had had described and sketched for him by seven of the men who had sold rings to the changer of twenty-pound notes in London! French's brain whirled. Surely, surely, it couldn't be!

Philpot noted the other's change of expression and followed the direction of his gaze. Then with a sudden gesture of rage and despair he dropped his glass, and his left hand flashed to the side pocket of his coat. French had noticed that this pocket bulged as if it contained some round object of fair size such as an apple or an orange. Philpot drew out a dark-coloured ball of some kind and began desperately fumbling at it with his right hand. And then French saw what the man was doing. The object was a Mills' bomb and he was pulling out the pin!

With a yell to Tanner for help, French flung himself on the doctor, and clutching his left hand, squeezed it desperately over the bomb. The pin was out, but the man's hand prevented the lever from moving. If his grasp were relaxed for even an instant nothing could save all three from being blown to atoms!

Philpot's mild and gentle face was convulsed with fury. His lips receded from his teeth and he snarled like a wild beast as he struggled wildly to release his grip. His right fist smashed furiously into French's face and he twisted like an eel in the other's grasp. Then Tanner also seized him and the three men went swinging and rolling and staggering about the room, knocking over tables and chairs and sweeping a row of glasses from the bar. Philpot fought with the fury of desperation. To the others it seemed incredible that so slight a man could show such strength. He strove desperately to free his left hand from French's clasp, while French with both hands tried for nothing but to keep it tightly closed on the bomb.

But the struggle was uneven and only one end was possible. Gradually Tanner improved his grip until at last he was able to use a kind of jiu-jitsu lock which held the other steady at the risk of a broken right arm. This lock he was able to maintain with his left hand, while with the other he took the pin of the bomb from the now nerveless fingers and with infinite care, French shifting his hands to allow of it, slipped the pin back into place. A moment later the bomb lay safely on the counter, while its owner sat faint and exhausted and securely handcuffed.

By the good offices of the barmaid French was able to wash the blood from his face, and a few minutes later a taxi was procured, and almost before the excited throng on the platform had learnt what was amiss, the three actors in the little drama had vanished from their ken.

20

Conclusion

The identity of the criminal known, it took Inspector French but a short time to compile a complete and detailed account of that terrible series of crimes which comprised what had become known as the Starvel Hollow Tragedy. Herbert Philpot, once he understood that the evidence against him was overwhelming and that nothing could save him from the scaffold, broke down completely and made a confession which cleared up the few points which from their nature it was impossible that French could have learnt otherwise.

The first act of the inspector, on lodging his prisoner in jail, was to visit his rooms in Glasgow. There in a battered leather portmanteau he discovered a large cashbox of hardened steel which when broken open was found to contain the balance of Mr Averill's money. With the £2000 which had been paid to Messrs Dashwood and Munce, no less a sum than £36,562 was recovered, no doubt all the old miser had possessed. Ruth Averill therefore received her fortune intact, and between the consequent easing of her circumstances and her engagement to Pierce Whymper, she found the happiness which had been denied her during her early years.

The history of the crime, as French at last presented it, made very terrible reading. Like most accounts of human weakness and guilt, it arose from small beginnings and increased stage by stage, until at last almost inevitably it reached its frightful consummation.

The trouble first arose in that house near the Ransome Institute in Kintilloch, when Dr Philpot discovered that he and his wife had nothing in common and that their marriage had been a fatal blunder. There is no need to recount the steps by which they drifted apart: it is enough to say that within two years of the wedding their hatred was mutual and bitter. Then Philpot became intimate with the nurse whom Roper afterwards found him embracing in the Institute shrubbery, and from that time the idea of getting rid of his wife by murder was never far from the doctor's mind. At first he did not see how this could be done, but as he brooded over the problem a method presented itself, and coldly and deliberately he made his preparations.

First, he selected a time when his wife should be alone with him in the house. Taking advantage of Flora's absence one afternoon, he made a pretext to get Mrs Philpot up to the bedroom landing. Silently he slipped upstairs after her and across the top of the lower flight he tied a dark-brown silk cord. Then, returning to the study, he called to her for Heaven's sake to come quickly for the house was on fire. She rushed down, caught her foot in the cord, and fell headlong to the hall below. She was stunned though not killed, but Philpot was prepared for this eventuality. Seizing the only implement he could find, a cricket bat, he struck her savagely on the temple, killing her instantaneously. As he expected, the blow made a bruise such as she might have received from the fall, and no suspicion was aroused by it.

But an unexpected contingency had given Philpot away. He had supposed that the servant, Flora, had really gone to visit her sick mother. But in this he was mistaken. It was to see, not her mother but her lover, Roper, that the girl had left the house, and this afternoon, like many another before it, she met him in a nearby copse. There, just after they had greeted each other, a heavy shower came on, and Flora had proposed an adjournment to the kitchen for shelter. To this Roper had agreed, and they had just settled down therein for their fifteen minutes' chat when they heard Philpot's shout to his wife, followed in a moment by Mrs Philpot's scream of terror and the crash of her fall. Flora involuntarily sprang to her feet and ran up the stairs from the basement to the hall. But she was transfixed by the sight which met her eyes and she stood rigid, gazing at Philpot. Roper had by this time crept up the stairs behind her, and both actually saw the doctor commit the murder. Flora was about to reveal herself, but Roper's grip tightened upon her wrist and held her motionless. Watching thus, they saw Philpot rapidly examine the body, and apparently satisfied that life was extinct, wipe the cricket bat and replace it in the stand. Then he ran upstairs and removed the silk cord, afterwards stooping over the floor on the halfway landing. They could not see what he was doing, but the evidence given later as to the hole in the carpet made his action clear.

Then followed a dramatic moment. When Philpot came downstairs he found Roper and Flora standing in the hall, and they soon let him know that they had witnessed the whole of his terrible proceedings. Philpot attempted to bluster, but he was quite unable to carry it off, and at last he asked Roper what he proposed to do.

Roper, in his way quite as unscrupulous as the doctor, had instantly thought how he might turn the affair to his own advantage, and he quickly stated his terms. If Philpot would increase his ten shillings a week to forty, thus enabling Roper and Flora to marry in comfort, the evidence against him would be withheld. Philpot protested, but Roper was adamant and the doctor had to give way. Had that been all that Roper required, the matter would have been settled in five minutes. But the attendant pointed out that unless he had some material proof of the crime, his hold over Philpot would be gone by the evening: if he did not give his testimony at once he would have to explain later why he had withheld it. He would therefore follow the precedent he had set in the case of the nurse, and would require from Philpot a signed confession of the murder. He swore solemnly to keep this secret as long as the money was paid, but with equal solemnity swore to send it anonymously to the police the first time the two pounds failed to materialise. Again Philpot blustered, but again he had to give way. But he pointed out that a confession would take some time to prepare, and that if he wrote it then and there the body would be cold before the police and another doctor were called in, which would give the whole affair away. Roper admitted this difficulty and proposed the following solution. He would give Philpot until nine o'clock that night to write it. If it was not forthcoming Flora and he would visit the police station with the yarn that Flora alone had seen what had taken place—but without revealing herself to Philpot; that she had been so frightened she did not know what to do; that she had consulted him, Roper, and that he had told her she must immediately reveal what she knew.

Philpot had perforce to agree to this, and by nine o'clock the confession was ready. But Philpot with perverse ingenuity found a way of tricking his adversary and rendering it useless. He was an extraordinarily clever draughtsman and had frequently amused himself by forging the handwriting of others. Now he forged his own. He wrote the confession out, and then copied it, letter by letter, *upside down*. The result was a passable imitation of his own handwriting, but one which any expert would recognise as a forgery. If the document were produced his denial of its authorship would be accepted without question.

But Philpot did not wish the document to be produced. It was too horribly credible, and inquiries by the police might easily lead to some discovery which would convict him. With all the appearance of reluctant good faith he therefore handed over the document and promised to pay the two pounds a week with the utmost regularity. Roper, believing in the value of his instrument and fearing Philpot might make an effort to regain it, rented a box in a safe deposit and stored it there.

Some four months later Philpot, as already stated, left the Ransome Institute and put up his plate at Thirsby. There he speedily made the acquaintance of Mr Averill. The old man indeed called him in, thinking that the fees of a newcomer who had to make his way would be less than those of a well-established practitioner.

When Roper was dismissed from the Institute he wrote to Philpot asking if he could help him towards getting another job, and it was while thinking over this request that the first idea of the crime entered the doctor's mind. His plan was if possible to get Averill to dismiss his servants and to employ the Ropers in their places. Then he intended to get the couple to join with him in the murder of Averill and the theft of his money.

At first Philpot's only idea was to obtain as firm a hold over the Ropers as they had over him, so as to free himself not only from the serious financial drain of their blackmail, but also from the terrible haunting fear that sooner or later they would betray him. But further consideration showed him a way by which he could get enormously more than this. By it not only would he achieve absolute safety in connection with his wife's death, but the whole of Averill's wealth might be his. It was no doubt a very terrible plan, for it involved committing two other murders, but fear and greed had by this time rendered Philpot almost inhuman and he cared for nothing but his own welfare. By this plan both the Ropers were to be done to death in such a way that suspicion could not possibly fall on himself. Even suspicion that a crime had been committed at all was unlikely, but if this by some unforeseen circumstance were aroused, it would certainly be believed that Roper had not died, but had committed the crime himself. After careful thought Philpot decided to put his plan into operation.

First, he sent Roper a note to meet him at a secluded point on Arthur's Seat, Edinburgh, and there he put up his proposal. Roper listened eagerly and accepted with alacrity. But in the course of conversation he made an admission and suggested a modification which amazed the doctor, but which, as it fell in with the latter's secret plan, he agreed to after some show of objection. Roper, it appeared, had also made a mistake in his marriage. He had also grown to hate his wife and would go to any lengths to regain his freedom. In the light of the doctor's proposal he saw his chance. Old Averill was to be murdered and to cover up the crime an accident was to be staged. Very well: Mrs Roper could be got rid of at the same time. The same accident would account for both deaths.

The two men discussed the ghastly details, and by the time they parted the whole hideous affair was cut and dry. Briefly, the plan was as follows:

Roper should first arrange his getaway, and while still living at Kintilloch should apply for a passport for Brazil. Inquiries about him would come to the local police, who would certify that he was the original of the photograph enclosed and that the matter was in order. Roper would drop a hint that he had a brother in Santos whom he had often thought of joining, a course which he proposed to follow now that he had left the Ransome. On receipt of the passport he would obtain the necessary visa.

Philpot in the meantime was to see Averill and try to get him to dismiss his servants and install Roper and his wife in their places. As a matter of fact he found this an easy task. Working on the old man's weakness, Philpot explained that having left the Ransome under a cloud, Roper would be thankful to take a job at a greatly reduced salary. This was enough for Averill, and he at once gave his people notice and offered their positions to the Ropers.

The couple thereupon settled down at Starvel, and by living exemplary lives sought to establish a reputation for integrity which would tend to support the accident theory to be put forward later. Philpot insisted that for at least a year they were to carry out their duties quietly, so that no one would think the 'accident' came suspiciously soon after their advent. 'We are going to make all the money we want for the rest of our lives,' he would say to Roper. 'No precaution is too great to be observed.'

Philpot told Roper quite openly that he wished to use the

crime to free himself from the other's blackmail. Roper on his part accepted the position, as he considered the money would be worth it, and also as he believed that his hold over Philpot would remain strong enough to protect him completely. The two scoundrels therefore concluded their evil compact, deciding to act jointly in all respects and so to bear equal responsibility. After the crime Roper was to emigrate to Brazil, the idea that he had lost his life being suggested by the dreadful expedient of leaving a third body in the house, which, it was hoped, would be taken for his.

The procuring of this third body was not the least of their difficulties. Markham Giles was to be the victim; in fact it was Giles' existence which had suggested the plan to Philpot. The man was known to be in poor health, and a few doses of a mild poison would make it poorer still. The result was that his death at the critical time excited no comment.

Philpot was to assist in the murders, and partly as a safe-guard against night callers, and partly to establish an alibi, he determined to fake illness. He therefore took to his bed on Thursday evening, telling his housekeeper he had influenza. The symptoms were easy to simulate and a doctor knows ways of raising the temperature. His housekeeper and the aged Dr Emerson were easily deceived, and on the two dreadful nights of crime he was able to leave his house unheard and unsuspected.

For the safe working of the scheme it was necessary that Ruth Averill should be got rid of. We have seen how this was done, but it unexpectedly involved drugging her uncle to prevent the fraud from becoming known. The plan was, of course, Philpot's. He supplied all the necessary forged letters and the ten pounds, but Roper carried out the actual details. Ruth left for York on the Tuesday, and that evening after dusk had fallen Roper and Philpot met secretly at Markham Giles' cottage, and there in cold blood the two miscreants murdered the unfortunate man by a forcible injection of cocaine. They left him in bed, Roper undertaking to 'discover' his death next morning. On that fatal Wednesday morning he arranged the funeral in such wise that the body would be coffined and left in the house that night.

The Whymper episode had been thought out to learn whether or not the numbers of Averill's notes were known. Roper would not murder the old man without Philpot's actual assistance, lest the doctor might evade his share of responsibility, so he kept him drugged to enable the £500 to be obtained. Whymper on that Wednesday evening was brought out to Starvel and made the accomplices' dupe.

On that same fateful evening Roper laid the foundation of the accident theory by simulating drunkenness in Thirsby. Of course it was a lucky chance for him that George Mellowes should overtake him on the way home, but even without this he believed he had arranged sufficient evidence of his condition.

Then came the hideous deeds of that tragic night. Under cover of darkness Philpot went out to Starvel and there with almost incredible callousness and deliberation first Mrs Roper and then Averill were done to death by throttling, their bodies being laid on their respective beds. Next the safe was robbed and the contents packed in two despatch cases, half for Philpot and half for Roper. The newspapers were burned in the safe, the latter locked, and the key replaced under Averill's pillow. Finally, petrol was poured over the house, ready to be set alight at the proper moment.

The next step was to bring over the body of Markham Giles. Philpot and Roper took the handcart from the outhouse and went across the moor to the unfortunate man's cottage. There they opened the coffin, with diabolical coolness took out the remains, laid them on the handcart, placed a suitable weight of earth in the coffin and screwed down the lid. They wheeled the body to Starvel, and carrying it upstairs, left it on Roper's bed.

All this time Philpot had carried out his part of the affair so wholeheartedly that any suspicion that might have lurked in Roper's mind as to his companion's good faith had been completely dispelled. But Philpot had been only biding his time until his dupe had given him all the assistance that he required with his own even more hideous plan.

As they turned to set fire to the house Philpot moved rapidly behind his victim and suddenly with all his strength struck him in the back with a large knife which he had secreted in his pocket. Roper, stabbed to the heart, fell and died in a few seconds.

There were now in that sinister house the bodies of no less than four murdered persons—Giles, Averill, and the two Ropers. But of these only three must be found. Philpot had foreseen the difficulty and quickly and methodically he proceeded to meet it. One of the four bodies must be buried, so that no suspicion of untoward or unusual events might afterwards be aroused and no investigation as to the identity of the fourth victim might lead to the truth. He chose that of Giles for two reasons. First, it was the lightest, and second, if identification of any of them should prove possible, it would obviously be safer to have those of Averill and the Ropers found. The interment accomplished, he transferred Roper's portion of the money to his own despatch case, set the house on fire and returned unseen to Thirsby.

Philpot was pretty certain that no suspicion would fall on

him, but to safeguard himself still further he adopted yet another subterfuge. Some months before the crime he began deliberately to lose money by betting. When the crime was committed he was known to be in low water, and he was careful afterwards to continue gambling, even to the extent of ruining his ostensible career and going through the bankruptcy courts. In this way he hoped to dispel any suggestion that he had recently come into money, and give a reasonable excuse for quitting Thirsby.

From what French had told him, Philpot realised that the numbers of some of the stolen notes were known, and French's announcement at the inquest he did not fully believe, fearing a trap. His ready money was, however, by this time exhausted, and he set to work to devise means not only to obtain more, but also to transfer a nest-egg to Brazil, to which country it had all along been his intention to emigrate.

The arrangements for this journey he had carried out with the same careful regard to detail which had characterised his other actions. Hidden in the cashbox with Averill's money French found a passport made out for Brazil in the name of Arthur Lisle Whitman, with a photograph of Philpot, vised and complete and—a forgery. The way in which this had been done showed the man's extraordinary ingenuity once again. He had obtained in the ordinary way a passport for himself for holidaying in France. Roper's passport with its Brazilian *visé* he had searched for and stolen before setting fire to the house. Of these two he had built up a new one, using certain pages from each. From his own book he took the description of himself, his stamped photograph and the vacant pages at the back. On certain blank pages from Roper's he forged both the printing and writing where he could not suitably alter his own, as well as obtaining a model of the Brazilian *visé*, which he also forged.

The wretched criminal's last move, the meeting with French at Waverley, was on his part a throw of the dice. On receipt of the wire to Whitman through the Edinburgh tobacconist he half-suspected a trap, and of course the plan became apparent when French's letter to himself arrived. He saw, however, that he was either quite safe or irretrievably lost. If French had no inkling of the truth it was evident that he must keep the appointment and continue to play his game. On the other hand, if French knew, nothing could save him, and he would make an end of things for all concerned with his Mills' bomb.

To bring this tale of the Starvel Hollow Tragedy to a close it remains only to be said that after a dramatic trial Herbert Philpot paid for his crimes with his life, while to turn to a happier side of the picture, Pierce Whymper and Ruth Averill were united in the bonds of holy matrimony where both found the happiness which at one time had seemed likely to be denied them.